SOUTH PACIFIC CUT
AN ECO-CRIME NOVEL

Joshua McKenzie-Brown

SOLWARA
PUBLISHING LTD.

This novel is dedicated to my beautiful daughter, Serena. If we all showed as much compassion, curiosity and wonder for nature as she had, then humanity would be heading in a better direction. Love, Dad.

Prologue

Cartons of frozen tuna swung out of the hold, stacked on pallets, condensation rising in the tropical air. Forklifts backed up as they took the load from deck cranes, alarms sounding. Next, hundreds of sacks came off the ship, mixed in with legal catch, lighter than yellowfin but worth far more.

Beyond barbed wire perimeter fencing, mangroves stood in black mud, choked with soda bottles, nappies and plastic bags. Raw sewage rode in on the tide, swirling in slicks around breathing roots that emerged from filth. Clouds of sandflies hovered above.

Ship's officers stood dockside overseeing the unloading, spitting tobacco juice. The cargo had travelled a long way under their supervision, starting in the Pacific Islands. They cursed at men operating the machines, unwilling to remain in port longer than necessary, heat increasing by the hour. The air reeked of fuel and rotten fish. The deck shook with engine vibrations, kept running to feed refrigeration units as the hold was emptied. Thin, dark port workers in jandals avoided making eye contact with the officers.

Several berths down, abandoned longliners sat ghostlike, paint peeling, flags of convenience limp in the still air. By the gate, an unattended security booth had its door ajar, the monitor screens unwatched.

Unannounced, the harbormaster appeared at the foot of the gangway, papers under his arm. The veteran captain came down from the bridge to meet him, signing the bill of lading with a shaky hand. He then slipped an envelope into the man's jacket, the real cargo accounted for without discussion.

A black hose lay across the dock, coiled like a cobra, feeding into the ship's belly. With no wind, diesel fumes made the eyes sting. Boxes of rice and beer moved up the boarding ramp in trolleys, brushing past women trying to sell trinkets to the crew. Deckhands moved fast, provisioning and unloading in the same breath, swearing when frozen tuna burned their bare hands.

Standing apart from the crew, two men chatted to each other, dark glasses hiding their identities. In leather shoes and suits, their presence was not subtle. Nor was it intended to be. One checked his watch, impatient. As his arm moved, the cuff of his shirt slipped a few inches to reveal the edge of a colorful tattoo.

Water beneath the massive hull of the reefer vessel contrasted with her white rust-streaked sides. Dark as coffee, it was full of plastic, foamy scum suffocating the surface. Rising bubbles broke the stillness. A teenage diver wearing swimming goggles popped up, having removed barnacles from the hull with a scraper. Risking entanglement, crocodile attack and bacterial infection for a handful of cash.

An unbalanced sack fell from the jaws of an old forklift, hitting the ground hard. Dried shark fins spilled out like cards fanned across a blackjack table. Egrets perched on the ship's gunwale watched with interest, necks turned, heads tilting.

Stiff grey fins landed at the boots of a uniformed customs officer, clipboard in hand. Laborers stopped moving, staring at the scene unfolding, interested in his reaction. The man looked around to see who was watching, then checked the shipping manifest.

He flipped the page, pretending to read, running a hand through his hair. His eyes scanned the columns, lips moving without a sound.

Frozen Yellowfin / Skipjack / Albacore Tuna – 18,600 kg Marine Oil (cosmetic grade), Beche-de-mer – 7,900 kg

He tapped the margin with his pen, then shook his head. After looking over at the men in suits for a moment, he walked off to another ship, visibly stressed.

Laborers dropped to their knees, collecting the fins. Sunlight reflected off something metallic amidst the sea of grey. It was a satellite tag, overlooked in the chaos, embedded in the flesh at the base of a hammerhead's dorsal fin. Still alive, transmitting confused data to a marine biologist in a lab somewhere. After the concrete had been swept, the bags were tied and unloading carried on as if nothing had happened.

Below deck, someone opened the bilge line, discharging tons of foul water into the harbor. An iridescent sheen curled around oyster-covered pylons. The holding tanks were next.

One of the suited men took a call, his voice lost in the clamor of cranes and forklifts. When it ended, he let the cheap phone slip to the ground. The screen cracked on impact, then he nudged it into the filthy shallows with his shoe. Job done, his colleague made a joke and lit a cigarette as they walked away from the dock.

Back in the booth, energy drink in hand, a guard waved as they approached. The barrier lifted to reveal their driver waiting on the other side. The trade had cleared another port.

By nightfall, the refrigerated vessel would be empty, her holds scrubbed clean and sealed once more, the chill never broken, ready for the next illicit consignment. Ready to vanish into the South Pacific.

Within days, shark fins would simmer in broth from Guangzhou to Singapore, each bowl paid for in blood.

Chapter 1

The kingfish shot past Leilani's face in a blur of silver and green, inches from taking her head off. Her spear punched through its flank, steel tip vanishing into muscle. Blood clouded the cold water, curling in red spirals. The sharks would come.

The reel screamed as the kingfish bolted, line running. Leilani kept her grip steady. The spear had set deep, but the wrong angle could rip it free.

Loose line whipped around her right fin, cinching tight. In an instant, she was dragged down. Salt stung her eyes as her mask slipped. Her lungs burned, screaming for air. Panicking, she heard her dad's voice. Slow the heart, find the surface.

Streams of bubbles rushed past as she was pulled deeper. Seconds before blacking out, her thoughts slowed; a sense of calm, reaching euphoria, overcame her. The change of pace allowed her to assess the situation. She had not been attacked. Blood in the water was not her own. Under load, nylon wrapped around her legs cut into her wetsuit, the kingfish's survival instincts kicking in.

Her vision narrowed, the edges blackening. Then the line went slack. The kingfish was alive but spent, its thrashes reduced to twitches. By muscle memory, moving fast, she worked the nylon free.

She planted her fins against the rocky bottom and drove upward, every kick a drain on what little oxygen remained. The lead belt around her waist needed to go. She ripped the buckle free, belt slipping into the darkness below. Without it, her body surged upward toward the light.

There was no one on the surface waiting for her. She dragged in air, chest heaving. This wasn't a freediving competition, with safety boats nearby. Far from shore in open water, rain slashed her skin, lightning building overhead.

The boom of thunder reverberated in her ears. Exhausted, she let herself float weightlessly on her back; the adrenaline ebbing, muscles relaxing. After a minute she realized the noise in her ears wasn't thunder, surf or wind; it was the sound of her own blood, amplified by a lack of oxygen. A passive tug on the line, still clenched in her bare hand, brought her back, reminding her the hunt wasn't over.

Recovered, she ducked beneath the waves, slack line light as she hauled it in, arm over arm. She was relieved to see the kingfish still impaled as it rose from the deep, but its fight was gone. Swimming in weary circles, tethered and broken like a captured wild horse, it came up without struggle. Once within reach, Leilani forced her fingers through the gills. Her knife entered the top of the head, spiking the brain. A humane, precise dispatch she'd perfected over the years. The fish convulsed, its body jolting as nerve endings fizzled out, suspended in winter-clear water. Leilani surfaced to breathe again, exhausted from the effort of dragging the kingfish's weight. If the bronze whalers were going to tax her, this was their last chance. Speargun in hand, catch in the other, she kicked against the swell, heading for the white sands of Pakiri Beach, knocked back at a rate of knots. From water level, she thought the coastline looked like nature intended it to, with no development, rugged, untamed, even in the rain.

Once Leilani felt sand underfoot, she stopped to catch her breath. Out of the water, the kingfish was heavier. She lowered it with care onto the beach, pushing wet hair from her eyes. Its color was already fading, tail twitching long after the brain spike.

Dad will be impressed, she thought. Last week it had been greenbone, small, sweet tasting from their seaweed diet. This fish was different. Blood still seeped from the spear wound, dark against the silver flank. There was enough meat here to feed half the bay.

Clouds blocked the sun. The tide pressed in, surf hammering harder now. She'd timed it right; another half hour, and she'd have been caught in the break. She'd never enjoyed the waves. The quiet beneath was her element. No doubt the local boys would arrive soon, boards under their arms.

Out of the water was colder than in the water. A wide rip across the shoulder of her 5mm wetsuit invited the wind in. It would need stitching. With adrenaline still in her system, she hadn't noticed. *Damn it.* Six months of working at Goat Island dive store had paid for that suit, top of the line.

She knew the walk home would bring the warmth back. There'd be no hot soup waiting; her father's fridge ran on beer and steak ever since he'd become a bachelor. Her fingers and toes were numb, needles of cold driving into them with every step.

Careful to avoid seabird eggs laid haphazardly in the rolling
dunes, Leilani eventually reached solid ground, her house in view.
An older Māori man was ahead, bending over to check a nest within
a stand of spinifex. In fisheries officer uniform, he stood and raised
his hand in greeting. He wore his thick hair back in a ponytail, with a
bone clasp.

She'd never told Hone, but his work was why she'd chased marine
biology. If she could have, she would've told him she'd graduated
from the Ocean Enforcement Academy. He'd be proud. The man
was always there for the community, giving his time, sharing his
knowledge. But the white Ministry ute made him a target. Gangs up
north didn't like him and made it known. In a community this small,
nothing stayed secret. Another sacrifice he'd made.

"That's a record, I reckon, Lani," he said, acknowledging the fish
carried on her back, breaking into a grin.

The walnut-brown skin of his face was etched deeply with faded
charcoal lines, whorls and korus. Carved into the skin, not inked into
surface layers like weaker men. The *mataora*, full facial tattoo for
indigenous men of status and *mana*. In the old days, he would've been
a respected chief, worn a cloak of feathers from kiwi that still existed
in the hills. Word was that the blood of legendary warriors ran in his
veins. Leilani remembered the primal fear she'd felt as a girl the first
time they'd met on the beach.

A radio on his utility belt crackled as a fellow officer called in an
abalone seizure, requesting backup. Hone ignored it; he was too far
away to be of use. Leilani noticed his knife, sharp end in a leather
cover, had a whalebone handle. Everyone in the North knew the law.
Natives had first rights when marine mammals washed up deceased
on the beaches. Sometimes even the right to decline necropsy, which
Leilani strongly objected to when given the chance to speak. She had
no friends at the Department of Conservation.

Replying to Hone's admiration of her catch, she said, "Thanks,
Matua," using the respect term for an older man.

"Nearly took me down with her. Bloody strong. You on your
way to the south end?" She asked, putting the heavy fish down onto
damp grass.

"Yeah, got a tip that the Asians are back. Greedy fellas."

"Got that right," Leilani agreed. "They were there earlier today
when I went out, too."

"I'll check it out, don't worry. Say hi to your old man for me. Papa still tells visitors what he did for us after the storm. Don't hear him praising white folk much, I'll tell you that."

Leilani laughed. This did not surprise her. Jake had always had a way with the locals, which was probably why they'd let him build on customary land.

"Give 'em hell", she called out as Hone returned to his truck. She looked down at the massive fish. Getting this deadweight over to the BBQ was going to be a mission.

* * *

Wondering if his daughter was due back, Jake leaned against the railing of the front deck, eyes scanning the wide expanse of wind-ravaged Hauraki Gulf. The water was dark under an overcast sky; and the air heavy with the threat of more rain. Tucked into the corner of a wet deck was his prized Weber, its bulk protected by a sunshade he'd installed last summer. This year it had kept more rain and hail off the expensive grill than sun. The table was spread with fishing magazines; pages curled and rain-damaged.

He wore the reading glasses she'd picked for his fiftieth, and boardshorts and jandals he lived in. When he saw Leilani coming up the path, fish in hand, his face lit up. Weathered skin folded at the corners of his eyes, teeth flashing through salt-and-pepper stubble. His shoulder-length hair lifted in the breeze, highlighted from years at sea. Most seasons he'd be in Fiji by now.

"Good timing. Dinners on you tonight, I see," he said with a smile.

"Least you can do really, since you don't pay any rent. No crayfish this time?"

"You know there's no crays left out there. At least we're not having steak. It's not healthy to eat that every night, Dad," Leilani said.

"By the way, might need your help to cut this fish up after my shower."

"Sure, no worries, darling. Let's see if your kingi tastes better than the last one I brought home."

Leilani rolled her eyes and disappeared inside. Jake put his glasses down and walked over to the corrugated iron shed, across damp saltgrass. Inside were an array of garden tools and endless fishing gear. A two-person blue plastic kayak rested against the wall. Filleting knives lay next to the smoker, a rusted aluminum box, layered with manuka wood chips. Oxygen holes had been drilled on both sides.

"Are we smoking this one?" he yelled.

"Nah, she'll go good on the BBQ," Leilani yelled back from the upstairs shower. Washing salt out of curly hair took longer than people expected.

With development subject to tribal approval, the area stayed quiet at night, broken only by birdsong and surf. There was one road in, one road out. The multimillion-dollar homes and golf courses were far enough away to feel like another world. Only surfers, fishermen, and horse riders came here, chasing escape and solitude.

At the edge of the road, where pine forest gave way to dunes, stood an imposing carving of Tangaroa, God of the Ocean. The New Zealand sun and salt air had bleached the timber, but his abalone shell eyes still caught the light, unblinking. Reminding every passerby where they were.

Moving north from the city a long time ago, Jake and Leilani stood out. When asked how he'd secured consent to buy here, Jake was vague. Leilani figured he'd done someone a favor they didn't want mentioned. As an architect, he had his ways around red tape. During the Covid years, the local gate had been locked to outsiders, supposedly to protect elders, shutting off the community and pissing off surfers. Old disputes had flared again, as they always did.

Warmed from her shower, Leilani emerged from the house in a hoodie and Northland rugby shorts, hair tied up. Light rain was falling. Jake was halfway through hacking up the kingfish, tired of waiting. The filleting bench he'd built from driftwood and scrap metal was slick with fish blood. As he sliced large steaks off the flanks, Leilani could see his faded Polynesian tattoo below rolled-up flannel sleeves. He told her once that the marks had been made with a shark tooth, then sealed with ash. Leilani believed him. Whatever else he was, he wasn't a liar.

It seemed like another lifetime when her mother, Asu, had disappeared. Leilani would never forgive the woman for abandoning them. While she still had questions, Jake said he no longer thought of her. Whether she'd run away after receiving the New Zealand passport or returned to Samoa was an unresolved family mystery. Jake had tried a few lines of enquiry over the subsequent years, but given up when all he received was silence. As he often said, his work and his daughter were more than enough to sustain the mind and heart.

The grill sizzled as flames melted kingfish fat. Jake worked the tongs, throwing around mock commentary, doing his best Gordon Ramsay impersonation. Beyond the BBQ's crackle, the only sound was the lonely call of kiwis in the dark.

On the deck, Leilani sat cross-legged, breaking down the fish head with her hands. "Shit," a splinter of bone stabbed her thumb. She'd need to find the tweezers.

"You're not gonna eat that, are you?" Jake said as he watched his daughter pop raw eyeballs out of the skull.

Leilani looked at him directly and put both eyes in her mouth, crushing them on the roof of her mouth. She spat the hard, chewy lenses onto the grass. Her father pretended to dry-retch.

"Your mum used to do that," he said with a half smile.

"I remember. Want the brain?" Leilani asked, offering a handful of sludge. "You need them more than I do."

Jake laughed. She wasn't wrong. It was hard to recall a time he'd ever seen his daughter study during her university years, yet she'd graduated with two degrees. Most of her time had been spent diving or beachcombing. Recorded lectures had been her saving grace. He remembered what the school counsellor had told him over the phone. To say Leilani was antisocial was an understatement.

As the weather app had predicted, southerlies had eased. Being outside in the evening was a blessing after days of nonstop rain. Jake cracked his third beer, handing a can over to Leilani. They sat on the deck in silence, eating, listening to the crickets. When they forgot to shut the sliding glass doors, the light brought in dozens.

"What's on your mind, Dad?" Leilani asked after a while, between mouthfuls of fish and salad. Jake looked frustrated, frowning.

"I forgot, sorry. You missed a call earlier. Think they left a message. You should call them back."

Leilani was not surprised. Since her thesis proving New Zealand's orca were calving off Kawau had gone public, the media interest had been hard to manage. Her photos of the newborn calves, watermark stripped, were everywhere online. Posted, shared, stolen. More people adored orca than she'd ever thought possible. Within days she'd abandoned the idea of retrieving control of her work. Scientific credit was all that mattered.

"Guess that new gear I got you for Christmas was a good investment after all," her dad joked.

Leilani ignored him and took her iPhone up to the loft. One corner looked like a film studio, with underwater rigs, waterproof housings and lenses stacked high. On the windowsill, gold freediving trophies gleamed beside sea urchin shells and fragments of whalebone.

Two framed certificates hung on the wall: Environmental Law and Marine Biology.

The expansive windows gave the illusion of floating above the coast. Sand stretched on forever, tide racing in. It was too dark to be sure, but at the far south end, a white dot might have been Hone's truck. She wondered if he'd fined the shellfish poachers or taken their gear.

She lay down on her bed and called the number back, first checking the time in Hawai'i. When she saw the US prefix, she knew who it was.

"Good afternoon, Leilani Brown from New Zealand, returning your call. Apologies, I was out spearfishing."

A deep American voice answered. He seemed pleased to hear from her.

"Agent Brown. Director Ventura. Good to hear you're keeping your diving skills up to date. Well, your ability under the water certainly made you stand out from the crowd during training. Now, the reason for my call. I have your first assignment."

"Thank you, sir," Leilani replied. They hadn't spoken much during her months of formal training at the Academy, but when they had, she'd sensed a connection.

"I'll be blunt, you seem to understand the ocean in a way that very few of your colleagues do. I read your thesis, by the way, after you survived the open sea challenge."

There was a pause as he looked up the title on his computer. *"Breeding Behaviors of New Zealand Orca (Orcinus orca): Insights from Local Populations."* I read it for a week straight. Wife thought I was crazy. Science is as readable as fiction in your hands, Agent Brown. Well done."

Leilani was taken aback by the feedback, also that he remembered her first name. There had been so many cadets.

She'd known of it by reputation, but the Ocean Enforcement Agency had felt beyond her reach until a surprise call-up last year. To say the Academy's initiation had been brutal would undersell the programme. Antarctic water drills. Days left adrift at sea. Boat chases that ran engines so hot she thought they'd explode. Dive training near seal colonies, always scanning for fins.

Saving the ocean via a courthouse had seemed a more likely career. Fate, or destiny, thought otherwise.

"Thank you, sir," Leilani replied to the director's praise. She struggled to hold back from asking questions about her first assignment. Ventura would reveal all when he was ready.

"I want you on board. The guys we had stationed in the islands gave up years ago and returned to the States. Couldn't hack it."

Between you and me, we've received a tip from a partner organization in the South Pacific. Sharks are washing up in Samoa without fins. Reports of tigers, hammerheads, whitetips. Maybe others.

Shark finning and export are illegal throughout most of the South Pacific these days, as you know, including Samoa. But here's the challenge. Either fisheries and police don't want to confront the issue alone or they lack the resources to investigate this. Potentially both. We're going to help them, and that's where you come in. The Ocean Enforcement Agency wants you to expose whatever the hell is going on down there. Document it, prove it, shut it down. Do you need to take the night?"

"No. I'm all in. Thank you …" Leilani replied, no doubt in her voice.

"Great, I'll send specifics via the app. You'll be on the island for a few months, longer if need be. Plane tickets and accommodation will be finalized this week, and then you'll leave Friday after. Appreciate your time, Agent. Keep your phone with you; I'll be in touch."

Leilani felt her heart beat as fast as when she'd been seconds away from drowning. She was about to say something when she realized the director had ended the call.

Jogging down the stairs, she looked for her father. She hugged him from behind while he watched Netflix on the flat screen. He was into red wine now.

He paused the documentary and turned to look at his daughter, raising his eyebrows.

"And?"

"I'm in!" Leilani couldn't hold back her excitement, a smile never leaving her face.

"Well done, darling. They've made the right choice. Always knew you'd get there," he said.

"The boss even read my thesis. Can't believe it."

"Neither can I, Agent Brown," Jake grinned.

"That was an 85-page document! But seriously, where are they sending you? It's not Invercargill, is it? Lots of great whites, but I'm not visiting you there. Too cold. Better not be England either."

"Samoa, Dad. It's Samoa. I'm gonna see where Mum came from," Leilani said, becoming serious.

"You remember where her village is?" she pushed.

Jake had not expected his daughter would be sent to the Pacific Islands, and it showed. He switched into father mode.

"Hang on. What about your PhD?" he asked, ignoring her provocative question. "Didn't I already pay for that?"

"I don't even know if I want to do that anymore, Dad. Maybe later. It's refundable, so relax. Anyway, think of this as practical experience. I can dive every day I'm there."

Her green eyes lit up at the thought of clear, warm water. Sunshine and palm trees.

Jake sighed in defeat. His daughter had inherited her mother's stubborn nature. Both women never took no for an answer.

"Leave your bikini at home. They don't like that in the village," he yelled across the house, half-serious, as she headed back upstairs to plan.

Underwater visibility remained good for the following week, but Leilani stayed ashore. Her daily ritual of walking the beach in the early morning, beachcombing before waves could take away treasures of the deep, continued. Sometimes a lone rider would trot by. Her mind was occupied with thoughts of coral and sea turtles. Late at night, lying in bed, she watched shark attack videos online. The ones made using AI made her cringe.

She stuffed a wetsuit, mask, and fins into a waterproof bag. On top lay her new staff ID, the photo catching her with messy hair, fresh from a dive. Soon she'd be in Polynesia, chasing shadows through reef and open water. Not just fish this time. Sharks, and the men trying to kill them.

The night before departure, Leilani tried to find the district she'd be working in on Google Earth. An encrypted message on her phone had given coordinates. Satellite maps revealed rainforest down to the ocean, with areas cleared for plantations and villages. There were a handful of buildings, tiny squares and rectangles. There seemed to be a church. Not much else; it was hard to tell. Turquoise shallows fading to dark blue drop-offs captured her attention. She pinched the screen, forcing the map closer, until the picture dissolved into blur. *No imagery available.*

Chapter 2

Customs should have been routine. Instead, an officer with thick makeup and tobacco breath pulled Leilani aside. Her New Zealand passport was not handed back.

"Come with me, please. This way."

She followed the officer. They entered a private room with cold air-conditioning and closed the door.

"I'm on assignment, not on holiday." Leilani pre-empted the questions to come and handed over her ID, visa, and letter of service. She could feel the eyes of security staff at the door boring into her back. She bit down on her lip, wondering what her next move would be if denied entry to the island nation.

Fake red nails tapped on the desk as the officer flipped through her documents, over-plucked eyebrows raised in surprise. For a moment, Leilani thought she might be detained and sent back. Instead, the officer smiled.

"Good for you, girl. Doing God's work. Sorry about the delay; first time we've had an agent here."

Leilani was unsure how to respond, so gave a tight smile and kept her mouth shut. It looked as if she were free to go.

The tall woman stamped her documents. As she slid them back, Leilani appreciated the tattoos on her large hands for the first time, delicate black lines and dots, tracing the officer's wrists, flowing down her fingers.

"Anyway, welcome to beautiful Samoa," the officer said, finished with admin. She took the hibiscus flower from behind her ear and gave it to Leilani. It was an uncomfortable moment. The scent of cheap perfume and vodka was overpowering, like when a man desperate to impress wears too much cologne.

Feeling awkward at the extra attention, Leilani mumbled thanks in Samoan, looking towards the door. The security guard who'd come with them was still standing outside. Using her phone as a mirror, the customs officer touched up her lipstick and makeup. Remembering that she represented the agency, Leilani waited patiently without saying a word. *What else did they need from her?*

Trying not to stare, she realized that beneath the foundation and lipstick, there was a shadow of stubble across the officer's jawline.

It was subtle, barely there, unless you were close. But it was there. She/he must've been on the overnight shift. Strong features, broad shoulders, the hint of an Adam's apple. Now it made sense.

Disappointed with her own perception, Leilani decided that the baggage handler who'd helped locate a missing camera bag had also been a man. Samoa's third gender. Called fa'afafine, 'to be and act like a woman'. There'd been one or two at high school. She wanted to kick herself for not knowing.

"Sorry, um, you can go now. Don't let them give you a hard time in the village, okay, hun?" the officer said, ignoring the waiting passengers outside at the main counter. There seemed to be no other staff processing check-ins.

"They always make fun and things like that, especially with outsiders who come and stir things up."

Leilani nodded, adjusting the flower she'd been given, her dark brown curls keeping it in place. The officer's advice remained in her mind as the guard opened the door, no longer in the way. Keen to get out, she looked for the airport exit. Joking and teasing she could handle.

She stepped out of the terminal and into a wall of heat. Humid air clung to her skin, thick and unrelenting. A typical day in the South Pacific. A prebooked resort van idled at the curb, wrapped in tropical decals, white frangipani and palm fronds splashed across its sides, jarring against the gray concrete of the parking area.

The shared pickup and drop-off area was alive with sound and movement, a kaleidoscope of humanity in motion. There was nowhere to take a phone call in peace. No chance of competing against the laughter, horns honking, car stereos, endless talking and crying in English and Samoan.

Most of the crowd were locals, brown skin used to the sun, pushing towers of luggage, balancing polystyrene boxes packed with village food, children trailing at their sides. A few white tourists wandered about, sunburned during resort stays, fewer than Leilani had expected.

Wondering if the van that had pulled over was for her, Leilani watched a man propped up against a warm airport wall, eyes closed, chest rising and falling. Somehow, he remained upright, experienced at sleeping on his feet.

Movement caught Leilani's eye. A boy in an All Blacks shirt darted onto the road, barefoot, hair wet with sweat. In his hands was a signed

rugby ball, his prized possession, rescued from under the wheels
of a taxi.

The driver leaned on his horn. But instead of yelling at the boy,
he laughed and called out in Samoan, his voice carrying above the
commotion outside. "Sole! That ball worth your life?" Other drivers
idling in the waiting area howled with laughter.

The boy grinned, embarrassed, cradling the ball like a treasure as
he ran back to his family. His father, a heavy man in a polo shirt and
lavalava, stepped forward to meet him. Without a word, he delivered
a smack to the back of his son's head with an open palm, not hard, but
enough to make a point.

A woman nearby on a bench wiped her cheeks with the hem
of her dress. Sobbing uncontrollably. A passing man with taped-up
suitcases clutched his daughter's hand and turned for one last wave.
Leilani understood the emotion. Many of these goodbyes would have
unknown timeframes., return flights from Australia or New Zealand
not yet booked.

After the driver finally waved her over, taking her seat in the van,
Leilani was thankful he had the air con running. After greeting him in
Samoan, she checked the seatbelt was functional. She'd heard stories
from her friends.

The man was younger than she was, eager to talk and,
with passable English, determined to make the most of what
time he had.

"Where are you from?" he asked, speeding through airport gates
and onto a narrow road.

"Niu Sila," Leilani said, translating her country's name, not asking
him questions to end their conversation. She was tired.

"All Blacks!" he said, his joy instant when he realized she was
a Kiwi. For the next thirty minutes, they discussed rugby, favorite
players, latest games, and the Samoan national team. The boy's
knowledge of sport was impressive, even if his accent made her work
to follow along. He reckoned Leilani was built like a rugby player.
Maybe a wing, he clarified, not a prop. His sisters loved the Black
Ferns too. Rugby for women in Samoa was higher level than in NZ,
but lower pay, he alleged.

Just when Leilani thought the young man was going to focus on
driving, he veered into other topics without warning. Religion, his
girlfriend's unexpected pregnancy, and plans to move to New Zealand

for fruit-picking work. He talked fast, without filter, as if unloading his troubles to a stranger might lighten the burden.

"School finished," he said with a shrug. "No money. Baby, come soon. I need go to New Zealand. Good money. Samoa life is too hard. Maybe you can sponsor me," he tried.

Leilani tried not to laugh at his bravado. She felt sorry for the kid. He was young, facing tough times. At least he had a part-time driving gig. As he reached for the volume on the radio, a flashy gold watch caught her eye.

Probably fake, she thought, although she doubted Temu delivered to the islands. Her gaze shifted to the dashboard, where an iPhone 16 rested in its hands-free cradle, screen lighting up with TikTok and Instagram notifications. That was not fake.

Sliding too fast around a tight corner, the van ran over what appeared to be a chicken that emerged at the wrong time from the bush. A bump and flurry of feathers alarmed their backseat passenger, who hadn't uttered a word since leaving the airport. Leilani glanced in the rearview mirror. A lean Chinese national in his forties stared back. He'd been so silent she'd forgotten there was another person in the vehicle.

At a brief stop outside a commercial warehouse on the outskirts of Apia, where the engine was left running, the man loaded heavy cardboard cartons into the trunk of the people-mover. The driver got out to assist. The boxes had brand imprints on them, tinned fish and breakfast crackers; the kind sold in bulk at every shop on the island. He spoke briefly to another Asian staff member who came outside to assist. Leilani wasn't surprised. These guys seemed to run stores all over the South Pacific.

Practicing Samoan with the driver was too awkward with a sullen stranger right behind her, so she decided against it.

About to doze off, Leilani realized a small camera was mounted on the dash, its lens facing into the vehicle. A red light blinked, confirming it was recording.

"Camera?" she asked.

"Yeah, for safety," the driver replied without hesitation. "Like Uber, I guess. Company policy."

The explanation seemed unlikely. He wasn't driving in Auckland or Wellington. Most taxi drivers here took cash.

As they left Apia behind, the road quality deteriorated, ageing buildings in the capital giving way to lush rainforest, hillside waterfalls and scattered villages. It was here that the driver became a tour guide, pointing out features on the way. Leilani half-listened, exhausted after the long flight delay at Auckland before the sun came up.

Stirring up dust that settled on the windows as he drove too fast for the conditions, the van avoided potholes until the inevitable occurred. Miraculously, after pulling over and doing an inspection, the driver decided the wheel had survived, and they could continue. Cartons in the back had moved around, some splitting open. The Asian passenger got out in a flash to check if his stock had been damaged, retaping boxes as needed. He seemed overly protective of basic store goods. As he worked, Leilani caught the metallic glint of a handgun in the mirror, tucked into his waistband. This man was not in Samoa on holiday either.

After seeing his gun, she forced herself to stay awake, wishing there were somewhere to buy coffee. The young man was not driving in a way that brought any peace. He needed another pair of eyes, if not total supervision. Then there was the man behind her, watching her. All on her first day on the job.

An hour into the cross-island drive, Leilani was jolted awake, forehead slammed against the glove-box. Her safety plan had failed; sleep had beaten her. A sharp bang, like a gunshot, split the air. The van bucked to the left before grinding to a jarring halt, kicking up sparks. *Had they been shot at?*

Concussed, she saw double, her head pounding worse than a hangover. The next sound she became aware of was barking, urgent, aggressive, and too close. She remembered her pre-trip rabies jab. According to the World Health Organization website, presence of the disease in Samoa was unconfirmed, which worried her. Rabies was not a good way to die.

She looked at the man now slumped over the wheel. Airbags hadn't deployed, if there were any. Shards of glass from the shattered windshield had sliced his face in several places, and blood seeped down his cheek from a head cut, soaking his uniform.

"What the hell happened?" Leilani asked no one in particular, spitting blood. She'd bitten her tongue hard during the crash. Immediate swelling made every word hard to pronounce.

Her best friend's advice played like a song on repeat in her mind: *"If you hit a pig in the islands, don't stop."* Leilani had assumed the scenario would never play out in real life, but now that it might have, she felt anxious. How much did a pig cost? She wondered if the agency would reimburse her. The unconscious driver wasn't about to pay up.

The sliding door of the van jammed, but gave way after a strong kick. Smoke outside hit her like a wave, carrying the memorable scent of burning rubber. She stepped with caution out of the wreckage. It didn't take a mechanic to see that where the front-right tire had been, was now an axle twisted into a 90-degree angle. A pothole beneath looked like a moon crater, full of muddy brown water.

"If these people look after the road, this not happen," the Chinese man muttered, stroking his goatee, keeping a safe distance away. He seemed uninjured. Anger and frustration were all over his scratched face.

The dirt road that had defeated their vehicle was pitted, like many on the island outside the city. Pothole depths were hidden by inches of rainwater, reflecting afternoon light. At the roadside, modest concrete homes, painted in colors that would never be permitted back home, were built next to traditional thatched huts and open-sided meeting houses. Man-made black rock terraces separated wandering livestock and gardens.

From a nearby house, a big man in a lavalava emerged, his toddler following close behind in a sagging nappy that dragged across the ground. He took in the scene, hands on head, then yelled at the dogs waiting around the wreckage. When they ignored his calls, he threw rocks until they whimpered and retreated.

"You guys need a better driver!" the man called out.

Leilani ignored his island humor. "Yeah, we know, but he's hurt badly. We need to get him out."

Upon realizing the Chinese man dusting himself off had not been the driver, the Samoan ran across and reached inside the wreck from the driver's side where the door had come off. He pulled the teenager out and over his shoulder like a sack of taro, then carried him into the house, out of reach from opportunistic dogs. When he reappeared, breathless but in control, smears of the driver's blood painted his bare chest.

"He gonna be okay. Don't worry too much," the man said. "We know his family. Let him sleep for now."

Villagers now gathered at the roadside, children clinging to parents, staring and taking photos on their phones. Leilani was about to press for an ambulance when she was distracted.

A group of solid men who'd been playing cards and drinking in an open-sided hut walked over to check out the scene. She could see numbers tattooed across their necks, machetes on their belts. Pupils wide, twitchy. She knew the look, amphetamine. Her gut tightened. They didn't look like taro farmers.

They paused at the smoking van, laughing with each other, sized Leilani up for a moment, then turned back to continue their gambling. Bass-heavy music rattled the hut from a massive speaker. Outside, a blacked-out Land Rover was parked, glass tinted darker than oil that spilled from the van.

"We were on our way to the Mormon church," Leilani said after a while to her rescuer, trying to forget about the intimidating men who'd just stared her down.

The man who'd come to their aid was unfazed by his neighbors.

"Huh? What church? That bus long gone. Stay here tonight. Tomorrow it goes the other way." He broke into a laugh. Leilani studied his face, unsure if he meant it.

The Chinese passenger had walked away from the crash site, phone in hand. He kicked the dirt when it failed to connect. An agency-issued satellite phone in her bag would've worked, but she thought better of it. The fewer people who knew about her valuable equipment in the suitcases, the better.

"What's their deal?" Leilani asked, nodding toward the Land Rover and the circle of men drinking in the hut, immersed in the game.

"Those guys? Deport from America. We don't want them, and they don't wanna be here, but they're living on family land. Not much we can do for now. Too many drugs, you know. Sell ice and ah weed. Stay away, and they not bother you," he said, lowering his voice.

Satisfied with his explanation, Leilani and the big Samoan worked together to retrieve her luggage. The camera in bubble-wrap was still intact, fortunate considering she doubted replacements could be found on the island. Calling rural Samoa a developing economy, as her father had, was a generous statement, to say the least.

Leilani?" the man said. He must've read name tags on her bags.

She looked up. "Yeah?"

"Flower from heaven," he translated her name. It wasn't the first time she'd heard that line.

"My name is Siaki. Jack, if you want in English. Nice to meet you."

His sons, in yellow shirts and green shorts, peered from behind the eggplant bushes.

A puppy waddled over and flopped at Leilani's feet, tongue lolling, fleas crawling on its fur. She kept her hands at her sides.

Siaki disappeared down the back of the property, then returned with fire-roasted breadfruit. He tore it apart with his fingers and passed her a warm piece. The flesh was smoky and dense. He dipped his into a coconut shell filled with cream and tinned fish, then offered it across.

The boys hacked open coconuts with a machete, pushing the drinks toward their guests.

"I've been to NZ for rugby. Food here is better, I reckon," he said, as he tossed a chunk to the dog. "Natural, fresher."

Leilani agreed through a mouthful. Once coated in the fishy cream, the breadfruit tasted good, but it was still an unfamiliar taste.

The Chinese man returned at last. He sat across from them on a tree stump at the back of the house. He said something in Mandarin under his breath, then asked, "When bus is coming? I am going to Apia tomorrow."

Siaki shook his head, smiling at the idea of rushing anywhere. "Bus comes when it comes. Stay here tonight, no worries. Tomorrow, we figure it out. Nobody hurt you, okay."

"Thanks again," Leilani said. "It's not every day a girl crashes in the middle of nowhere and finds a good person willing to help."

Siaki looked surprised. "What are you talking about? This is paradise, Leilani!" He gestured to the towering palms, the wide-open spaces. "Simple life. People help here. This is how we survive."

She agreed to some extent. It was an agreeable change from the 1970s vibe of Apia.

Drifting in and out of conversation, her mind was full of Final Destination-type scenarios and hypotheses. The crash, the van driver, the deportees who had now driven away, there were too many red flags, the type she'd been taught to avoid in the Academy. The sooner she got to the church to meet the minister and his wife, who were hosting her, the better.

As the sun cast shadows across the clearing behind his home, Siaki's wife arrived with bingo papers and her blotter pen. She smiled at Leilani and the Chinaman, then disappeared into the house, yelling at her husband. The kids, emboldened by their mother's presence, moved closer to Leilani.

"You're like a movie star to them," Siaki explained, slapping one boy who got too close. "They think you a Palagi. White woman."

Leilani nodded, unsure if he was flirting with her. Finishing the last of her coconut, she stood and brushed dust off her shorts. "I reckon I'll get an early night. Not feeling hungry, just tired. See you in the morning."

Siaki nodded. "*Seki*. Sorry, my house, it's no good. Should be a mat and a pillow in there, kids will help you find it."

Inside, the concrete floor was covered with vinyl, ripped in the corner. Portraits of family members, decorated with artificial wreaths, hung on nails in the wall. There was only one bedroom, with a mattress. Hinges and splintered wood showed where the door had once been. The driver of their van was inside, lying on his back, chest still rising. His breathing was labored.

Out of sight and alone, Leilani tried the satellite phone. It was not right to leave an injured man in that state. Maybe she could get a doctor from the nearby clinic to come out. The driver's injuries were well beyond her paramedic abilities. The line crackled, but failed to connect to anyone.

She'd slept on the floor before during training, but not for a while. It took some getting used to again. An hour later, a burning sensation in her legs woke her. It was not muscle cramps.

"What the hell!" Leilani jumped up in shock from the mat she'd been sleeping on, smacking her thigh.

A golden-brown centipede, as wide and long as a school ruler, crawled down her calf and tried to escape to safety underneath a pillow. The segments of its hard, jointed body shone as though freshly varnished. The oldest boy, half asleep after finishing his homework, reacted in seconds to her scream, slicing the visitor in half with a machete. Using the flat side of the blade, he gathered up the halves, still writhing. Outside, the moving pieces were tipped into residual embers of a coconut husk fire. Leilani followed from a distance, watching. The centipede sizzled as it was cremated, air bubbles escaping from between armored plates, withering down to ash.

"Akoloa," said an elderly woman now sitting beside the fire, whom she guessed was Sione's mother. "Centipede".

"Not good. Maybe you die." Her expression was deadpan.

Among the hundreds of charred coconuts surrounding the open island-style kitchen, Leilani noticed empty sun-bleached *Tridacna* shells, over three feet wide. Giant clams, a protected species. Siaki mistook her shocked expression for trauma.

Sensing a drink might resolve the situation, he returned with more coconuts under his arm and half a bottle of Jack Daniels. He smashed the coconuts onto a metal spike driven into the ground, then stripped the husk away with his teeth, grinning through the effort. With the air still near ninety degrees, the cocktail was welcome. There was more liquid inside than she remembered from childhood holidays in Fiji and Hawai'i.

"Cigarette?" the Chinese man enquired from the shadows, where he'd been sitting, brooding.

Siaki checked his watch.

"Sold out now. For sure."

The man spat audibly on the ground in the dark, disappointed.

As Siaki bent over to stoke the dying fire with more husks, flashes of light caught the necklace he wore. Natural cord, adorned with a shark's tooth that would've fit in Leilani's hand. Unblemished, porcelain-white. Older teeth yellowed over time. The rooster comb shape gave it away. There was no other shark it could've come from than a tiger. Another protected species in Samoan waters. She knew she was right, but decided against asking questions this early on.

The family prayed together before the meal. Leilani bowed her head, trying to follow along but unable to keep pace. When the prayer ended, Siaki served boiled corned beef over white rice. Overhead, fruit bats stirred, rising from the trees where they'd slept through the day, their black shapes silhouetted against an evening sky.

A lavalava sarong was placed in Leilani's hands by the old woman. She'd seen men and women wearing them everywhere since arriving. The material was lightweight, cotton soft against her legs. She thanked the woman and walked away from the glow of the fire to tie it over her bike shorts. Siaki smirked. His mother was only offering the clothing because she considered Leilani's tight shorts to be immodest in the presence of strangers.

The local store was closed, but as a host, Siaki was well prepared. He set down a pallet of beer before the group. 7 percent alcohol. He offered a quart bottle to both guests. Leilani took one, always thirsty in the heat and keen not to test the water out. As she drank, the best comparison she could think of was warm methylated spirits or petrol. Even though she had no idea what either of those liquids tasted like.

"Good try," the big man said when he noticed she was wearing the lavalava.

"Huh?" Leilani asked, confused.

"Men tie in front. Women to the side," he said. The darkness spared her embarrassment. Her mother should've told her that. Maybe her father too, since he still kept a few lavalavas at home. Mostly for the memories.

After sharing stories for a while, Leilani went inside. The old woman had retired earlier, asleep on the low-framed corner bed. Beside her on the floor were her grandchildren, all sharing one pillow. Leilani felt safe with the family around, despite the open sides of the house and grunting of amorous pigs outside. The deportees next door had not returned.

Ten minutes later he stumbled in. "Lani, my friend. Your bus leaves early tomorrow, so I go fishing. No bus on Sunday, tomorrow is your last chance," he slurred to no-one in particular. There was a clatter as he knocked over an empty Vailima bottle with a glowing red mosquito coil affixed to the top.

Six bottles of strong beer had caught up with him. From her mat, eyes half-shut, Leilani watched as he flicked on the naked bulb in his room. Its light fell across the blood-stained mattress. He stared for a moment, then collapsed onto it, drunk and oblivious. The van driver was gone.

Chapter 3

The rooster's crow woke Leilani up long before the bus was due. The radio was on, but no one appeared to be inside the house. A whole fried fish was beside her sleeping mat, along with a banana, and hot chocolate.

She looked through glass shutters with dead flies on them. Everyone was already on the move, even the neighbors.

Fixing her messy hair in a broken shard of mirror, she re-tied her lavalava, then took breakfast out back. No-one was waiting around. The early sun felt replenishing after the trauma of yesterday. Ripping apart the fish with her hands as locals did, Leilani realized her host must've gone fishing during the night, as he'd said he would. Sure enough, his pole-spear and mask were drying on the roof of the outhouse. *Hell of an effort for a man who was drunk after midnight.*

The hot chocolate was unlike any she'd had before. The gritty drink had a kick to it, like dark chocolate. But any potential health benefits of the plantation-grown cocoa were canceled when the diabetes-inducing sugar rush hit her. A family-sized, dented metal pot in the outdoor kitchen was available for refills.

She felt uncomfortable standing around while everyone was completing chores. She knew this was standard from Polynesian girls at school, their busy lives full of responsibility and obligation, but Jake had never made her do much at home. He preferred to hire a housekeeper. Walking around the side of the house, she found women sweeping fallen leaves away, but they refused to accept help.

Leilani felt a wave of relief when the bus finally pulled up, an hour later than scheduled. The old vehicle, splashed with every color imaginable, was hard to miss. If you didn't see it coming, you'd hear it coming, the music so loud she found it hard to think. All the windows were open. She wondered if they could shut when the rain came. Unlikely. Looking around the property, she tried to locate the family to say goodbye and thank them for their hospitality.

The young boys were working with their grandmother and mother, all bent over a mountain of laundry. Wet clothes hung on a line strung across from the bathroom to the house. Nearby, the curly-haired baby was enjoying herself in the sun, giggling as she chased bubbles of laundry liquid, chickens darting out of the way.

Siaki was inside an acre of taro plants, his bulk hidden from view as he tended to his plantation. The leaves created a curtain that shielded him from the sun. He noticed the bus and waved from a distance before wiping sweat from his face with his singlet. He returned to digging, preparing for the next planting cycle. Leilani waved back before stepping onto the bus, ready for the last leg of her journey to the coast.

"Morning, are you going past the Mormon church, to Sapunaoa?" Leilani asked the driver, handing over ten dollars. There was no indication of what the fare should be, but he wasn't offering change.

Relaxed behind the wheel, the man wore an All Blacks t-shirt stretched to the point of ripping. His lavalava looked at risk of becoming tangled between the accelerator and brake. He'd been driving with bare feet.

"No, we not going there," the driver laughed. "But it's okay for me. I take you. Not too far. Everyone here, just go to the city."

The volume of the auto-tuned island music playing inside the vehicle made it hard to understand him. Walking down the aisle between some of the widest women she'd seen in her life, Leilani tried to forget the headlines. ***SAMOAN BUS DRIVES OFF CLIFF, BUS WASHED AWAY BY RIVER, NO SURVIVORS***. She wondered how many more years the bus had left before it ended up in a scrapyard or abandoned on someone's front lawn.

There were a few bench seats available, with no one on them. No seatbelts, though. The bus wasn't full, which came as a relief. An older woman smiled from behind shopping bags, and Leilani smiled back. At the rear, three men winked. One patted his thigh in invitation, laughing too loudly when she ignored him and turned to face the window. Until the bus moved, inside was a cloying mixture of perspiration, perfume and cheap cologne.

There didn't appear to be any speed limit signage, but the driver was not taking any chances, moving along at a rate she was sure she could beat on a bicycle. They passed several more villages, then a calm lagoon came into sight, waves breaking far out on the reef. She spotted a gap, maybe natural, maybe cut by hand, where canoes could travel through safely. A dilapidated jetty stretched out into deep water. In view of the white stone church where Leilani would stay, the bus stopped, the idling engine coughing black smoke.

The obese driver turned around to look at Leilani, pointing toward the village.

"Sorry, my friend. Bus is not allowed in here. You have to walk."

People moved out of the way for Leilani to get off the bus, then helped to unload her four suitcases. An old Samoan man dressed for work also got off the bus. When the dust clouds disappeared, he was left spluttering, leaning over, hands on his knees.

"Excuse me, sir, are you okay? Did they leave without you?" Leilani asked, concerned. There was no way the bus driver would stop again if she tried to flag him down.

"Thank you, thank you. I'll be fine," the man said, brushing the dust from his pants. "You have enough to carry, young lady, don't worry about me. The bus comes again tomorrow, same as always." He smiled, genuinely wanting to help a foreigner in need.

He took two cases and dragged them across the clearing, wiry muscle flexing in his forearms. The bags jolted over the dirt, wheels bouncing, fragile camera gear clattering inside. Leilani followed close behind, pulling the rest, wondering if he was expecting a tip. *No, it would've been mentioned in her assignment notes.*

A heavyset, pale woman with rollers in her hair stood outside the church, arms folded. She snapped at the old man. He patted Leilani's shoulder, shook his head at the woman's rudeness, and began the long walk back toward his village along the roadside. If she'd had a car, she would've driven him herself.

The church that was to be her home for the coming months was near the ocean. A volcanic rock wall ran the length of the shore. On one side was a black sand beach; on the other side, the village. Lines of slender palms split the two like no-man's-land. The wall, she guessed, had been built to hold back storm surge, to protect against wave action. As in the last village, the settlement looked to be a semi-organized collective of concrete houses, well-planned gardens, palm-thatch huts, and overgrown plantations.

"Welcome to the islands," said the big woman, whom Leilani assumed must be the minister's wife. "Blessed to have you with us, Miss Brown. Perhaps we'll see you leading Bible study one night soon, God willing. My boys will take your bags."

She whistled, and two teens rushed over, trailing behind as the woman led the way through the grounds. Leilani offered to carry her own bags, or at least some of them, but the boys just smiled and shook their heads.

The woman casually mentioned that the church dated back to the early 1900s, once hosting German and New Zealand officials during wartime services. Looking at the building, it was hard to imagine. Whatever grandeur it had in the colonial era was long gone.

Across the road was a red corrugated-iron store. Outside, Chinese men sat at a table shaded by an umbrella, overalls peeled to the waist, boots caked in grime. Between pagers, bottles of rice wine, and cigarettes, they played cards, laughing and yelling at each other. Their white trucks were parked out front.

Leilani kept her eyes ahead, the men barely glancing at her. To the workers, she was just another village girl.

"It's not the Sheraton, but you have your own bathroom and lock on the door works," the minister's wife said, unlocking a sparse, white-tiled room. They entered the church accommodation from the outside. There was no decor other than an oil painting of Jesus and a single bed.

Leilani wondered how many people had declined the assignment before the Ocean Enforcement Agency had asked her. Older agents told stories of five-star hotels and private planes, butler service and champagne. Maybe they'd been joking, or those perks had been left in the days of James Bond.

"Hope I'm not inconveniencing any missionaries," Leilani said, thinking of something to break the awkward silence. The two women were shut in together; the boys waited outside the door.

"Unlikely," the woman said flatly. "You know, I have a strong feeling about this year. Better you finish what you came for before the winds arrive. Oh, and missionaries are still on the far side of the island, if you're that keen." The way she said it carried more judgment than hospitality.

Leilani had spent hours reviewing the Agency's cyclone-track charts; no storm had ever made landfall directly over the village. She had no time for local superstition.

"Here's your key. And remember, as I told your boss on the phone, when you are here, no men are allowed inside. This is a place of God."

"Right, thanks," Leilani replied, taking the key, waiting until the woman left. She took her time, scolding her sons first.

Eventually, the teenagers hauled the suitcases inside without making eye contact, then disappeared.

Left alone to unpack at last, Leilani sat on the bed, looking outside. The room had its own private entrance, a side door opening onto gardens full of pineapples in spiky crowns and clusters of green papaya, bending over. The ocean was mostly hidden, with only glimpses of blue showing through the palms. An electric purple butterfly flittered inside through the still-open door.

Watermarks scarred the walls of her room, paint stripped back to the coral composite beneath in places. She touched the bubbled, damaged surface. It wasn't hard to tell the sea had been inside, an uninvited guest of the church.

She pictured the tsunami wave, a wall of water tearing through, wooden pews rolling, villagers screaming. Her skin prickled with heat and fear. On the drive in, it had been hard to miss the blue sign, with its white arrow pointing uphill. She'd need to find out where to go, just in case.

Sand in the sheets would not have been a surprise, but the bed itself was beyond fault, clean resort-style linen and pillows awaiting her arrival. Above, a plastic fan rotated at a lazy pace, as if even the building was on island time. A Mormon edition Bible lay on the bedside table. Leilani wondered how different it was from the version she'd been forced to memorize verses from as a child.

There was no safe to store her passport and laptop in, but there was a small refrigerator, humming louder than it should've. Leilani enjoyed the rush of cold air that greeted her when she opened its door. Midday was beyond humid. Inside the fridge were the expected water bottles of accommodation worldwide. Not usually a fan of plastic, she felt an odd relief at the sight of the bottles. The travel forums had been clear; local tap water was crawling with giardia and campylobacter.

With an hour to kill before joining her hosts for lunch, Leilani locked the room and walked down to the beach for the first time, keeping a lookout for stray dogs. A massive cockroach scuttled to safety as she slid her jandals on outside the door. At the right angle, looking past a home that seemed abandoned, she could see boats being tied up at the end of the pier.

Fragments of coral, bleached of life, littered the wedge of black sand that she walked on. The rock wall she'd had to climb over had finger-like leaves growing inside its cracks that looked like aloe vera. Crabs darted into crevices once they felt her vibrations. Leilani closed her eyes and enjoyed the feeling of warmth that emanated from the

basalt rock on her face and body. The warm iron sand massaged her
bare feet. The ocean was like glass, a sea breeze yet to develop, the
surface only pierced by pinnacles of coral able to survive low tides.
Checking first for rays and stonefish, Leilani rolled her lavalava
up to the knees and walked into the shallows. There was almost no
difference. The saltwater was as warm as the air.

A green coconut rolled around at the waterline. Leilani jogged over
and picked it up. After an hour in the room's fridge, it could be good to
drink. She examined the exterior, rotating it. *Damn it, bloody pigs.* One
side had been ripped open. She threw it back into the ocean. If the pigs
had got in first, then it was no longer safe for human consumption.
That wisdom had come from her father when wild boars had destroyed
the sweet potato patch she'd planted back home.

For the first time since descending the face of the beach wall,
Leilani noticed a woman and children sitting together in the water,
eating something.

Minutes later, she could see the family had a palm-frond basket
sitting in the wet sand, wavelets flowing over the contents. Long,
purple-black spines jutted out through the sides at all angles. It had
to be some kind of sea urchin. Where Leilani was used to diving, the
smaller New Zealand species blanketed the rocks like a plague. Her
dad smashed dozens whenever they went under together, drawing
hungry fish in closer. Standing beside the family, the small children
giggled when the hem of her lavalava got wet. Unafraid to use her
knee as a board, their mother cracked the urchins open with the flat
side of a wood-handled machete.

"Try," the woman said, looking up from her task, offering half a
broken shell to Leilani. The children stared, waiting to see if she was
brave enough to try the local delicacy.

"Thanks, never tried this type," Leilani said, examining the watery
contents, careful not to get pricked.

"My husband, he get from out there," the woman said with pride,
pointing towards deeper waters. Close to the waves breaking on the
reef, Leilani could just make out a person in an outrigger canoe.

"You know, the hospital is so far. Please be careful. Eat like this,"
the mother instructed, concern in her voice. She scraped the orange
roe from inside with her fingers, avoiding touching the needle spines
or inadvertently eating the intestines and digestive tract. Then she
indicated for Leilani to copy her. With longer spines than the New

Zealand kina, it took some getting used to. The fresh taste made it worth the struggle, reminding her of the caviar Grandma had let her try at Christmas. Full of brine and creaminess.

Thanking the woman for the experience, Leilani promised her children chocolate and lollies the next time she saw them, then continued beachcombing. Checking her watch, she realized lunch would be ready, so retraced her steps along the beach. There were no footprints other than her own.

From the water's edge, she had a straight line of sight to the minister's house. He appeared to be a Celine Dion fan; the music carried from a mile away. One of the boys saw her looking up and gave a wave. Time to head back.

Halfway along the beach, something near the high-tide line made her stop. It was a plastic grocery bag, sun-damaged, encrusted, but still bearing the logo of a Singapore chain. She hated finding them here, in what was supposed to be paradise. Ocean currents had their way of transporting rubbish to all the untouched corners of the Pacific she'd been to.

Leilani knew better than most how the bags looked underwater, translucent white, pulsing like jellyfish. A turtle without human-level eyesight could easily mistake it for food. One meal, and the plastic would lodge inside, tricking the animal's stomach into thinking it was full. Starvation disguised as sustenance.

She pulled the bag out from where it had stuck, the surrounding sand like cement. Removing plastic from coastlines when she saw it was an impulse Leilani had no intention of controlling. Maybe it was full of trash, but the bio-fouled bag felt heavier than it should have. After having to brush away a writhing mat of sand-hoppers and tiny crabs, she pried it open. She gagged at the smell of rotten fish, caught by surprise.

Inside were half a dozen triangular shapes. They'd been in there for a while.

What looked like blood pooled at the bottom of the slimy bag. She reached inside, pulling out the first object she touched. It felt firm as rubber, lightweight. The skin was rough as sandpaper. Liquid dripped from its pink base, like a rare steak once cut into. There was no doubt in Leilani's mind. These were shark fins. The reason the Agency had sent her to the South Pacific. The tip-off had been right.

Chapter 4

The church room smelled like a tuna cannery. The shuttered windows were open, but even tropical flowers outside did nothing to mask the smell of decomposition.

Leilani had taken the shark fins from the beach, tucked under her shirt. They were evidence; she rationalized; it would've been unprofessional not to. They probably should've gone in the fridge overnight, though.

After washing each fin in the sink, wearing her blue gloves, she took a step back and took a deep breath. The bathroom looked like a scene from a 90s slasher film. All the fins were dorsal, the most valuable. She photographed each side, recording scars and nicks that could help with ID. Without DNA analysis, there was no way to make a case in court, but her gut told her they came from hammerheads. She took a scalpel from her kit, cut a circle of flesh from the largest fin, and slipped it into a zip-lock evidence bag. The skin was tough, the meat rubbery, even with a fresh blade. She wanted nothing more than to ship the sample to a lab in Australia or New Zealand, but in a village this remote, that was unlikely to happen anytime soon.

After an hour of scrubbing shark blood from the bench and sink, Leilani felt drawn back to the beach, like a killer returning to the scene. Anything to clear her head, to ease the anxiety twisting inside her. Maybe the breeze and sunlight would help dry the fins. Leaving them outside was not an option; birds or dogs would find them in minutes. Her hands ached, and vomit pressed at her throat. She needed to get out now. The smell was worse than tuna sandwiches left in the backseat of a hot car.

Perhaps the ocean would offer further explanation. She was tempted to get in the water, but her first dive could wait. A reef pass channel was draining hard with the tide, a wide ribbon of fast water cutting across the otherwise still lagoon, dragging debris and foam with it. One or two canoes were still out there. Locals dived in all conditions if they needed food, a more pressing reason than research.

A man broke the surface in the whitewater and looked her way as she sifted through coral and shell fragments with her toes. He carried a New Zealand-brand speargun in one hand and a parrotfish in the other. His old-style dive mask rested on his chest, the rubber strap looped around his neck. Ink covered the curve of his right bicep, Samoan patterns running up to the shoulder, shaped to the muscle. The lines were darker, sharper, than the faded tattoos on her father's arms. Done by a machine, not chisel or shark tooth. She judged him for it.

"What are you looking for?" the man asked, confident as he walked towards her. He'd noticed her eyes on his body. His accent differed from others she'd met, more Australian than Islander. Saltwater had curled his long black hair, reminding her of young Maui from the movie *Moana.* She'd loved that movie, the first time she'd seen someone like herself on a big screen.

"Just having a look around," Leilani said evasively. "Shouldn't kill parrotfish. They look after the reef."

The man looked at his fish, embarrassed. In death, its vivid green, yellow and blue had faded.

"Eh, you're right. I try not to, but food ain't easy to come by here," he said, extending his hand.

"Sione. My father is in charge here, high chief," he said, pointing beyond the village.

"You a missionary? Mormon?" Word must have traveled that a foreigner was staying in the church.

"Marine biologist. Here to study coral, climate change and all that. I'm Leilani, by the way," she said, careful not to give away too much.

"Husband waiting back in New Zealand?" He smiled, trying his luck. He'd assumed her nationality based on accent.

Leilani cracked a half-smile. Sione wasn't the first man to make a move on her, and he wouldn't be the last. From what she'd seen, unmarried women without children were hard to find on the island.

"I live with my dad, but I travel for work a lot these days," she continued with the ruse.

"I get it. Dad sent me to university in Melbourne. I graduated, but couldn't wait to come back, live a simple life. Plenty of work now, different from how I remember it. Cousins hit me up me about the tuna fishing. We get paid well; beats picking kiwifruit," Sione said.

Leilani was intrigued. Wages on the island lagged far behind Australia or New Zealand. Most families seemed to scrape by selling taro or reef fish, some dependent on money from overseas. Even that came at a cost: hours on a crowded bus into town, just to queue at Western Union. So why were these men on a higher rate?

"I work for the owners of the trade store, the red one," Sione said. He almost continued his sentence, then reconsidered. An educated man, he was aware their job descriptions had now crossed a line far past tuna fishing. He'd seen his father catch and cook sea turtles as a child, so was what he was doing any worse?

"They run a family fishing business," he said after an uncomfortable pause. "Got two longliners out there. They only hire from within the village, young guys. Anyone who lives here wants to work on those boats. We take shifts. End of the day, all comes down to money, I guess."

"Reckon they'd take me on?" Leilani asked, taking the initiative. She could read Sione's mind; he knew more than he was telling her. He could be a valuable asset to the investigation at a later date.

"No chance. But we're going out again on Thursday, I can ask?" he said.

It was obvious he was trying hard. The man was handsome, but it wouldn't work; their lifestyles and dreams were incompatible. And after what had happened to her mother, a relationship on the island was never going to happen.

"Um, we're having a celebration tonight to mark the start of the taro harvest," Sione continued. "You should come, meet everyone, have a feed, island-style. You'll hear us from the church."

"Thanks. I'll be there." The alternative was reading alone in her room, so the invitation was welcome. Any chance to blend into the community was a win, personally and professionally.

* * *

Sione was not lying. At 9 pm, someone plugged in a commercial speaker. Auto-tuned love songs thumped across the South Coast, the bass running through the sand.

Refreshed after a cold shower, Leilani chose casual attire for the evening: a black sleeveless blouse, a lavalava from the South Auckland markets, and comfortable jandals. Most of the men she spotted in the distance were barefoot, so she would fit right in. Dressed and ready, she followed the sound of voices and laughter toward the gathering.

The smell of a pig on the spit reached her before she could see it. It was small, only a juvenile, but the crackle of skin in the flames made her hungry. Not eating before coming out had been the right decision.

She'd let the minister and his wife know where was going, out of courtesy and safety.

She had a similar skin tone to women in the village, but Leilani felt out of place. She reminded herself she was here for work, not socialization. Sione was nowhere to be seen, despite promising he'd be there. Men and women moved around the fire, bodies moving to the music. It was a very family-friendly event, not like shed parties back home. A few people attempted to speak with her, pleased to have a visitor to their village. Though most knew only a few English sentences, their laughter and warm smiles conveyed a kindness Leilani appreciated. No wonder her father had overstayed in the country decades ago.

Not wanting to draw attention, she sat alone on the steps of a meeting house and drank from the warm beer bottle an elder had pressed into her hand. *The taste of Samoa*, according to the wet paper label on the glass. Knowing what she was in for this time, she tried to ignore the taste of petrol in her mouth. *Mojitos from a hotel would be great right about now,* she thought. Looking around before taking action, she tipped the bottle upside down, thinking no-one would see in the dark, when Sione appeared. Sitting down beside her on the steps, he avoided the pool of alcohol she'd made. He had no shirt on and a lavalava that looked shorter than usual, soaked in sweat or covered in baby oil. Without any context, it was hard to tell.

"Don't worry, I know the beer's not great," he laughed, looking at the wet sand. "Try this, promise it's better."

He passed over a paper plate overloaded with food, soaked with grease. Big chunks of pork with crispy skin lay beside cooked green bananas, covered in fresh coconut cream. Cheap sausages and a side of vermicelli noodles doused in soy, with fatty lamb and ginger completed the meal. She examined a piece of pork skin in her hand, turning it over. Even in the dim light, she could see dozens of singed, bristly hairs. The dogs could have it.

"I was hoping you'd come tonight. You look beautiful. So, ah, welcome to the village," Sione said, white teeth flashing in the firelight. His hair was tied back with a cowrie clasp, an unlit fire baton in his hand. He hadn't mentioned a performance. She caught envious stares from other women as the chief's son gave her all his attention.

"Thanks, appreciate the invite. You know, I've never seen a necklace like that," Leilani said, looking at his shining, broad chest.

Some men wore pigs-tooth necklaces, like she'd seen in Hawai'i, but Sione wore a shark's tooth. It looked like it came from a tiger shark. The shape was a giveaway to any marine scientist or fisheries official. She wondered if it was aligned with his status in the community, then remembered she'd seen another man wearing one.

Self-conscious, he held the tooth flat in his hand. They admired it together.

"A gift from my father, when I was young, after they cut my …" he said. She got the drift. To her trained eyes, the tooth looked fresh, not ten years old. So he was lying. She played along for the sake of the investigation..

"Please, Leilani, can you wait for me? I have to unload this truck," he said, jumping up to his feet mid-conversation.

A white ute, the same model she'd seen in the trade store carpark, rolled up in the dark, engine revving to draw notice. Several men drifted over. The driver stayed hidden, speaking through a half-lowered window. Leilani caught only the orange flare of his cigarette, never his face. From the tray, Sione and the other young men wrestled steel drums to the ground, two at a time, muscles straining. One after another disappeared beyond the edge of the firelight. When they came back, breathless, they blended back into the celebration, drinking and singing as if nothing had happened.

"Bringing in more beer," Sione explained as he returned to Leilani's side. "We go through a lot here".

"I can see," Leilani replied, with a hint of sarcasm. There was no way that had been beer. Beer was transported in trucks, on pallets, or in crates. She wondered if she'd watched a shark fin transfer in real time. Sione pulled her up by the hand for a dance. Concerned he might try to move in for a kiss, she sat back down and changed the topic.

"What kind of fish do you catch here?" She asked innocently, spearing another chunk of savory banana onto her plastic fork.

He paused, translating local names of the different species into English in his head.

"Mahi mahi, octopus, lobster, wahoo, tuna. Dive for sea cucumbers too. Most gets exported, some sold to the resorts and restaurants. Tourists love fresh fish."

Leilani nodded, still chewing. On the surface it sounded believable, a cover story rehearsed since day one. But Sione had slipped, dulled by drink. She'd already traced the trucks' plates to two offshore vessels licensed only for tuna. The mixed catch he described was a nonissue among the crew, but to her it was everything.

Talking about seafood made Leilani reminisce about fish and chips from home. Battered, never crumbed. She liked to bring her own catch in newspaper, for staff at the local takeaways to fry. It tasted better that way. Lemon pepper seasoning was a bonus, if they had it. She tried to eat only what she caught, but it was hard during the winter. Even if she ate calamari, she felt guilty, thinking about sea lions caught in the nets.

"You ever catch sharks?" Leilani asked an intoxicated Sione.

He looked taken aback, as if she'd asked where to buy meth in the village.

"Ahh, they take fish off the line. Can be a problem. Didn't you say you study coral?" Leilani knew he'd understood her question, but she held off on an interrogation. He might be a fisherman, but he wasn't an easy mark.

A woman approached, smiling at Leilani before murmuring an apology and leaning close to whisper in Sione's ear. A crescent of mother-of-pearl rested on a cord around her neck, catching the light against her modest dress. Lines traced her skin and silver threaded her hair, yet she wouldn't have been out of place on an old South Pacific postcard.

"Dad's not here tonight," Sione translated. "Mum says he'd like a meeting with you. How's tomorrow before lunch?"

"I'd love to," Leilani replied, as if meeting the head chief was optional. "Anyway, I better get back to the church. I wanna video call home. Couldn't find anywhere that sold SIM cards till now. Thanks for a great night. "

"You're gonna miss the fire dance, but it's all good. I understand," Sione said. The celebrations would go on without her.

He took Leilani's hand to make sure she made it safely through the village. At election time, they promised solar power, but it never came. Not one to fear the dark, she still appreciated his chivalry. Dogs barked and growled as they moved past, then settled when they saw who it was. Those who chose to make half-hearted lunges from the shadows ended up with a kick in the ribs and harsh words directed their way. After watching Leilani cross into the well-lit church grounds, Sione waved and went back to the party.

Across the road, she noticed a figure standing outside the trade store. A tall shape, inhaling from a pipe, mumbled as he moved amongst the shadows of palm trees dancing over the building. His gait was unsteady, but different from that of a drunk, as if he was recovering from a hip replacement or injury. As Leilani passed through the private side entrance to enter the church, she felt his eyes following her in the dark. This was the first time she'd felt unsafe since arriving in the village. The man ignored her 'good evening' and hawked onto the path opposite. Shaking, Leilani turned the key to her room as fast as she could, double-checking it was locked once inside.

Switching on the lights, she froze. The floor was wet; the curtains drawn tight. Someone had been in here. She checked her bags; they were untouched. Bottle of rum still on the countertop. Camera, laptop, passport, all in place. But the bathroom had been cleaned. Surfaces wiped to a shine. And all her shark fins were gone. She opened the cabinet drawers with trembling hands. Empty. The DNA samples she'd prepared so carefully had been taken.

Sitting down on the toilet seat lid, Leilani closed her eyes, running her hands through thick hair. She still had photos, but without hard evidence, early progress meant nothing. Rules of Evidence lectures played in her mind. *Where had she gone wrong?*

Checking her phone, she saw her dad hadn't been online for hours, but if her calculations were right, it was daytime in Hawaii. She selected the clearest images she'd taken of the detached fins and emailed them through to the boss. Cellphone signal was weak, but the photos went through. At least she'd confirmed the tip-off about the island. The Agency's investment in her assignment was worth it. Sharks were definitively being finned in local waters. Now, all she had to do was prove who was doing it.

Chapter 5

Loaded down with fresh catch, outrigger canoes were paddled into shore from beyond the reef, as Leilani's ancestors had done for generations. White-capped waves crashed onto the barrier of coral hidden beneath the surface, protecting the coast, offering a tranquil lagoon once they made it through the limestone pass. Threading the maze of hull-splitting coral was a feat only a local could achieve, she thought.

Her first sunrise in the village was as dramatic as she'd hoped, the sand still wet underfoot from the last high tide. Overhead, she could make out silhouette of frigatebirds against an orange sky. She'd seen the M shape of their wingspan in the tattoos of village men. The water barely rippled, with just a whisper of wind present.

The skiffs were still tied up at the end of the barnacled pier. She'd get closer at night, when fewer people were around. Shallow-hulled, built for minimal draft, the boats looked off balance with twin 120-horsepower outboards bolted to the stern. They'd be support craft, probably, ferrying crew and gear to the commercial boats offshore. There were at least two long liners anchored beyond the drop-off she could see in the distance. Allegedly chasing tuna, no doubt closer to shore than their permits allowed. Their flags of origin were too far away to identify, even with binoculars.

Looking to the sky, she saw blood-red blended with the orange-hued banks of cloud. She recalled her dad's words: "Red in the morning, shepherd's warning." If sailors' lore was right, incoming weather would bring storm clouds and rain. It could be awhile before the boats could go out again, but she'd monitor their movements, since Sione had shared an intention to fish.

She'd tried to call home, but the connection had cut out enough times to make even the most determined daughter give up. WhatsApp was no better. Considering father and daughter had spent months at sea on the family yacht since she was four years old, Leilani knew her father had faith in her ability to make good decisions, wherever she was. He'd understand the lack of contact. Walking the high tide line made her think of him. His work had taken him overseas for much of her teens, but they'd stayed close. No matter where they were, the beach walk came first, a tradition they'd started when she was a toddler. He had the photos to prove it. She'd never missed a morning, except during her time at the Academy.

"Leilani!"

Daydreams were interrupted by a man's voice. She looked up at the man-made rock wall above the beach. Sione was standing on the edge, looking down. He had a rugby league jersey on, with a lavalava wrapped around his waist, tied in front.

"Chief is ready to see you. He killed a pig too ..." he said, beckoning from a distance for her to climb up and join him.

"Help me take this apart first?" Leilani called out, kicking at a stack of driftwood and seaweed that had been assembled on the beach. The village council signage was clear: no unauthorized fires on the beach. It wasn't the rule breaking that bothered her, but the odor. The stench reminded her of the time a power cut back home had knocked out the freezer while she was camping up north. The lobsters had rotted, leaking through the trays; the smell taking days to clear. Here, purple blowflies sparkled in the sunlight, and biting sandflies swarmed the structure, thick in the still air. Something had been hidden underneath.

Sione hesitated, not wanting to get involved, but took off his jandals, jumped down and came to her aid. The wood was waterlogged and heavy. Leilani was right; this was a two-person job at least.

"Since when did you become the beach police?" he asked, pulling away another layer from the pile. The blowfly cloud rose, disturbed. Leilani pulled her singlet up over her face, only half hearing him.

He laughed at her, and their eyes met for a second, then both looked down, not acknowledging the moment.

Following her lead, Sione stripped off his shirt and tied it around his head, covering all but his eyes. Leilani had seen boys coming back from the plantation do the same, coconuts lashed to thick branches, shoulders burning. Anything for relief from the relentless Polynesian sun.

As debris was cleared aside and heavy sand brushed away, it became clear why locals had built the oceanside lean-to. It was a shallow grave. Partially buried beneath were malnourished bodies. Laid to rest side by side.

Decomposition was underway, with internal organs exposed beneath the flesh. Heaving with maggots and lice, at times it appeared the limbs were moving post death. Within the eye sockets of a fist-sized skull, Leilani watched several species of marine worm digesting soft tissue.

Crouching down, trying not to gag, she pried open the jaw of the body closest to her side, as if in the necropsy lab at university. Matted fur around the mouth felt greasy to the touch. The sharp, curved teeth were whitish, unaffected by the ravages of time and a nutritionally deficient island diet. Along the pink gum line, she noticed remnants of a meat she didn't recognize at first, stuck between the molars. A recent meal, dried, gummy and pale. It looked like sliced turkey, but that made no sense out here. She checked the other carcasses; all were the same.

It was hard to tell the breed, but they were juveniles. Volunteering at the SPCA back home had taught Leilani more than the basics. They looked like any other stray roaming the roads, barking at tourists and chasing cars.

Sione watched her, as if she were crazy for touching. He took a step back.

"Sorry," Leilani said under her breath, feeling guilty. More for the dogs' sake than his. It felt *tapu,* disturbing the resting place of any animal. Forbidden. They covered the site, packing it down with their feet, using seaweed to bind the sand, hoping the next tide would hide their interference.

"Better down here than in the village," Sione said after a while, leaning on his knees, out of breath.

"Some of the others are so desperate they'd dig these up and cannibalize them in a heartbeat. Even if they grew up next door to each other."

"Damn, it's too early in the morning for that," Leilani replied, feeling sick. As a biologist, she'd witnessed plenty of death, but so many young animals in one grave had taken her by surprise. She needed a cold shower, a minute to compose herself.

"Sorry, I thought it might've been something else," her voice trailed off as she caught herself. "Vitamin A poisoning for sure." *From eating toxic shark organs,* she wanted to add, but Sione was still to prove where his loyalties lay. He nodded as if he understood the cause of death.

"Anyway, we better get outta here." Leilani said, ending the uncomfortable moment.

Aware the chief had been waiting for longer than he was used to, she ran down to the water's edge to wash her hands in the bathwater-temperature ocean. The gritty sand worked as an exfoliant, but they still didn't feel clean.

Walking together through the village, Sione confessed something that had been weighing on his mind.

"I can't get you out on the fishing boats Lani, I tried, but Zhang said crew only. Sorry."

"All good, honestly. I appreciate the effort," she said with a smile. The answer was not a shock. She would've been more surprised if the captain *had* agreed.

"I'll make it up to you soon, promise. We can go out in my canoe. I wanna show you something. The Chinese would never have found fish without us. That's why they hire from within the village, I reckon."

Leilani was intrigued. He seemed conflicted, openly sharing insider information.

She'd suspected local involvement in the shark fin trade since day one on the island. The juxtaposition in wealth between those families who had members working on the tuna boats and those who didn't was jarring. Remittances could not be responsible for that alone. She pretended to play along in the role of a naïve PhD student.

"Yeah? Let's do it, never been in an outrigger before," Leilani lied. Sione looked amazed she'd accepted his offer. *Did she need to clarify that this was not a date?*

"Great, by the way, boss says he knows you," he continued, changing the topic nonchalantly. "Zhang, I mean."

Leilani stopped walking. *What the hell did he mean by that? Was the captain the man who'd been waiting for her after the feast?*

A circle of grandmothers sat in a hut by the dirt road, plant fiber in their hands. They paused their weaving, assuming an argument between lovers had spilled into their corner of the village. Drama beat social media every time. Sione waved and called a greeting. Leilani hesitated. She'd learned from experience it was often the people you least expected who played a part in trafficking.

"So Zhang knows me, what does that mean?" she pushed after an awkward silence.

His revelation made her head spin. Honolulu would need an update. *Surely the Chinese had not figured out the nature of her assignment after being in the country for a few days?* That was a record she'd rather not hold as a rookie agent.

"Don't worry about it; the man's not right in the head. One minute he's smoking his pipe, next he's throwing boys overboard to teach them how to swim. Makes them go all the way to shore too. He told us don't talk to you."

"It's best if you don't talk about this with the Chief," Sione cautioned.

"People you don't know yet are not your friend here."

Leilani nodded in understanding as they walked.

This was an unexpected development. The fishing crews assumed she was spying for the competition or worse. *Better than the truth, but at what risk?* She'd call the agency in the evening for guidance.

"Zhang ruined my brother's life," Sione shared, to Leilani's surprise. "Supplies him with, ah, we call it ice in Samoa. Dad wants to deal with it the island way, you know, but my grandma needs a hip replacement soon," he said.

His expression gave away his confusion: the money versus the situation his brother and other young deckhands faced. Now it made sense why he saw an ally in Leilani.

He led her off the main village road without a word. The path was unmarked. They walked a few hundred meters beneath coconut palms, then turned onto a narrow track that cut past a row of ramshackle homes, hidden from the road and buried in the rainforest.

After a while, Sione pointed to a vast cleared property ahead. The chief's land stretched for a mile in every direction, his white concrete house set in a valley of banana, taro, and cocoa. Mud-caked pigs roamed freely across the fields.

He looked down, avoiding eye contact, as they approached. A middle-aged man built like a rugby player was waiting for them in the shade of a concrete meeting house.

The open space was empty, other than plastic chairs and a table, well-suited for ceremony or business without distraction. A wet Land Rover Discovery was parked beside the main house. A high-school girl with oiled plaits washed her hands in a soapy bucket of water in front. Her shirt and lavalava soaked, she seemed exhausted from working in the morning heat but managed to smile for a visitor.

Removing his jandals, Sione entered the building via the front steps. Unsure of protocol, Leilani followed. Her mother had failed to teach her the customs of her islands as a child, which she'd resented from the day she'd arrived.

A red seed necklace marked the chief's status. He wore a formal black wrap and an open white shirt, his broad chest inked with faded lines that wrapped around his flanks and back. Even his navel carried ink. Leaning on a carved stick, he fixed on Leilani's green eyes, ignoring his son. His clean-shaven face was grave, his gaze edged with concern.

"This is not a tourist area, young lady; this is customary land," he started, in a deep, confident voice. "Private."

"If you're from the Ministry, then you know the process for speaking with *matai*," the chief said. His words carried a threat behind them. Leilani wondered if he'd been investigated before. The New Zealand accent was a surprise.

Sione stood to the side of their conversation, eyes averted. He seemed reluctant to come to her defense, scared of the older man.

"I'm not with the government, sir." Leilani hesitated, unsure if that was the right way to address a chief. "I'm a marine biologist. Here to study coral, sponsored by Auckland University." She stuck to the cover story. For a second, it felt like she was back in high school, standing in front of the principal after skipping class to go diving.

He said nothing, considering her argument.

"This is a beautiful property," she offered, hoping to ease the tension.

"My father's land, thank you," he said, softening. "Where are you staying? There's no hotel here."

"The Mormon church over there." Leilani nodded toward the ocean.

The chief chuckled, her interview apparently over. He seemed amused. When he grinned, she noticed a gold tooth.

"I haven't been inside that church in ten years. Be careful there," he said.

"I don't trust that minister's wife any more than I do the Chinese. She was raised in New Zealand, spent too much time around the natives."

"So then, you're not from here, from Samoa?" he clarified, taking in her broad nose, caramel skin, green eyes and waist-length Polynesian hair, frizzier than usual, thanks to the humidity of the tropics.

"Half-caste. NZ father, Samoan mother. She was born here, in this district, I think. Her last name was Sapunaoa?"

The chief seemed like he would have a heart attack when he heard her surname, as if he'd found a missing child. He looked at

his son, raising his eyebrows, seeking confirmation. Shaking his
head in disbelief, he conferred with Sione. The young man bowed
his head when he answered his father's questions. Leilani could not
understand the words, but she could tell Sione was in trouble. She felt
apprehensive; the big man's face was hard to read.

"Sapunaoa ay. I thought maybe you from one of those Apia
families. Mixed with German."

"No, sir. Fa,asu was my mother's name."

"Mmmm, *sa'o,* I knew your family well. Even your Kiwi father, he
was a builder back in those days, working on a hotel."

"Do you know why your mother left for New Zealand?" He paused
as Leilani shook her head, lost for words. Her father had been vague
about that part of the story.

"It was because of you," the chief said.

Leilani didn't know what to say, that she was responsible
for her mother's trauma had never crossed her mind. She tried
to hold back emotion in front of the chief, willing him to share
more family history she was hearing for the first time. *Never
show weakness to people you don't know,* she remembered her
instructor saying.

"Your mother was a teenager, a schoolgirl when they met.
Unmarried, pregnant to a white man twice her age. Her actions
brought shame to the village, her family. After that, your grandparents
didn't want to know her, or you." His voice changed as he recalled the
difficult episode from the past.

"But it was a different time. Now, most families would be pleased
if their daughter married a foreigner," he mused.

"Sir, is my mother still on the island?" She asked the old man, self-
control subdued by her desire to find out the truth. The tremor in her
voice was obvious, even to her.

Leilani's head ached. She needed a Xanax. In her imagination,
this conversation had ended with the head chief confessing his
involvement. No doubt his approval had been bought by the shark fin
traders, but his familiarity with her origin story had thrown her off.
He had no interest in talking about fishing or foreigners. Now that he
knew her identity, he wanted to talk about her.

She was unprepared. There was too much information to process
in one conversation. *How much had her father kept hidden? To protect
himself, or to protect her?*

The chief had not expected her direct question. He was used to controlling the narrative. Looking straight at her, he laid all his cards on the table. Leilani wasn't sure to take it as a threat or a sign that he was a fair man.

"I know where to find her. My son has been there too. It's a long way from here, but I'm sorry, I will not share village secrets with someone I don't know."

"That being said, Leilani, enjoy your time on our island. If you last a month, come back to me and we'll talk more," he said, as he ended the discussion by turning his back on her, retreating down the side of the home, to an outdoor kitchen where a pig was roasting on a spit. She was not invited to eat.

The aggressive humming of an electric fan made her look through the open front door as she made to leave. Several people slept on the floor in front. One of the younger men caught Leilani's eye and held her gaze, as if pleading for help. He looked familiar, nursing a bandaged leg with stitches across his forehead. It was the inexperienced driver who'd crashed on her first day. He rolled over, pretending to be asleep when the chief passed. A boy scared of his father's return.

Chapter 6

The canoe trip had been postponed to the following morning by mutual agreement. Leilani wasn't sure she could trust Sione anymore, but he deserved a chance to explain. And she missed being out on the ocean.

He was there at dawn as promised, standing in the shallows, hand on the canoe. The craft was a rough-hewn outrigger, lashed with coconut fiber, hardly seaworthy to her eye. A palm frond catch bag and coconut shell bailer lay in the stern. The same unchanged design his ancestors had taken across oceans.

The hull was carved for gliding across shallow coral-dominated waters. Naively, Leilani had expected a version of the modern, multi-person fiberglass canoes that surfed the waves of Waikiki to turn up. Years ago she'd been invited by a surfer who looked like Jason Momoa to join his paddling crew for a morning session, after already having spent the weekend diving with manta rays.

Other than a confirmation text that their planned trip was still going ahead, Sione and Leilani had not spoken since the encounter with his father, the village chief. That both men knew where her mother was and had kept it from her was difficult to push to the side.

Leilani had lost sleep over whether they meant her grave or that she was still alive. However, Sione was currently the only viable way to infiltrate the island fin trade. Alienating her best source of information would be career suicide. She took a deep breath and reminded herself – this was an OEA mission, not a family reunion.

It was said that locals held secrets of the island close to their hearts, maintaining sacred knowledge and methods for their own people. With that in mind, it seemed hard to believe that the environmental harmony their ancestors had maintained for centuries had been corrupted in less than a year by the prospect of fast cash in hand. There was more to this story, she felt.

Her assignment supervisor, Director Ventura, had not been as supportive in his last encrypted message as Leilani had hoped. There was no leeway given to first-assignment agents.

The opposition hadn't challenged her outright yet. Instead, they'd built a wall around her, locking her out while disregarding her capability, entrepreneurs playing poor in a developing nation.

The Asian man from the van crash had become her shadow. Each morning he trailed her down the beach, chain-smoking, eyes fixed, saying nothing.

He stood watching as she stepped into the hollowed canoe. It lurched under her weight, nearly capsizing before Sione steadied it and slid in. They paddled out, with the reef ahead. She turned her shoulders enough to see the minder light another cigarette, phone pressed to his ear, spitting in the sand. The canoe rocked again, and she was forced to look forward.

After thirty minutes of consistent paddling across the shallow lagoon, Sione passed the paddle backwards over his shoulder. Sweat and a crust of ocean salt blended together on his face and muscular torso. He was a big unit, but his puffing gave away how unfit he was.

"Your turn. Over there." He pointed towards the break in the reef. The swell was gentle; it seemed to be a good day to make a safe passage. Sione had been the one to insist they leave at dawn. Later in the day, he said, the wind and waves would build with the afternoon sea breeze. Leilani had no issues with an early start; this was his backyard, not hers.

She grabbed the shaft of the paddle, concentrating on making sure she had the curved side of the blade pulling water towards her side and not the flat side. The Hawaiians and Maoris had taught her well, although she still struggled with the rhythm when multiple people were paddling at once.

At ease after a while with the instability and movements of the canoe, muscle memory stepped in. The water felt easy under her blade. Six strokes on the right, then a smooth switch of the shaft between hands in front, and six strokes on the left, then back again. The pace became second nature. The *paopao* glided without resistance, responding to her every move.

As she paddled, Leilani's mind wandered to an intense dream tableau of a war canoe fleet chasing her, before the days of Christianity and colonization. Tattooed men with long flowing hair, armed with carved shark-tooth edged weapons, intent on capturing her to be a wife. The saltiness of the ocean snapped her back to reality as a wave sent drops of spray into her eyes and mouth.

"Hey, relax your shoulders; it's not a race." Sione advised, twisting around to observe her technique. He was impressed. Not only could she maintain a good pace, but very few of the village women would use the canoes at all. On the water, she seemed as natural as he was. In a way, she looked happier at sea than she was on the land.

Several kilometers offshore, they'd slipped through the intimidating reef passage without incident. There were no other vessels in sight other than the distant silhouette of another unknown ship sitting on the imaginary line where international waters began.

Sione was spending more and more time peering over the edge of the canoe as they traveled further offshore. The rising sun backlit the water, making it possible to see down through the transparent water column to the white sand seafloor 30 feet below. In contrast to the shallows in front of the village, there was no live coral out here, only a carpet of algae that smothered the aftermath of Cyclone Bola. Acres of smashed, bleached coral that could take generations to regenerate. Together they stared at the devastation below, saying nothing. Both ocean people, they needed no words.

Eventually, the canoe glided over bright, healthy spirals of coral. Sione raised his hand in the air, palm open, without saying a word. Leilani lifted her paddle out of the water and laid it across her knees. The canoe slowed itself down until it was near still in the swell. It was harder to balance when it wasn't moving. Sione looked at the land for a minute, then back down to the water.

"We're here," he said, looking back at the distant shore, then at Leilani. "Can you see your church?" he asked.

Leilani strained her eyes against the sun's reflection on the surface of the ocean, but could just make out the distinctive color of the village church. White coral stone set against a background of verdant green.

"Kind of. Why?"

"Line up the church on this side and the headland over there that kind of looks like a fish, then you know you're in the right place," he said confidently.

"What are we looking for?" Leilani asked.

"This," he said, pointing at a few barrels lashed together, ropes descending beneath. After a while, she realized it was anchored.

"This is where the Chinese make their money," Sione replied, without looking up at her.

"Without us, they'd still be diving for sea cucumbers."

He took a dozen gray mullet out of a woven bag in the canoe's stern and began hacking them up into chunks with his machete. He'd netted the fish in the mangroves before paddling along the coastline to collect Leilani. Rivulets of fish blood and entrails ran down the interior of the hull.

Pieces of oily fish were thrown overboard in every direction. As the current dispersed most of the meat, a thin rainbow film, like fuel leaking from a wrecked ship on the reef, extended for as far as they could see. In the right location, chumming the water was an effective way to draw in sharks. Leilani didn't necessarily agree with the practice, but diving operators did it all throughout the Caribbean. She could already see small fish darting out from under the shelter of the FAD.

Sione leaned forward to clean his greasy hands, rubbing them together over the port side of the canoe in the water. As he did so, the *ama* support lifted into the air. Leilani felt her sense of balance leave her body. Next thing she knew, she was plunged headfirst into the warm ocean.

The *ama* splashed back down, and the canoe remained upright, thanks to Sione's fast instincts. Acting from experience, he grabbed his paddle and extended it to Leilani. People always fell out during the annual outrigger races in Apia Harbor. She could smell the sun-warmed fish at water level and see pieces of bait bobbing around her.

"Not the best time to swim," he said, half seriously.

His expression revealed the balance of the situation Leilani faced, despite trying to keep the moment light. She freestyled over and grabbed the wooden blade, concerned about swimming in a bait ball. He pulled her closer, where she gripped onto the side of the canoe. The ocean remained calm, yet the sides of the hull were steep and buffed too smooth. An experienced spear fisher, she knew every splash, every movement she made underwater now they'd chummed the area increased her risk. Sione too was risking his career by taking her out here, exposing the waters he worked for a living. Leilani struggled to haul herself up. She was strong enough, but the sides were steeper than she was familiar with. A disturbing memory entered her mind – the time she'd watched a tiger shark crunch through the shell of a sea turtle like pork crackling during a training mission in Micronesia.

"I can't; it's too high," Leilani said, in between deep breaths. She tried again to use her fit upper body to pull herself over the side into the canoe, but the design made it difficult. Sione tried to pull her in, but when he shifted his weight, the canoe threatened to capsize. Both of them in the water would make the situation worse.

Eventually, he grasped Leilani under her armpits and hauled her upwards in one strong motion. All the sinew and veins in his biceps and shoulders popped under the strain. Lying horizontally across the long canoe, she carefully shuffled her legs inside and sat up. As she caught her breath, still in disbelief, water cascaded off her rash top and hair.

"Can we get on with this now?" Sione asked with a grin.

The words to a smart reply were on the tip of her tongue when he started slapping the surface of the water loudly with his flat paddle.

"Use your hands," he told her. Following his lead, Leilani began slapping the surface of the ocean with cupped hands. After a few minutes of disturbing the water, he stopped and slumped back into the canoe.

"Wait," he said, as Leilani looked down through the crystal clear water again, in expectation. As a freediver, sharks were nothing new to her, but this was the first time she'd voluntarily drawn them closer.

Thirty minutes later, the burly trail of fresh mullet in the lazy current worked its magic. Large dark silhouettes ascended to the surface in vast numbers. The instability of the canoe was once again at the forefront of her mind. Sione seemed bored, like it was just another day at sea.

At one point, there were ten adult tiger sharks beneath the hull. Given the clarity of the ocean, Leilani counted them through the water with ease. Black-and-white striped pilot fish swam below and to the side. At least a dozen bull and gray reef sharks sulked around the edges of the melee, barreling in at times, seeking an opportunity.

She imagined the fear of prisoners or captured warriors as they'd been thrown into the water here all those years ago. Being inside a traditional canoe above masses of predators felt different from being underwater, armed with a spear gun. Being onboard the million-dollar University research vessel and observing sharks was another experience altogether. Here, she felt vulnerable, but also natural. This was the most organic way to study sharks in nature she'd ever experienced, minus the ethically ambiguous practice of fish feeding.

Half of Leilani wanted to put her dive gear on and get back into the water with a camera. Shark diving had been part of the curriculum at the Academy. Not with baited sharks unfamiliar with humans in the water though. Aggregations of this size were uncommon, rarely documented. The footage would sell overnight. She reckoned National Geographic would buy it, or Discovery Channel for Shark Week.

Cruising back and forth, over and under each other, Leilani realized there were now layers of reef sharks below. The chunks of fish were long gone, but they had worked themselves into a frenzy. The surface of the water churned like wind against tide as dozens of dorsal fins and tails thrashed around. Once in a while, a worked-up tiger would collide forcefully with the hull, the blunt head creating panic as the canoe became unstable. Ever the waterman, Sione would adjust his weight when it happened, laughing at her fear.

"We used to feed them chickens. They love those," he said with a smile. He spoke as someone might when talking about their pet Labrador. Then, his expression changed. He looked down at the water, as if in shame. He couldn't make eye contact with Leilani or look at the sharks he loved as he spoke. His long tied-back hair covered part of his face when he bowed his head.

"It's not right what's happening here. Sharks are guardians. Our stories say they carry the spirits of warriors who have passed away. We never harmed them until now. Our people should not be lured with easy money. But it's so hard to say no. It's us that do the ugly work, but the Chinese make the real money," Sione explained.

The conflict of interest playing out in his head was clear in his voice. Not only was he exposing the fact that his community was complicit in shark finning operations, but admitting the shame that his people had let cash come before culture.

Leilani stayed silent, listening with respect. She could read between the lines. Not everyone involved in the wildlife trade was equally guilty.

"Maybe one day God will punish us for what we have done. We are gonna kill the reef that kept us alive for so long"

Leilani understood what he meant. It was a complicated situation. The villagers were not her primary suspects in the investigation. They were being exploited, willingly or not. She needed more evidence to ascertain the truth. Arresting taro farmers who'd been lured into crime would not stop the trade.

Sione shared more of his feelings about the subject. Samoan men were being used for local knowledge and labor; but it was the Chinese immigrants who had started the violence. It was their fault; he said. Until their arrival, there had been no value in killing sharks.

The meat tasted like ammonia if not prepared well. Even cats would sniff it, then refuse to eat, he claimed. The fish market in Apia would not accept sharks or their parts for sale, keen to avoid legal issues. The cartilaginous fins were worthless on the islands.

That was until entrepreneurs and exporters arrived, with a demanding, superstitious Asian market of billions waiting for fresh shark fins, delivered on ice from the exotic South Pacific. The source location increased the value of the fins as well, the region marketed as pristine to consumers who couldn't find the islands on a map if they tried.

The hottest time of the day came and went before Sione made the call to turn the canoe around and head back to shore.

"Go in front, but don't fall out again, okay?" he teased.

"From there, you should see the turtles before they see us."

Leilani agreed, eager to spot the first turtles of the day. Sharks were still milling around, but most had swum away to deeper waters as the sun rose higher in the sky.

As she made her way to the front of the canoe, her eyes scanned the horizon for any sign of movement on the surface. The lapping of waves against the hull as Sione's paddle dipped in and out of the water was the only sound as they glided across the lagoon towards the beach.

As if on cue, a table-sized green turtle gracefully propelled itself through the water beneath the canoe, its flippers moving in smooth, unhurried strokes. She'd seen hundreds over the years, but always felt a deep appreciation to witness an ancient creature in its natural element. Its shell reflected the dappled light above, a mosaic of greens, yellows and browns.

Near shore, more turtles circled the outrigger, surfacing, watching, then gone again. She wanted it to be from friendliness, but the scientist inside her knew it was curiosity, nothing more.

After they hit land, Sione lifted the *paopao* onto his shoulder and carried it up the beach face. Leilani walked behind, wondering if she should help, maybe carry half. He spoke to her without turning around, as if not looking at her made it easier to confess. "Lani, the fishing boats are going out tomorrow. Wish I could tell you when, but they're changing it up; we don't get told now until it's time to go. Try looking through the gap in the palms from your window; that's the path the crew takes."

Inwardly, Leilani congratulated herself. *Keep it up, Agent Brown.* She'd turned her first asset. In a way, he hadn't volunteered so much as given in, guilty about what he'd become involved in, and by the sight of his brother's future being stolen from him by criminal outsiders.

Chapter 7

The support boats still hadn't moved by late Thursday, their engines cold. Each hour that passed made Leilani more certain the fishermen were stalling for a reason.

She declined dinner with the minister's wife. If she were being watched, the men would head out while she was eating.

As Sione had guessed, one end of the pier could be seen at an angle through the slatted window, past the palms. Nothing was happening. Frustrated, she stepped back to give her strained eyes a rest, the first pulse of a dehydration headache throbbing. The local water was already turning her stomach.

The Agency was pressuring Leilani for an update. She considered the unthinkable. What if Sione had been compromised, the chief leaning on him? But if that were true, he'd never have led her where the lines were set, never spoken of what his ancestors had done there, of how resistance fighters had fed dead Tongan warriors to the masses of sharks. She forced the doubt down. No, he wasn't the problem; he was her Trojan horse.

Close to giving up on the solo stakeout, it was male voices that gave away the men as they were heading out. Footsteps followed, with laughter. In a village without traffic, nightclubs, or background noise, sound carried with unsettling clarity. Leilani froze up, then moved under the window. She'd kept the lights off inside. Peeking through the glass slats, she saw silhouettes of boats against the darkening sky. Friday evening, this was it. *Better late than never.*

Kept awake by a cheap energy drink she'd found in the store, Leilani had been expecting action. Sweating up a storm, she already wore her 3mm black wetsuit, including hood, to conceal her identity. She'd be in the water tonight.

She checked her agency phone. No GPS signal yet. Sione had agreed to plant a tracker on the longliner he was allocated to crew for. It would be awhile before the tracker would ping; the fishing vessels were far from shore.

Keen to gather intel before heading out on a small boat the Agency had arranged for her to use while in country, Leilani crept down to the water's edge undetected by the crew of rowdy men boarding the support vessels.

There was more chance of the nosy minister's wife catching her sneaking out at night from the church than these men noticing anything amiss. Evidently, drinking was the only thing to do whilst waiting for their shift to begin. Both Chinese and Samoan were spoken with no concern of being overheard. Some of the inebriated locals let out a loud cry of "CHEEEHOOOOOO", as if supporting a rugby game from the sidelines. Dogs barked in response from nearby, risking waking village elders not on the payroll. Leilani wondered what the captain would do then.

Hidden by thick rainforest that came down to the sand, she watched in shock as an annoyed captain pushed his way through the group of deckhands towards the individual he believed had led the chanting and forced a 9mm black Glock pistol into the back of his open mouth. With his other hand, he grabbed his hair and jolted the man's head back. The villager began shaking in fear, which made the captain laugh. This must be Zhang, Leilani thought. He'd clearly done the threatening act before and enjoyed the effect it had on his subordinates. The group was now silent. The captain paused for effect, staring at the shocked crew members, then holstered his weapon and continued preparing the fishing boat for departure as if nothing had happened. Leilani prayed Sione was among the men. In the dark, it was hard to make out faces.

With blinding spotlights on the bow unashamedly switched on, the boats were untied from their moorings and driven skillfully at 5 knots to the northeast, where Sione had paddled out to the day before. The skippers knew what they were doing, maintaining a slower speed to avoid collisions with hull-slicing coral heads. Operating at night made sense, from a criminal perspective and an ecological perspective. Under moonlight, sharks would hunt closer to the surface, harassing schools of feeding baitfish. The tuna heads on the longlines would prove irresistible.

Leilani waited until the boats were yellow dots in the dark, then began the walk along the beach, to where black sand gave way to a shallow river mouth, fresh water blending with salt. Only a single shack was built near the estuary banks, with no lights on. Thick mangroves choked the waterway, hiding her small, stripped-back, ex-Fisheries boat, tied up where it was meant to be, to a rotting jetty that looked like it had been around since German occupation of the island. The agency's partner organization had come through. Knee-deep in mud, harassed by swarms of invisible mosquitoes, she climbed over the side, relieved to see the keys in the ignition had not been taken.

The boats were out of sight, but Leilani set course in the same direction, the light of the full moon just sufficient to get out through the reef pass without issue. The tracker still had not been activated. Regardless of whether Sione delivered on his promise, she'd find the boats, having programmed the GPS position of the aggregations into her dive watch. The longlining captains were men of habit, usually setting the lines within a similar area, according to her informant.

She laid a shark prod down into the starboard side tray of the boat, where old rods, a gaff and a scratched measuring tape were already rattling around. The lightweight prod, designed to mirror the version made for cattle, remained charged and unused. For now. Nighttime on the reef had the potential to create life-threatening scenarios. 20,000 volts would deter an inquisitive large shark long enough to allow her to escape, without long-term harm to either player.

Intentionally strapped and hidden behind her right calf muscle was a dive knife, useful for cutting lines entangling marine mammals. Rolling inside the port-side trays was a red and white bottle, about a foot long. An emergency oxygen tank, for when her breath hold was not up to the task. This one Leilani *had* used. After every dive during Academy training, she would check the level as part of a list of safety checks burned into her memory. Being captured at the surface was as foolish as approaching an exploding harpoon head-on.

The tracker came to life with a soft ping. Leilani looked at her phone screen, one hand still steering the boat. She frowned. *Why were they not slowing down by now?* She could see the larger fishing boats on the horizon. They continued offshore at pace, well clear of coral and rocks. After a while, they killed the engines and rafted up beside the larger longliners, giving her time to catch up. Keeping the boat in neutral, approaching from behind but still far enough away to remain unseen, Leilani watched through thermal night-vision binoculars as the captains and crew climbed up rope ladders to board the rusted, commercial fishing vessels. Hydraulic winches were mounted on the stern decks, ready to haul in miles of line. The support skiffs were secured alongside the grey hull. There was movement on board both tuna ships, but they were not preparing to set the lines.

The larger of the two vessels was being loaded with large rice sacks, men forming a human chain from hold to hold. The bags were packed full; crew straining under the weight. As they worked, the drunken revelry of the wharf resumed, only interrupted by commands from Zhang, the tall captain overseeing the operation. His cigarette glowed yellow in the thermal imagery Leilani saw through her binoculars.

Far in the distance, floodlights were suddenly turned on, illuminating a Navy-sized ship against the night sky, waiting close to international waters, but certainly breaking the law by being inside Samoa's Exclusive Economic Zone without permission. Leilani's heart raced as she checked her location. 2am. Close to 12 nautical miles offshore.

This had to be a reefer. The ghost ships that transported illegal wildlife contraband around the world, never seen or caught. Most agents had never witnessed one, only followed paper trails. She'd heard the stories, the legends.

The lights were a signal; they were ready. The larger longliner, heavily laden with rice sacks, reversed from its embrace with its partner and motored out towards the reefer. Some men stayed onboard the smaller boat, but most were needed.

Leilani followed behind, thankful for her low profile in the water and that she'd checked the extra red plastic petrol tanks at the stern before heading out. This was a lot further offshore than she'd counted on.

After what felt like an hour of motoring across calm seas, the longliner pulled up short of the intimidating, grey steel fortress of a warship towering above. Through her binoculars, Leilani could make out human figures on board the ship at the gunwale, untangling what looked like a rope and pulley system.

From the shadows, she watched as thick rope dropped from the mothership's crane, swaying above the deckhands like an executioner's noose. One by one, heavy rice sacks were slung into a harness and winched up into the darkness, disappearing into the hold without a trace. No paperwork, no inspection. There was no doubt about what she was witnessing.

It took two men to throw the sacks into the sling. After they relaxed into a rhythm, a deckhand in jandals slipped. The sack rebounded back onto the longliner, where the fabric split. Coarse plastic weave ripped with a dry tearing sound, and a cascade of shark fins spilled out mid-air, curved and unmistakable. They bounced off the side of the longliner as they fell, some sinking, some recoverable, some drifting like fallen leaves, floating on the water.

The entire transaction took less than fifteen minutes before the lights were extinguished again, but Leilani could not lower the binoculars from her eyes. It was hard to process what she'd witnessed, only a few hours away from the nearest tourist resort. Her first mission under contract was testing her, as the Agency had promised it would. With the small boat bobbing on the surface of the ocean, she took a few long-range heat signature photographs and a short blurry video. The reefer was too far away to make out the name on the hull.

Ahead of the poachers on the return journey, close enough to see the village, Leilani realized the longliner was not taking the same path it had before. It was headed right for her at twice the speed. Free of its illegal cargo, the tuna vessel was lighter, covering ground at pace.

There was no choice, no other decision to make. If the crew spotted the boat and captured her, she'd never see her father again. The captain couldn't afford to let a witness live, not when exposure risked a multi-million-dollar operation with players stretching from Apia to Asia. She wouldn't make it back to shore; this was not a hostage scenario playing out.

Reaching beneath the side tray, she grabbed a cord she'd stashed earlier. Prepared for anything, one end was already tied off to a rusted D-ring welded to the inside of the transom. She looped the other end around her waist and cinched it tight with a quick-release knot, just enough to hold her position. Masked, she slipped silently overboard, letting the dark water swallow her. With luck, they'd speed past, never noticing the 15-foot boat drifting, abandoned miles from shore in the early hours of the morning.

* * *

The coral reef at night, lit by the new moon, contrasted in every way with the rainbow playground of daytime. With nothing to do but wait on the sea floor until the longliner passed overhead, Leilani took in her surroundings, slowing down her mind and body as she'd perfected, to conserve air.

Not only were the colors muted at this depth, but the entire reef had shifted into a different pace, one few tourists ever saw. White-tip reef sharks cruised in silence above the coral, then burst into motion like torpedoes, sending clouds of sand and debris spiraling upward as they struck. Leilani stayed still behind a fridge-sized brain coral. She watched the translucent tentacles of a thousand polyps reaching into the current, each one trying to snare something tiny and drifting.

Moray eels, thick as her calf muscle, slithered out from within the reef skeleton, unafraid. Without the heat generated by swimming, the lukewarm water at depth seeped into her core, and she was glad for the thin freediving wetsuit. Tourists came to the island for the bathwater warmth of the ocean all year round, but down here at night, it wasn't quite the same.

The reef itself was far from silent. The clicks of pistol shrimp hunting, the scraping of urchins mowing down fields of algae, the hushed crackle of life and death in motion. It was a brutal beauty, Leilani thought. A reminder that paradise wasn't always peaceful.

She waited to see white water, shadow overhead and the loud buzzing of the longliner's prop, but it never came.

Eventually, her lungs burned, signaling the need to surface. She kicked off from the sandy bottom with her fins, careful not to damage branches of decades-old coral around her, and ascended slowly. Getting the bends out here would mean death. Breaking the surface, she intentionally breathed in the warm night air with the control of an experienced diver. Within seconds her trained mind betrayed her surface protocol, racing to analyze the implications of what she'd witnessed offshore. The dive watch said she'd been underwater for 9 minutes. On a single breath hold, it had felt like forever. The emergency oxygen tank she'd left in the boat, an error of judgment made under pressure that could have had serious consequences. A mistake she would never make again.

The tuna vessels were long gone, anchored somewhere further down the coastline until their next trip. They must have changed direction. Leilani treaded water, scanning the horizon for any sign of the warship. By now it would be in international waters, on its way to Asia before returning to collect another shipment. There was nothing to see, only a smattering of stars above and the distant glow of one or two village lights.

The anchor rope to the boat had worked, but only because there was no swell. She'd got lucky. Climbing back onboard, fatigue settled into her muscles as the adrenaline of the dive ebbed. Soaking wet, she lay on the deck of the small boat on her back for a minute, re-adjusting. Hawaii would be online by now, expecting to hear about the night mission. She'd briefed the team earlier in the week. But first, she had to make absolutely certain she wasn't followed back to the mangroves. On such an exposed coastline, there were very few other places to hide a boat.

Driving into shore on autopilot, her mind went into overdrive. The mothership's involvement suggested China was turning a blind eye to what passed through its own ports. *No surprises there*. The reefer had emitted no sonar signature that Leilani could detect, and its AIS had been deliberately deactivated. Even the Agency struggled to track ghost ships like these. The shark finning captain and his officers weren't independent operators chasing profit in a developing nation, as she'd first believed. They were enforcers, following orders from marine crime lords hidden overseas or anchored in lawless waters. Leilani vowed to find that ship again. One day.

As she approached the river mouth, she killed the motor and let the boat drift forward at will for the last hundred feet towards the rotten wharf. As soon as she guessed her feet could touch the bottom, she jumped out and tied the boat securely back to its post. Even on windy days, the dense mangrove forest kept it safe, absorbing any wave impact. The ramshackle hut she'd seen before on the riverbank had a light on, but no one came outside.

She walked back along the tree line, above the beach, playing it safe. Dawn was underway, so she'd be seen down on the sand. The walk felt a lot longer this time around.

At the end of the pier, the support craft were already tied up as they had been the night before. They'd beaten her in. The crew had disappeared, leaving only two men standing, talking by the boats.

Hidden behind a wall of ocean-facing palm trees, Leilani located her binoculars. She didn't need the night mode on now. Engaged in hushed conversation, the men stood close together. One of the pair was clearly the bony Chinese operative, who she'd seen on the longliner during the night, Captain Zhang. The other appeared to be a Samoan, his broad back to her, with long hair tied back, exposing neck tattoos. Lip-reading had never been Leilani's forte, but body language said enough.

A plastic bag was handed to the bulky crew member, who opened it. He seemed frustrated with his employer. Hands still red with congealed shark blood, the man pulled out thick stacks of bills, bound with rubber bands, and counted. *Was this money all for him, or was he a delegate for the deckhands?* It was more than she'd ever seen in one place at the same time. Although the transaction took place at a distance, she was certain the notes were not Samoan tala. From the brief glance she got, it was obvious the designs and colors did not match. These looked like US dollars, greenbacks. The global currency of wildlife trafficking.

Chapter 8

Between daily freediving expeditions, part of her cover as a coral researcher, Leilani monitoredd expected the trade store. It gave her something to focus on, a way to maintain her sanity. The neighboring families had plenty to say about the Chinese owners, though sorting racism from fact proved more challenging than she'd anticipated. Everyone had a story, the truth buried beneath layers of rumor and jealousy.

The neighbor to the right, who seemed to spend most of her days in a rocking chair nursing babies that may or may not have been her own, claimed the CCTV camera mounted in the store's corner was a fake.

"There's no way that's real. I used to work in security, for the hotels in Apia. Maybe they used to make the kids think twice, you know." Not that any youth from the village were likely to steal. Leilani had winced as she'd watched how parents disciplined their children in the community.

For one of the most recent new builds in the area, the store's construction was subpar, even by village standards, built on leased customary land within a matter of weeks. Local builders hadn't asked questions, just pleased to get the work, paid in cash. Wooden shelves offered only imported tinned and dry goods, no better or worse than other stores nearby. Yet, refrigerated supplier trucks arrived every week, unusual for a business without a fridge or freezer. No fresh fish, no meat, no eggs, no vegetables.

Prices were set too high without reason. Leilani checked the other local stores to confirm. There could only be one reason they were pricing themselves out of the market. They didn't want many customers in there. It had to be a front. The store was their laundromat.

Inside, the place felt like a warehouse, with concrete floors and blank walls. No Coca-Cola posters or Bluebird chips advertisements. A plastic shower curtain, printed with red dragons, divided the public aisles from the modest living quarters in the back. Leilani had heard voices back there before; sometimes it sounded like an entire extended family was crammed into the space; other times, the store seemed to be run solely by a quiet, older man. Captain Zhang. Tall and serious, she recognized him as one captain involved in the midnight rendezvous.

The store made no effort to attract customers. Its one flourish
a dark-red exterior, a jarring paint choice in a village dominated
by cheerful blue and yellow houses surrounded by tropical flower
gardens. Corrugated iron roofing completed the cheap aesthetic, one
step up from palm thatch.

* * *

With no fishing boats heading out because of the forecast, Leilani
began to get in her head. Overthinking, replaying scenarios, missed
opportunities. There was no doubt in her mind that a full-scale illegal
wildlife trafficking operation was going on here under her eyes.

The team back in Hawaii were impressed with her baby steps.
Photos and videos she'd uploaded, when the Wi-Fi wasn't acting up,
were solid enough to build the framework of a case. The Agency had
already started drafting a report to the Samoan government, citing
irrefutable evidence of shark finning in the region. For now, it was
enough to keep the operation alive and its backers happy.

Bored and boxed in by the heat, she wanted caffeine. At this time
of day, Coke seemed like the only option. Better than nothing. The
man behind the till nodded as she entered, but did not smile. Inside, the
store felt more like a sauna than it should've, the owners too cheap to
install ceiling fans.

The shelves were stacked with overpriced, dented tins and
packets. She saw nothing on the shelf she wanted, other than some
dated Oreos. They crumbled inside the blue foil when she removed
them. Disappointed, she walked back down to the far end of the store,
intending to return the biscuits, when she heard angry, raised voices
inside the store. An argument between two men, from behind the
plastic curtain.

At first, Leilani assumed it was another tense argument between
the Captain and his son. At dinner, the minister's wife had admitted
the young man had come to her, wanting support to escape and to go
back to China to continue his university. Their screaming matches had
become a weekly fixture. Village women loved the drama, the obese
woman said between mouthfuls of home-fried chicken.

This argument sounded different, louder, like domestic violence.
Half-expecting a blade to be thrown, Leilani ducked behind a stack of
Weet-Bix cartons, watching through the gaps.

Zhang had stepped into the store. He was shouting in Mandarin, not caring who heard him. His face was pale, eyes bloodshot, pupils blown wide.

Meth, she thought. It was handed out like beer after a rugby game on the tuna boats, according to Sione and the crew.

Zhang wasn't alone. A second man stepped out from the back , younger, broader, with an air of authority. His eyes were bloodshot too, but not as bad. He wore white overalls streaked with grease and blood, unzipped to the chest. Sweat soaked his skin. The heat and the drugs weren't mixing well. When he spoke, his Mandarin sounded strained, like he was searching for the words, not a native-born speaker.

It was then that Leilani noticed his gun. The unmistakable outline of a semi- automatic handgun strapped to his waist, barely concealed under the overalls.

Remaining calm, she slipped into a freediver's mindset, total focus, measured breathing, and silence. No panic, only control. Authorized to carry a defensive weapon, of course, today of all days she'd left it behind.

The exchange was rapid-fire. She didn't understand a word. No cellphone signal meant no translation app, no backup, whatever that would have looked like. All she could tell was they were not arguing about corned beef on the shelves. The fury in their voices was at a level Leilani hadn't heard in years.

Eventually, after exiting the store in a huff and rummaging inside the cabin of his Ford truck, the visitor returned with a heavy package, swaddled in oil-soaked cloth. The size of a freshly slaughtered sheep, he carried it under one arm and then slammed it onto the countertop. Thick liquid seeped out, the color of canola oil. They exchanged a few more words, then he turned and walked out for the last time.

Leilani stayed in place, frozen, her heart hammering in her chest as his truck pulled away, its sides emblazoned with **"Cui Delivery Ltd",** a line of Chinese characters beneath. The tray of the vehicle was overloaded with green plastic barrels. She swallowed hard. Whatever was in that package, it was not food.

After the visitor left, the captain stared at the greasy bundle for a while, as if it were still alive. His bodyguard stood behind him, with arms crossed, observing in silence. First, the old man wiped away the excess liquid from the bench.

Leilani moved silently across the aisle and crouched behind a stack of tinned mackerel, close enough to catch the rancid stench coming off the package.

There was no risk of the captain spotting her; his eyes were clouded with untreated cataracts. The village women loved to argue about whether he was truly blind or just faking it. Either way, he could still steer a boat at night, half-drunk on homemade rice wine. The real threat was the man behind him. He was alert, and if she slipped up, he'd see her.

Zhang unwrapped the package fold by fold. The cloth was soaked through, stained like a newspaper that had fish and chips inside it.

The smell hit the room fast, warm tuna and mayonnaise. Leilani's stomach turned, but she held her breath, motionless, as if she were waiting on the seafloor for the perfect head shot on a big fish. Just as the last knot came loose, footsteps approached. The captain froze, dropped the cloth back over the package and stepped back.

A young Samoan woman entered the store, balancing a baby on one hip. Her child clutched a plastic bottle of milk, his chubby cheeks sweaty from the heat. The mother wore a dirty oversized t-shirt and a lavalava, bare feet sandy from the walk over. The captain leaned over the package to hide it from her line of sight. He forced a smile for his customer, an unnatural cheeriness that didn't suit his disposition.

"Talofa lava," Zhang said, proud of the few Samoan words he'd bothered to learn. "You need find something, I find ok?" he switched to English. She glanced at him and nodded.

Leilani had heard the village teenagers doing their best impressions of the man outside his store as they waited for the school bus. His language skills left a lot to be desired.

The young mother grabbed a packet of knockoff crème biscuits and a single Stayfree pad, the kind sold individually under the counter when they weren't supposed to be. She paid in coins, then hoisted the baby above her head and sniffed his nappy. Grimacing, she swore, blaming the child for the stench rising from somewhere behind the register.

The baby started wailing. Annoyed, she gathered her things and hurried out to the family van idling by the roadside. Her husband sat behind the wheel, four other kids squashed in the back without belts or car seats. As the van pulled away, the suspension groaned as tires dipped hard into muddy ruts gouged into the road outside the shop. Once his lone customer had disappeared, Zhang returned to the delivery.

Before revealing what was inside, he turned and spoke to the bodyguard behind him, who, with resentment showing on his face, retreated to give the Captain privacy.

Underneath lay a slick mass of raw flesh, glistening tissue the length of an adult's arm and as thick as a thigh. The organ was lobed, as if it were an oversized human kidney, its unwashed surface creamy brown and streaked with blood like a placenta.

Zhang cut into it, checking inside as if it were rare steak. The knife sliced cleanly into the rubbery mass, yellow droplets of oil oozing out, trickling down the side like sticky tears.

Initially at a total loss, Leilani now realized what was going on. The grotesque organ in front of her was a shark liver; so the oil had to be squalene, used in cosmetic and pharmaceutical products worldwide.

Given the size of the organ, she guessed it had been cut from a tiger shark or an oceanic whitetip. The shark would have been gutted alive, its belly slashed open from gills to caudal fin. To the untrained eye, the bleeding mass was a horrible sight, but nothing more than dog food at best. To those in the know, the liver was a hidden prize, an unlikely treasure coveted in Asian markets. Not as valuable as fins, but a profitable side hustle.

She calculated the illicit profit in front of her. Assuming the black market rate of $150-$200 per liter held steady, there was at least 45,000 US dollars' worth of squalene seeping out on the countertop, and the ageing captain knew it. He also knew as well as Leilani did that to get that price, he'd need to have somewhere local to process the squalene before export. Raw, the oil was worth much less. The powerful odor now dominated the small store, a nauseating mix of rancid fat, rotten fish and ammonia that even a hardened slaughterhouse worker would have struggled with. Leilani wondered if he knew he was running out of time to make maximum profit. As a biologist with years of experience in the fisheries lab, she recognized the telltale smell of degradation. The liver was on borrowed time already, internal fat and proteins breaking down in the heat.

She thought about the delivery man. This was not a fishing trophy – it had to be a subliminal order from those who ran the industry. With more shipments these days being intercepted by Customs, maybe the holds full of shark fins were not as profitable as they used to be. The organization was trying something new, adding value to their illegal activity by cutting out the livers of sharks they'd finned.

Commercially, it made sense. Maximum profit, minimal risk. *Where were they processing the* oil, *though? It had to be local, even with refrigeration. Squalene doesn't last that long,* she considered.

The captain punched a few numbers into his calculator and jotted them down in a ledger. Then he barked something to his crew, his voice rough from years of chain-smoking, likely telling them to get the liver out of sight before anyone else walked in.

From there, the organ was loaded into the back of a truck and driven away. To where, she had no idea. But it needed to be purified soon, refined to a clearer, more valuable state. Once natural impurities were removed, the shelf life and market value would skyrocket.

DIY purification in the village seemed easier, but without industrial-grade equipment required like a centrifuge, the Captain would get a product unfit for sale. Involving a third party seemed to be his only workable option.

More men emerged from the back room as the captain addressed his team, ordering them to follow the cargo in the other vehicles. The protection detail seemed more appropriate for gold than raw shark liver, but he was taking no chances on a new opportunity, not on the first delivery.

The distraction gave Leilani the break she needed to slip out unseen.

Once out in the clean air, she breathed in and pushed her hair back from her eyes, heartbeat winding down as she walked along the quiet dirt road as if nothing was out of the ordinary. "Ska lolly," the voice of a child who had been hiding behind a tree broke her train of thought.

She laughed, her eyes still adjusting to the brightness outside the store. The boy was confident and smelled of soap. Chubby girls in handmade Samoan-designed dresses stood beside him, looking grumpy. They had been wanting to go into the store to buy boiled sweets, but the loud arguments had scared them away, they explained to Leilani. She noticed there were no adults with them, only the diseased family dog that loped a long way behind.

"Sorry, I didn't see you guys before. Share with your sisters as well, okay?" she said, handing over a handful of Eclipse mints from the metal container in her pocket. The kids seemed pleased with the trade-off. The store didn't sell mints; these were from NZ. There was no way Leilani was walking back inside to buy lollipops.

For the next few days, while strong winds kept the fishing vessels anchored offshore, Leilani stayed close to the church grounds. With little else to do and no sign of movement on the water, she day slept, something she'd never done until seeing the locals do it, air thick with humidity and clouds of kamikaze sandflies rising outside the grated window. A brave few somehow made it through the mesh to the inside.

When the tropical temperatures became unbearable, she moved to the open-sided fale nearby, where the occasional breeze passed through and cooled her damp skin. From there, lying on her front on the rough-hewn wooden floor with a pillow, she watched village life move at its slow, predictable pace, children hauling buckets of water, women scrubbing laundry, the distant buzz of chainsaws, falling coconuts or hedge trimmers being used around the church gardens. She kept a low profile, conserving energy, waiting. The lull in action would be temporary; it always was.

The minister's wife was relentless, coercing her into attending Sunday service. It was a condition of the room, the heavy-set woman insisted, no exceptions. She would knock early, uninvited, standing in the doorway with arms folded over her enormous bosom, blocking any excuse before it was spoken. "We all make sacrifices, Miss Brown," she'd say, as if dragging a stranger to church was some shared burden. Declining did not seem like an option.

Reluctantly, Leilani gave in and sat through a sermon, unable to grasp most of the biblical concepts in Samoan, but enjoyed the schoolgirl choir. She tried to focus on the music, on the harmony of their voices, but the reading of individual donations, each family's contribution announced with reverence by the minister, even the shameful zero tala, annoyed her. It had been years since she'd set foot in a church, and now she remembered why.

A light-skinned chief from another political district in formal attire introduced himself to Leilani after the service outside, his smile kind. He told her the sermon's focus had been on honoring one's parents. She'd understood that much on her own. Although they spoke about her research, Leilani felt his sermon translation was deliberate, as if he knew her origin story. Maybe he'd even known her mother. He was of a similar age to the local leaders, after all. His subtle dig aggravated her, but she tried not to let it show.

The Agency was a family now too, but Leilani missed both her parents more than she was willing to admit. Her father, Jake, had always been her closest friend, the person she could rely on without question. Three months on his own in Pakiri... she wondered if he'd kept up their ritual of early morning beachcombing. He was probably sitting on the deck right now with a beer in hand, reviewing the building plans for his next project. Hopefully, he'd still be in NZ when she returned. With the entire village asleep on Sunday afternoon after lunch, she typed up her latest report for the Agency, keeping her distance from the red store but never losing sight of it. The routine was tiring, but necessary. Familiar faces like Sione and the injured van driver teenager, came and went from the store, oblivious to her covert surveillance.

She photographed men she'd seen on the fishing boats, open envelopes stuffed with cash, right outside the store as they smoked and chatted. She wondered how much the men were paid to make it worth it. By now, all the deckhands knew they'd not been hired to catch tuna, as originally promised. Ignorance was no longer a plausible excuse.

There was one question on her mind at all times: *when would the boats next head out?* If she could catch the fishermen in the act, fins on deck, everything documented, it could be enough to shut the operation down there and then. Local police and fisheries squads, already briefed and working with the OEA, would have no choice but to move.

Until then, Leilani had nothing to do but wait. The forecast looked good. Lighter winds, no swell. The boats would go out soon enough. Baited lines would go down, and she'd be ready to catch them.

Chapter 9

Every day, Leilani looked for a way in. Into the community, into their world, inside their heads. Small talk with fishermen, conversations with women searching the reef flats for shellfish at low tide, anything or anyone that might lead to a break in the case.

Her window was closing. In a few months, cyclone season would shut everything down, boat trips, longlines, finning. She had to move before that happened.

She had the training. In science, law, fieldwork, she could hold her own underwater or in a courtroom. But nothing at the Academy had prepared her for what was to come; she could feel it.

Her friend in neuroscience alleged there was a point where the human brain would decide enough was enough, death, corruption, blackmail, environmental destruction, silence where there should've been life. Older agents had stories. Not everyone completed their first assignment. She imagined the embarrassment of handing over the gold badge upon returning to headquarters.

That would not be her. She'd rather go home in a body bag than quit.

The fishing crews had become acquaintances, no longer seeing her as a threat; just another researcher, another foreigner at work. She spent hours with them and their families, sipping sugary tea in open-sided fales, playing cards, learning and listening.

It was challenging to convey the risk the commercial fishermen presented to the village - to taro farmers, stay at-home mothers, mechanics, painters, builders and security guards. Hardworking men and women who were not involved in the fishing industry.

"Long term, no sharks means less fish," Leilani explained. "Bigger fish, *gatala, lupo,* they take over. Eating all the fish that scrape algae off the reef. Without those cleaners, the coral suffocates and dies. Eventually, the whole reef turns into a mat of green slime and bare rock."

She paused, letting it sink in. "After that, everything leaves. Nothing left to hunt."

After translation, faces changed. No one had ever explained it in terms they understood before. She stopped just short of accusing their chiefs of being on the take. Having the community turning against her was not an option this early in a mission.

Although they were complicit in the finning, spending time with the men and their families gave Leilani an understanding of why they continued to work on the tuna boats. The hardships here confronted her every time she visited. Inconsistent supply of unclean water. Regular power cuts. One meal a day for some families. Fish and taro, or white rice.

Family members of all ages slept side by side on mats on the floor. Outdoor bathrooms came with resident cockroaches below and rats above. Floods of silt in the cyclone season killed seedling taro plantations they'd invested weeks into planting. There was no government support other than a stipend for pensioners that barely kept starvation at bay. On this side of the island, time and life moved at its own pace, dictated by tides and storms, crop cycles and the size of the fish on the spear. But in recent times, there had been a change.

It didn't happen overnight. The shark fin trade arrived without causing a scene, like everything else foreign that eventually took hold in the islands, a new offer that promised more than any sermon ever had.

Cash was hard to come by in Samoa. Businessmen pulling the strings of the operation were counting on that. Wages hadn't moved in decades, sitting between desperation and survival. The newcomers had done their research, figuring out exactly how little it took to get results.

Families here were under pressure. School fees, power bills, water tanks sitting dry because the account had lapsed. Remittances came in, but they didn't stretch far. The village was cracking, and the traffickers had timed it perfectly.

International non-profits – analyzing data from afar – reclassified the level of threat the fin trade posed to Samoa's biodiversity and food security as in the red zone. There was no category more concerning.

The trade arrived via Asia, establishing itself within the community like Covid. High school students dreamed of being recruited onto Chinese fishing vessels. Several parents Leilani had spoken to privately supported these plans. Killing sharks, although it went against centuries of tradition, would keep their younger brothers and sisters' stomachs full at night. Pay for nappies, bus trips to the city, funeral contributions as the older generation slowly passed on. Those who remembered the days of living in harmony with nature.

Over more cups of tea, both men and women shared hard times with Leilani: days when swells were too rough for the canoes, when rain ruined the taro, when there wasn't enough to feed the family. Bank loans from Apia kept growing, and no one could see a way out. Those who had been selected for fruit picking in NZ and Australia were lucky, they said.

Far from the sleepy island constabulary Leilani had originally assumed she would find – police didn't ask questions. They came in Ford Rangers, taking away loan defaulters, tracking them down even without street names or numbers. Bail was too expensive. Extended family stood back, watching, smoking, saying little. They would wait until relatives overseas stepped in. Sometimes social services would turn up months later, forcing children to live with aunts and uncles.

It sounded crazy when she considered the thought, but the attraction of shark finning as a viable career was making sense to Leilani. If there was any chance of stopping the trade, there had to be an alternative option for these men. None of them would voluntarily return to working the land for half as much cash.

According to those she'd spoken to, everything changed the day Captain Zhang arrived via cargo ship from Shanghai, China.

Sione had confided in Leilani. After a few too many beers ashore after setting the lines one night, some officers had eased up. They'd come to know the local crew well. Many were of similar ages. Without their boss around, they weren't all ice cold. They liked Sione because he spoke English, whereas the other Samoan deckhands had only a few phrases between them.

According to the men's' tales – Zhang had been moonlighting as a wildlife trafficker during his Navy years, when he was caught with forty Asiatic black bear paws in the back of an old refrigerated van. Packed between boxes of frozen squid and soft-shell crab, all bound for the Vietnam border. At 90 degrees outside at a truck stop, the heat had been his downfall. One of the freezer units had failed. There had been no way to mask the stench at short notice. That and a rookie customs officer who'd refused a cash bribe and insisted on opening all the crates to prove his ability.

Following precedent in the courts, as China pretended to be on side with Western nations, Zhang should've been imprisoned for a decade. Instead, he vanished from the mainland. When he returned, his back was never the same. The pain hit him so hard some days that he passed out. Hard liquor helped to heal his body and his mind.

There was no trial, no press release. Only a silent discharge from the navy and a sealed internal memo. Someone high in the Chinese Communist Party, family maybe, had made a few calls and cleaned it up.

The man came back months later wearing civilian clothes and working for a company no one had heard of, or was supposed to have heard of. A private seafood export firm with government ties and no online presence. Orders were completed through the encrypted app, WeChat.

He never talked about what had happened. But rumors followed him in Asia, like a bloodstain that wouldn't wash out, so he'd agreed to leave. Sent to an island he'd never thought of.

In Samoa, most of the crew kept their distance, even his countrymen. The deckhands followed orders to avoid consequences but never looked him in the eye. On the surface level, Chinese officers showed him respect, but they watched their backs when he walked past. Men under his command in the Solomon Islands had disappeared before, a story well known in the fishing industry, shared from port to port.

Zhang never smiled and usually drank alone, sipping his whisky straight whilst sitting on the concrete step outside the red store in the evenings he wasn't out fishing. He spent too much time on his black satellite phone. On the island, he was the industry's top man. The man who made decisions, enforced discipline, kept the locals in line. Chinese longliners throughout the South Pacific answered to him, along with others in senior operational leadership. Processors on the island would open or close facilities based on his texts, or his mood. But Zhang still answered to a higher power, cold, hard millionaires living beyond the reaches of Interpol or the OEA who moved product by the ton.

Under the captain, local operations ran with military efficiency. No missed opportunities, no loose ends. In truth, he was not respected by his men; they lived in fear of him. Coming from China, they knew more than the locals did of his past. They had a right to be scared.

Amongst themselves, the Samoans called him '*Aitu*-the ghost'. Because of his habit of appearing out of nowhere, soundless on the steel decks of the ships, catching deckhands off-guard during smoke breaks or leaning too long on a rail staring at the ocean. Sometimes he would yell abuse and spit in rage, but most days he would cuff them on the back of the head and move on. In recent years the drug use had caught up with him, ravaging his faculties. He was an unstable man on the best of days.

In reality, Zhang was more than a ship's captain or an overseer; he was Beijing's insurance policy. A smooth operative placed in the South Pacific to remind the locals that the CCP was always watching. His naval pedigree was window dressing. What counted was his unwavering loyalty and the Party's determination to claim the Pacific piece by piece. Shark fins were just the entrée.

* * *

There was no direct evidence, but Leilani was under the firm impression that chiefs of the village council had been bribed. She fought the impulse not to return to to talk to Sione's father, the paramount chief, but one month had not passed. She needed him on her side.

It would have been a verbal agreement, she imagined, between Zhang and the men who controlled the area. Cash changed hands, a generator arrived for the church, a few school-leavers were offered jobs at a processing plant. That was all it took.

It was unlikely all of the chiefs had agreed, but they didn't need to. Majority consensus ruled. No meetings, no *fono,* only a shift in what they tolerated . When questions came from outside agencies in Apia, the chiefs defended the foreigners. Said they were here for tuna, providing employment for locals. Their permits were in order, as were their work visas. The village had no issues with support boats entering the customary inshore zone.

Leilani had witnessed bribery before, during her internship at CITES, Convention for the Trade in Endangered Species. Bribes came in the form of a truckload of roofing iron, a scholarship to university in Beijing, a pig delivered before Sunday. But it always bought the same thing: silence.

Inside 1 nautical mile were customary waters. The tuna vessels weren't fishing inside this zone, but the support boats currently tied up to the pier crossed this imaginary line every night they went out, weighed down with local crew to reach the longliners anchored offshore in domestic waters. Those old boats were not intended to act as liveaboards for months at a time for a dozen men. A skeleton watch crew on rotation remained offshore.

Approval from the council was the last green light Zhang needed, in addition to his commercial tuna fishing permits that had been simple enough to procure from the Ministry of Fisheries and Agriculture office in Apia. There, cash under the table had avoided questions around the vessels' flag state of Vanuatu, a country no one on board had ever been to.

Most of the local men had signed on believing the job was tuna fishing, legal, steady, no questions. They knew tuna well, strong fish that hit hard and ran fast. They sold as as they were caught, from outrigger canoes, trolling bright plastic lures in the wake. Some days on a homemade handline and a prayer.

Expectations of the deckhands changed as fast as fish came aboard the longliners at night. By the time the men realized they would be finning sharks alive, the lines had been set and retrieved, the hooks baited with fish heads and the money and drugs were beginning to flow.

The money wasn't life-changing, but it was enough. A few hundred dollars here and there, always in cash, no paper trail. Not enough to fix everything, but enough to make a difference. More than they'd been making selling taro.

At first, some of the locals tried to back out, including Sione and his younger brother. Zhang made it clear that wasn't an option. Ordering the full crew to watch, as a show of force two armed officers stripped a shaking man to his underwear and pinned him down on the deck, face pressed into the wet metal, while another man kneeled on his back and slid a used needle into his inner elbow. The rocking of the vessel meant he missed the vein on the first try. The officers acted in silence, leaving the man alone and sobbing in the rain once they'd finished urinating on him. His colleagues were forced to walk away from the scene and return to baiting hooks at gunpoint.

No one asked to leave the boats after that.

In denial and morally conflicted, fishermen tried to change the narrative, explaining to Leilani they were the ones benefiting from the relationship. Only Sione told her the truth, his allegiance to no-one, horrified at what he and his brother been subjected to onboard. In a moment of honesty, he confessed to wishing he'd never returned from

Australia. His brother hadn't even wanted to come back, he'd been doing well at high school.

The men focused on the positive because they had to. It was more money than they were used to, paid every fortnight at the red store in cash, no ID required. An easy win, but they didn't control the boats or set the rules. And they couldn't walk away.

* * *

She'd had no intention of bringing up old memories. But there it was, tucked inside her A4 notebook on the table, a wallet-sized album Jake had recovered after her mother disappeared. The only piece of home Leilani carried on every trip. It'd been months since she'd looked through it.

As she sifted through the faded Polaroids, her eyes welled up. There was her mother, curly black hair oiled and plaited, standing barefoot on a palm-fringed beach, maybe even the same stretch she'd walked earlier that morning.

The woman in the photo looked so much like the memories Leilani had. A shade duskier, a little broader in the shoulders, with a softer face and a flatter nose. She was taller than she remembered. There was no shame yet on her mother's face. No reason to leave.

She ran her thumb across a torn edge of the photo, taking it out of the plastic sleeve. Her mother had been the village's best swimmer once, or so Jake said. At a time when most women in the village didn't know how to swim, she used to race boys across the lagoon and win, wearing a t-shirt and shorts. Could dive deeper than anyone too, he'd said. Bring back huge clams from the reef for dinner, carrying them underwater in her arms, like the legendary warriors of Hawai'i. *Guess it sometimes is really nature over nurture*, Leilani thought ironically.

It wasn't hard to imagine her mother laughing, standing waist-deep in the clear water, before it all went bad. Before the pregnancy. Before she'd been told to leave, to hide her growing stomach, forced to raise a child between two worlds.

Now, all these years later, her daughter had come back on assignment at random. Maybe there was a chance to fix something here.

She resolved to follow up with Sione now they were back on good terms. He knew where her mother was, or at least where her grave was. The Ocean Enforcement Agency had added him to the payroll as an undercover informant, off the books for now, on Leilani's word alone.

He wasn't cleared for enforcement work, only intelligence. Vessel movements. Crew changes. Names. Times. Dates. He sent encrypted GPS pins from his phone when the AIS was turned off, enough to track the longliners' patterns without tipping off Zhang's officers.

Leilani trusted Sione, but believed he was holding back. Whether it was out of fear, guilt, or loyalty to the crew, she wasn't sure yet. But he'd seen more than he admitted, for sure. And when the next move was made, she needed to know. The only crack in her confidence was his father. To say he was a complicated man was an understatement.

No matter how hard she'd tried to keep it professional, the secondment to Samoa had become personal. She accepted that. Maybe Director Ventura and the Agency team had seen it coming, how her connection to the land and culture would turn into leverage.

Protecting these waters felt like more than policy. It was her responsibility, she realized. Her ancestors had caught fish here, raised families here by the ocean.

Her mother had left the village in fear and shame, carrying her inside. Now, all these years later, there was an opportunity to bring something back. To restore honor to the Sapunaoa family name.

A text pinged, coming through from a blocked number. She wiped away tears of emotion and checked the phone screen. Only two bars of 3G signal were showing.

'Lines set and baited. 12 HOUR SOAK. wait BEFORE HEADING OUT. You know where.'

Chapter 10

Leilani needed exercise, and the church room was too hot to work in, so she walked the beach. The sea was wild again, green and foamy, early warnings of cyclone season. Diving was off the cards but at least the sea state kept the shark-finning boats at anchor.

Waves crashed against the black sand, throwing the scent of decomposition into the air, assaulting the senses. *Probably another dog that's been shot,* she thought.

She was wrong. Right on the waterline, below beach-cast seaweed, embedded in the sand, was a massive 24-foot carcass, unmistakably a female tiger shark. *Galeocerdo cuvieri.* Not what she'd expected to find on a last-minute evening walk. Theoretically found in these waters, a tiger was an uncommon sight around the island. Most inshore fishermen would never have seen one from their outrigger canoes.

Others had arrived first. A pack of dogs, all inbred, skin and bone. She hurled clamshells and handfuls of white coral fragments at the animals that had beaten her to the scene, trying to drive them off. They snarled and snapped aggressively at her, considering whether to attack, wolves sizing up a lamb separated from the flock. Leilani stood her ground, advancing a few steps towards them, yelling as the men in the village had taught her. This was a standoff she had been actively trying to avoid since arrival.

The dogs formed a circle around her, forgetting about the shark carcass. When she bent over to pick up a heavy rock, the leader of the pack lunged forward; she'd broken eye contact. Yellowed fangs passed close enough by her ear in a blur of movement for her to smell the rotten, warm breath of the dog. It missed and grabbed a mouthful of hair in its jaws instead, yanking her down to the wet sand by the roots. Her head burned as if she'd been scalped, her heart palpitating, beating in overdrive. Once her back was flat on the ground, the pack advanced with confidence, hissing and barking. They were close enough for her to see fleas riding on matted fur coats, bones and ribcages sticking out through the skin, saliva dripping from open jaws. Out of options, her hand reached for her dive knife.

When it seemed as if she were going to be the first foreigner eaten by dogs on the island, a gunshot rang out across the coastline. Loud and ear-splitting, a bang like a firecracker. The animals whimpered,

high-pitched and afraid, scampering into the bush, abandoning
their meal.

Still sitting on the sand, in disbelief, Leilani brushed herself off and
looked around. An old man standing outside a hut looking at the ocean
waved to her, a sawn-off shotgun in his other hand. He'd been on his
way to dispatch pigs for an upcoming weekend celebration. Amazed at
his timing, she waved back to her savior.

At that moment, she cursed the dogs, wishing they'd eaten the
shark. If they ate the wrong parts, they'd die from toxicity, like the
ones she'd found buried beneath the sand before. Blowflies were thick,
loud, unrelenting. Birds and ants wouldn't be far behind.

She hoped locals wouldn't find the meat, or give it to their
children, but knew better. At least the next high tide would take it
away, continuing the cycle of life.

Shark meat was a valuable protein. Someone would take it. Slice
it thin or smoke it. Bury it overnight in a charcoal fire pit. Early onset
decomposition would not put them off; Leilani had seen these men eat
raw fish from the canoe without even an iki spike to the head. Tiger
shark would at least be a change from tinned mackerel. She tried her
best not to judge, having never experienced real hunger.

There was mercury, ammonia, toxins concentrated in dominant
predators with health repercussions. She could warn them about
parasite risk, share stories of salmonella, slow gut rot from bad
flesh. But it wouldn't change anything. She knew Māori back home
who still smoked and ate bronze whalers when they got tangled in
mullet set nets.

The health directive needed to come from a chief, from someone
with respect in the community. It wasn't her place to say anything.

When it came down to it, in choosing between a shark carcass on
the beach and an empty dinner table, she knew which option most
people would choose. They would be unlucky to die, but pregnant
women eating the rotten meat risked miscarriage, and children could
end up in the hospital on IV fluids. It was unwise.

The box-shaped head remained intact. Jaws engineered to crush
turtle shells and bone would be cut out and stolen. Undamaged,
they sold well on the dark web, on the black market to collectors.
One beady eye stared skyward, fixed as if mid-attack. The body was
bloated with gas, dead one or two days. Its skin had turned duller than
in life, trademark dark stripes along its flanks faded. The underside

was smooth and snow white, counter-shaded to blend into the surface sunlight when viewed by prey from below.

All fins were gone. Given the size of her, traffickers were in line to make a lot of blood money.

Her prized dorsal. Her smaller second dorsal. Her broad pectorals used for steering. The pelvic fins. The powerful twin-lobed tail sliced clean off. This shark had been butchered, and not skillfully. Likely with a dull machete or hacksaw.

By now, the fresh fins would be in the hold of tuna vessels, or transferred across to the spacious, refrigerated hold of the mysterious reefer ship, waiting near international waters with its AIS switched off. Ready to unload at Asian ports, and then return for the next shipment.

Leilani wondered how many more of these disturbing scenes of mutilation would be found around the island in coming weeks. The resorts were so close to here. She wanted to set up a tip line where concerned members of the public called in, reporting what they found. That tactic had worked well during her research years in New Zealand, when she needed to know where the orca were. But it wouldn't work here; the all-seeing shark finning industry would shut down citizen vigilantism on the island within a day. Allegedly, corruption on the island ran deep. Maybe the shark-tooth necklaces she'd seen on the men came from these washed-up bodies. Somehow she doubted it.

She nudged the waterlogged carcass with her jandal. Without fins, it rolled enough to show her the liver was gone too, ripped out through an open cavity now occupied by a carpet of heaving, creamy maggots. Perhaps this was the unfortunate shark that had donated the organ Zhang had been so proud to show off to his officers inside the store.

Leilani crouched beside the bloated body, the volcanic black sand harsh beneath her bare knees. *Where were cargo pants when she needed them?* A grey-white Pacific reef heron descended from a nearby branch, landing near the corpse in a flurry of loud wingbeats. It watched her work with one eye, waiting its turn. It would ignore the tough skin and meat, preferring to spear with its sharp bill insects and larvae that burrowed within machete wounds.

She snapped high-definition photos from multiple angles as she'd been taught during practical sessions, head, pectorals, the exposed cavity where the liver had been taken. Each photograph could end up as an exhibit in court. Not for her own records, it was evidence. She reached into her field kit, pulled out a sterile swab, and worked quickly to collect tissue and blood residue from a jagged cut near the pectoral base. DNA samples, contamination-limited and time stamped. Once locals arrived, as they always did, the crime scene would be compromised.

If the body had been washed up on a beach back home, the Department of Conservation would have put yellow hazard tape around the scene by now, as if it were a murder. An overzealous staff member in a khaki polar fleece with a clipboard would stay by the site as long as he could, keeping dogs, children and seagulls away. Local tribes would've made a claim for the teeth, claiming cultural significance. If they felt like it, they'd try to close the beach for a while, say a few prayers. Leilani got along well with the natives but had no time for anything spiritual. She'd made that clear over the years, despite losing work relationships and opportunities because of her stance. For larger sharks, like the great white, local media back home would try to get a report into the newspaper, winding up public hysteria. Even more so in summer, when everyone was in the water. She hated the media too, another unpopular opinion that made her less welcome in certain scientific circles.

The remains of this specific shark, however, were significant. The finless body was confirmation of the shark fin trade's existence in the South Pacific, evidence of what was happening only a few miles offshore. Close enough for tourists at Saletoga Sands resort to watch from their balconies, if they had night-vision binoculars. Leilani really hoped they didn't. *This island needs all the tourists it can get,* she thought.

It was only the second tiger she'd ever seen. The first had been in South Carolina, years ago, during school holidays. Her womanising uncle had been invited to a game fishing tournament by a high school buddy who'd done well in cryptocurrency. He had the flashy boat, but needed a crew. The tournament had been a loud event where drunk, overweight, white American men in wraparound sunglasses and tight rash shirts dragged dying sharks up onto the back deck of luxury sport launches for prize money and social media clout.

There'd been next to no catch-and-release, mostly weigh-ins. A strong rope was looped around the shark's tail, then the crane lifted it slow and swinging into the air, blood still dripping, cameras and cellphones flashing. Tigers, hammerheads, makos. Blues had been thrown back, dead. She remembered trucks with lifted suspensions

displaying the Confederate flag in the rear window and men firing
bullets at the sky that night after winning the giant cheque. She'd
been too young, hadn't known what to expect. In retrospect, it was
unbelievable there hadn't been an age limit. The reality had been a
wake-up call to the cruelty and waste of humanity. Never again.

Village fishermen had different reasons for killing sharks, more
valid ones, but financial pressure had led them down a dangerous path.
They'd made a deal with the devil, and now the price was being paid
in more than just the blood of sharks.

Leilani recalled a case study from her marine biology lectures that
had never left her: **a shipwreck has more biodiversity than a reef
with no sharks**. After a while, there'd be no point in even trolling
a lure. Remove apex predators, and the whole system collapses.
Scientists had proven it; elders had seen it happen within their lifetimes.

She wanted to tell the village the truth, that their reefs were on the
edge of collapse and illegal fishing vessels were raping their traditional
waters. But one dead shark does not equate to ecological meltdown.
It would take time. She wasn't ready to make her case yet, and locals
weren't ready to listen. She needed more.

After finishing documenting the shark's body, she heard footsteps
behind her. She turned, expecting to see one of the Chinese traders
holding a knife towards her throat, but it was Sione. They hadn't
spoken for a few days, since he'd found out they were cousins and
romance was off the table. He walked towards the deceased shark,
looking it over.

"South coast reefs will die if this continues," Leilani said, admiring
the beauty of the animal too, even in death. The solid, thick build and
length gave away her gender.

"You check the lines?" Sione asked.

"Tried to, but tides were wrong. Thanks for the tip anyway. Boat
was stuck in the mud."

Sione grinned at the mental image of Leilani knee-deep in clinging
mangrove mud. Clouds of droning metallic blowflies arose from
inside the body cavity of the shark when he jumped back to avoid an
incoming wave set.

He ran his hands through long wavy hair like a nervous habit,
unable to keep his eyes off the mutilated remains of the tiger shark. It
was as if seeing the deckhand's work in the light of day was different
from at night, when it felt like they were just doing their job.

"My crew's on again tomorrow, maybe the night after," he volunteered, clearing his conscience and earning his informant money at the same time. "Always at midnight. You know where the lines are."

Leilani thumped him on the back as she did with old friends. His admission was valuable. He was earning his keep, as hoped.

Sione sensed she was still uneasy about something. For a man of ambiguous morals, he was good at knowing when people were having a hard time.

"I'm on your side, Lani. You know that, right?"

She nodded. He lowered his voice.

"Truthfully, we had no idea they'd stay this long. Samoa has a long coastline. We thought they'd move on after one season."

A pause. Then:

"I don't know if anyone told you, but not all the village council supports the Chinese. Some chiefs feel they were tricked. Used."

He glanced toward the pier, functional but in need of repair from years of cyclone action. Transport boats were tied up to the post at the end.

"We need to get the members to revoke their consent for the Chinese to be here. Until that happens, I doubt the authorities will step in. They'll say it's a village matter. Internal, to be handled by the council."

He met her eyes, noticing for the first time the jade-green sparkle when the light hit them.

"Trust me, as the son of a high chief, I've heard it all before."

"I believe you, mate. Relax. And what about Zhang?" Leilani pushed, curious to know what the captain made of her.

"The captain? Drunk half the time, barely knows what island he's on. Thinks you're too young to be a threat for now. Sometimes reckons you work for the opposition, whoever that is."

Sione laughed at her mock horror and wandered down to the shallow water to pee, adjusting his lavalava around his waist. They were the only two people on the entire beach.

Leilani knew local fishermen had been sold a lie. Once the localized shark aggregations were fished down, their bright future wouldn't be looking so flash.

A surge of impulsivity rose in her chest, hot and electric. Her vigilante side. But she forced it down, remembering her training. Strategy first, then action. Hotheaded actions would only result in jail time. The police were onboard with her assignment, supportive even, but there were still limitations.

She turned to continue talking to Sione about the tiger shark, but he was already gone, thirty feet offshore in the clear water. His lavalava and jandals lay on the sand.

"Don't you know sharks hunt in the evening?" She called out, teasing him.

From a distance, it looked like he was pointing back towards the low rock wall that overlooked the beach. Leilani spun around to see a line of cute preschool-age children standing barefoot on the warm rocks, staring at the dead shark. Some of the younger ones were wearing only nappies. They seemed afraid to come down onto the sand, concerned that the shark would come back to life and bite them.

She beckoned to the group, wishing they'd come over. She wanted them to feel the skin, open the mouth to see the teeth, run their fingers over the gills, talk about what had happened, why the shark had washed up here. Teaching the next generation to love and respect the ocean, to understand shark biology and the marine environment, was a blessing she took whenever she had the chance.

* * *

Chapter 11

Sione's confirmation that the men would be finning again set everything in motion. There'd been other nights, but weather patterns had been unstable. Relayed by satellite phone to Hawaii, the suggestion of an active sting to be undertaken that night reached the top brass fast. The young man's tip-off was believable. He was embedded in the trade, racked with guilt for involving his brother and going against the ways of his ancestors.

The Agency gave the green light. Senior officials had seen enough to confirm the existence of illegal activity in Samoan waters. The tiger shark carcass further supported the narrative. In the early hours of the morning, before daylight, they would move. There was no time to fly in a backup squad.

Director Ventura would rely on the Samoan maritime police and Fisheries Department. These were the men and women who had first reached out to the OEA, asking for help to expose the operation. Captain Sina Leua had been on the phone in Apia for over an hour. She assured the director her team was ready. The trap was set, GPS coordinates had been shared. Leilani knew her role inside out.

The investigation moved faster than she'd expected. A video call came in at 4PM, as agreed. Inside the room, the video feed was blurry, but voices came through clear enough.

Ventura wasted no time; his orders were direct. He wanted Leilani in the water first. The plan was straightforward: once the longlines were hauled in and finning began, she'd trigger the silent alarm via phone. Deckhands would be too busy manhandling sharks that came aboard and sorting through bycatch to notice any distraction. Although they were not the targets of the operation, it was too risky to warn them.

Captain Sina's voice cut in from Apia with an update. Maritime police and Fisheries were standing by in the next bay over. The moment Leilani sent the signal, they'd move in, fast and unannounced in the dark, from all angles, surrounding the long liners.

In theory, the plan was a strong one. But as everyone involved in the sting was aware, under pressure even the best strategies have a way of coming undone.

The humid evening dragged on. Leilani watched the clock, counting down to 2am. This time, she'd get there first. By 1am, she expected to see spotlights racing through the dark as they sped toward their submerged catch.

* * *

The water felt colder at night. The marine scientist in her knew that wasn't really true. At tropical latitudes, the water temperature only fluctuates by a degree or two diurnally. It still felt colder. That was what mattered.

Fisheries had zipped offshore in thirty minutes in their RIB, straight to the GPS coordinates, miles beyond the fringing reef, where longlines waited 90 feet beneath the surface, and left her in the water. The skill set she would deliver tonight was why she'd been chosen as an Agent for the ocean. The sea was inky, silence pressing in around her. She touched the dive knife strapped to her thigh and the shark prod, minor comforts in an endless expanse of darkness.

Floating on the surface of a black ocean beneath a black sky, without a horizon, was an uncomfortable sensation, disorienting, weightless. Only the swathe of stars overhead gave Leilani any sense of direction, their weak glow illuminating the slow rise and fall of swell on the reef. She hesitated to switch on her underwater torch. If ships were milling around in the distance, undetectable to all three agencies monitoring the area, it would be a risk that could cost her life.

With minutes to go before skiffs loaded with crew were expected to roar through the reef passage, she prepared for the dive she'd visualized all day. She floated with no effort, legs moving back and forth in the water, eyes fixed on where she imagined the horizon to be. Two minutes of slow, measured breaths. In through the nose, out through the mouth. Low into the belly, no chest movement. Intentionally slowing her heart rate.

Then quick, forceful exhalations followed by fast, full inhales, clearing CO_2, oxygenating fast. Three, maybe four. Now was not the time to risk hyperventilating.

She pulled her mask on and checked the weight belt for the last time. Enough to make her neutrally buoyant at 30 feet, one third of the way down to the lines. Too heavy, she'd sink uncontrollably; too light, she'd waste energy kicking down.

One last full inhale, deep into the diaphragm, up into the ribs, finished in the throat. As her coach had taught her, the freediver's three-stage breath hold.

She tipped forward, arms outstretched, and dived beneath the surface without making a splash, long fins trailing behind like a mermaid tail. This dive was essential. Without visual confirmation, the operation had not begun.

The lines were there; she could tell. Her torch beam confirmed it, reflecting at her, the light bouncing off hundreds of large steel J-hooks suspended in the water column.

When she switched on her torch, the dark water came to life. Plankton swirled like dust in an abandoned room, drifting through the beam. Particles twitched and vanished. Tiny clouds of shrimp darted sideways, compound eyes catching the light for half a second. Below her, larger shapes moved, out of reach, just beyond the glow. At 90 feet, there was no knowing what to expect.

As much as she wanted to reject the idea, she could see the lines had been cleared. She swam as far along as she could to double-check. It had been done in the last few hours, for sure. There were fragments of bait remaining on the sharp barbs, but no sharks hanging lifeless on the line, no bycatch of any kind. Only a nylon mainline, thin steel leaders and spaced hooks for as far as the light of the torch could travel. Looking closer, she saw some hooks were missing; the line cut too high in haste.

"Fuck," Leilani swore to herself as she surfaced, removing the mask and spitting out saltwater. Her lips felt numb; she'd been biting down too hard without meaning to. Either Sione had lied straight to her face or someone on the inside had tipped off the Chinese about the operation. *Who else had he told*? How the crews had outsmarted the Ocean Enforcement Agency, Police and Fisheries, escaped her. Both ship captains had remained onshore for the entire night, as far as she could tell. Maybe another officer had run the men out to the tuna boats, the old men being a decoy strategy to cause delay.

For the first time in years, she wished she had scuba gear. Her dad had made her get certified, even though she could free dive deeper than he could with oxygen tanks on. But at 90 feet, she was limited to two minutes. Not long enough to follow the line all the way. *What if they'd baited the other half? What was she missing here?*

Her dive watch showed the seafloor at 1500 feet, far beyond human limits. She watched the sonar field on the small, illuminated screen and immediately wished she hadn't. The circle was filled with moving shapes, lit in bright green, similar to a thermal camera. To a casual observer, the signatures meant fish were present. To Leilani's expert eye, the shapes below were unmistakably sharks. They appeared to be jolting around in a movement pattern she'd seen a hundred times during field research. A feeding frenzy.

They were cannibalizing their own who had fallen victim to the lines of death, cut free when the Chinese realized their plans for the night had been compromised. The timing was off; it didn't make sense. With no time to remove the fins, somehow officers had been alerted to incoming law enforcement, cut their losses for the night and run. Were there locals in other beachfront villages on the payroll? She took a deep, calming breath and forced her eyes away from the device. It was time to make a call.

If the operation went ahead, she would be held liable, maybe even for costs incurred. These longlines were over the legal length and breaking other domestic fishing regulations, but that wasn't the court case the Agency wanted. Either the intel had been unreliable, or they'd been played. She'd find out; Sione would answer for this.

For now, the immediate step to take was a humiliating text to the Agency, who would advise Samoan police and Fisheries to stand down, return to Apia. A two-hour drive, their New Zealand-funded patrol vessels bouncing around on trailers as they inched along the potholed main road. If there was one thing Leilani could count on, it was that there was always someone awake in the village, day or night. They would've been seen, and tomorrow morning, stories and rumors would begin.

Leilani floated on her back and tried to appreciate the uninterrupted view of a night sky unaffected by light pollution, waiting anxiously for a text reply. Instead of worrying about the feeding frenzy directly beneath her, she wondered how many sharks had been killed during the night. At least the fishing captains had received a warning; she was on to them.

Talk when back on land.

Director Ventura's brief text implied he was frustrated and embarrassed. Leilani had never met Captain Sina in person, but it was a safe bet the Samoan police captain was also angry at being duped and wasting resources.

Ashamed, Leilani waited until 1.30 am before calling Fisheries for pickup. Waiting made no sense after seeing the lines cleared, but Sione had never lied to her. *Was he playing the two sides against each other*? He was collecting two paychecks after all.

Reluctantly, she climbed the ladder at the back of the RIB and was handed a dry towel, instantly wrapped around her shivering body. Being cold was her own fault; she'd stayed in the water too long. There were only two uniformed Fisheries officers onboard. They had not taken part in the sting, having been woken up and sent out from another coastal location. Over the outboard engines there was no need for conversation, but the silence spoke for itself. They'd been informed on the radio. At full throttle, the men raced back across the obsidian lagoon towards the beach. There was no one to observe the wake.

On shore, her wetsuit felt like dead weight. The stress on the body from a 90-foot freedive at night was catching up to her. Waving thanks to the men who had come to her aid, Leilani crashed onto the beach, breathing hard. Soaked, exhausted, and angry. Her curly hair clung in strands to her clammy face. The operation was a failure. The shark finning industry was still in business on the island, her employer was losing patience, and Samoan police would think twice before answering her next call.

The girl who cried wolf. That's what they'd call her, she imagined. Another false alarm, a waste of limited resources. And when the actual wolves finally came, when blood spilled into the water, no one would be there to stop them.

Walking back to the church in defeat, on the lookout for aggressive dogs, she noticed a man standing amongst beachfront palm trees in the dark. A nearby backyard fire, burned down to embers, gave off enough light to make out his features. Tall, broad chest, sea breeze blowing his long hair. It had to be Sione, waiting for her.

Why? Leilani felt a shiver up her spine, and goosebumps appeared on her already stiff arms and legs. It wasn't the wind that caused it. She remembered bedtime stories her mother had shared in the years before disappearing. Tales of spirits, or *aitu* as they were known, haunted the village.

Was the apparition ahead Sione coming to explain, or something more sinister? As an academic, Leilani did not play into the superstitions of locals and never had. But not everything she'd witnessed since arriving in Samoa had a rational explanation.

"Anyone there?" she called out.

Her feet caught on thin vines running through the sand, like roots. She stumbled, then reached down to detangle her foot from the powerful grasp of the plants. When she stood up, Sione was gone. Blinking cleared her eyes. *Was her exhausted mind playing tricks on her?*

Trails in leaf litter beneath the palms told her she had not been hallucinating. Written beside deeper footprints, where he must have stood for a moment while using a stick to carve his message, large words were scratched into the ground.

SORRY. FORGIVE ME. HELP US PLEASE!

She shivered as the light wind hit her wet skin, trying to decode the message. She knew the village fishermen, including Sione, resented Zhang for not letting them leave. But they were still paid relatively well for their work and had given no signs of a mutiny. Until now.

Had the captain and his officers been torturing the men? Threatening their families? Or were they all bound by something far darker, trapped in servitude to the fishing captains for a lifetime?

It made sense now. Officers had intercepted Sione's text messages, revealing the betrayal. She'd had no replies all night because they'd taken his phone. He was lucky to still be alive.

* * *

Dawn would reveal more answers Leilani was seeking.

She awoke to the sound of loud sobbing inside the Mormon church. Mostly from women. Concerned, Leilani opened the door of the room a crack.

Inside, sitting in the front pews nearest to the altar, were a group of men and women.

The men were formally attired, supportive hands resting on the backs and shoulders of their partners and daughters. The minister and his wife were there, offering quiet words of comfort. A girl entered with cups of instant coffee, handing them out to the elders. There was no laughter or song, as Leilani was so used to hearing from inside the building, only the sound of sniffling and loud, unapologetic wailing.

The sound cut deep. In her heart, Leilani knew she recognized it, but her brain refused to accept reality. It was a unique cry that only a parent who has lost a child can produce. A rawness that transcended species. All mammals are capable of it.

She'd hoped never to hear it again. Not from human nor animal. But here it was, in paradise, ringing deeply in her ears.

Her first experience with the cry of death had been with humpback whales. Diving off the eastern coast of Australia to save humpback whales from ship-strike, she'd come across a mother with a six-month-old calf. The calf had been cleaved in two by an overpowered drug-running vessel, using known whale migration corridors to avoid detection.

Leilani had kept her distance, heart pounding as she'd watched through her dive mask. The mother had nudged the deceased calf upward, desperate, instinctively, forcing it to the surface to breathe. But there was no breath, only blood spilling from the gaping wound beneath its pectoral fins, clouding the water in dark, crimson swirls. The mother stayed. For over an hour, she stayed, lifting the dead weight of her calf, fighting exhaustion, refusing to let go.

Leilani had wanted to believe it would end differently, that there was something she could do. She'd even asked God to intervene, something she never did. But when the mother humpback finally faltered, her energy drained past the point of survival, she'd let go. The juvenile body had brushed past her, skin against skin for the last time. Leilani had never forgotten the sound that followed.

As her first-born calf descended into the abyss, the mother humpback had watched on and sung her song of death. A high-pitched, haunting melody that carried through the lukewarm summer water to rescue divers nearby. Deeper below, out of sight, a mournful cry from the father echoed. A melody that stayed with you forever.

She closed the door to her room, locked it, and turned the shower on. The cool water came from above, initially in stops and starts, then in a consistent flow after a minute. It was still early, but daylight was penetrating into the bathroom through the louvered window with mesh behind it. The light warmed the tiled floor underfoot. Salt was hard to wash out of her hair. Overnight it had clung to her thick Polynesian curls, stiffening them into wild knots, the tangles resistant to fingers and combs. She reached for the Protex, rubbing it between her hands before massaging her scalp. She tilted her head back, letting water cascade down, removing the last traces of the ocean.

A ritual done a thousand times after a dive, but this morning, it didn't bring the same relief. Sione's nighttime warning in the sand still burned in her mind. Sleep had come fast when she'd returned from the unsuccessful dive, before she'd even washed off. And as much as she wanted it to be, the weak flow of running water was not loud enough to drown out bereaved family outside her door, inside the church.

Dressed modestly in slacks and a blouse, she took a deep breath and forced herself to confront the situation unfolding inside. Her profession required it. Whatever had happened, the OEA were allies of the village. They needed the relationship as much as she wanted it.

All eyes turned as she stepped into the church through the side door. The minister's wife, the one person who was always unafraid to speak the truth, walked toward her with tears welling in her eyes. The sarcasm she expected from the woman was gone.

"Lani. Sit down," the big woman said softly, gesturing to an empty pew.

Leilani complied, waiting for what would come next.

"Sione's brother, Ioane, has been killed."

The words hit like a blow. Leilani had only been in the village a month, but the physical closeness of the homes, the tight-knit nature of the community, made her feel like she'd known the boy for years.

Then there was the aspect of her involvement. *Was she responsible?* This was not the first time people associated with an OEA investigation had become pawns for an industry, sacrificed to protect the wildlife trade.

"How? Why?" she whispered.

"The captain," the minister's wife replied. "Sione blames himself. He said it's his fault, that's all I know."

They both turned to look out the window. The red trade store was closed, its door padlocked. If they had killed the boy, they weren't running. Inside, through barred windows, Leilani could see their pigtail-wearing children playing with dolls.

For a moment, she felt envious of the children's innocence. Those girls didn't know the first thing about what their fathers did for a living. It wasn't hard to guess why Sione felt guilty. His younger brother had been killed as a warning, to teach the community a lesson, to show who was really in control. That he was the son of a high chief only made their statement stronger.

Chapter 12

The beach had always been her place to think. Staring at the ocean, with no one else around. After her mother had disappeared, after her grandparents had passed away. She'd walked right down to the far end, with only a spoonbill hunting in the shallows and restless terns for company.

Today was the same. Sione's brother was on her mind. Initial reports from the coroner, which Director Ventura had got his hands on, suggested the boy had drowned. Toxicology reports showed sky-high levels of impure methamphetamine. Blood work showed Hepatitis B and secondary tetanus from the rusty, unsafe vessels. Even if he hadn't been pushed overboard, it was a lot to process.

By killing a Samoan fisherman, one of their own employees, the Chinese had shown their hand. The village would not forget or forgive. Retaliation would come.

Over the following week, men spoke out, breaking the code of silence. Openly sharing stories of forced labor, of drugs pushed on them to endure endless numbing shifts at sea. Fear of death had kept them silent. Now the death of one of their brothers, pushed overboard after an argument, led them to the door of the village council pleading for help.

The fishermen wanted out. Even the last who had been holding onto their dream of fast wealth were coming around. Without labor, they doubted the shark finning operation could continue. There were not enough Chinese men on the entire island to bait, set, retrieve and remove the catch from those heavy baited lines of death. Immigration Samoa had been briefed; these ships were not to be flying in replacement crews.

A crew meeting had been called in the early hours after the death. Sione had advised the men to act natural around their employers, to play it safe. As next in line to be high chief, he held their respect. Ending the trade could not be done in the heat of the moment. It required a plan.

Leilani had brought her notes down to the beach. With no wind and plenty of sunshine, she'd moved her office outside for now. She couldn't work in the room. People were still coming to the church to pay their respects, day after day. Wreaths of flowers, artificial and fresh, were everywhere. As a place of community, coming together there made sense. Official communication via the village council suggested police would return the body in the coming days, pending investigation.

She had just unbuckled the clasps on the faux leather satchel when a rotund man in his sixties approached from behind and sat down at her side, cross-legged. He smoothed out the black fabric of his *i'e faitaga*, the formal wrap-around garment for men.

Leilani found her hand drawn to the concealed handgun she'd started carrying. Until the death in the village, she'd left the Agency-issued firearm under her bed most days, sealed in a nondescript ukulele case. At the outset, Samoa hadn't seemed like somewhere she'd need it.

After a tense moment, she realized precautionary action was unnecessary. The quiet, somber man to her left on the sand was the high chief. Father of Ioane, the teenager who had been killed. He had two brown coconuts in his hands, tops already severed by machete. He handed one to her; heavy, full of fresh water. Enough to sustain a shipwrecked sailor for a day.

"Miss Sapunaoa Brown. You and I need to talk," he said in monotone. His eyes stared out to sea in contemplation. No eye contact. He looked older than when she had last seen him. Grief and stress can do that to a parent.

Leilani swallowed nervously. *Did he blame her?*

"But first. Let me make amends."

"Amends, for?" Leilani questioned. She wanted to call him sir, but felt uncomfortable. She took a deep sip of the thirst-quenching coconut water.

"I was wrong to threaten you, to drive you away like my people did to your mother. I allowed my boys to work for those men. I chose not to oppose the village council vote."

"You couldn't have known," Leilani said.

"No, not everything. But I knew what they were doing. My sons told me. Killing sharks. Cutting the fins off and throwing them back into the moana to drown. Species that have been protected here since I was a boy, all for a quick buck."

He paused, then shook his head in shame and sighed.

"I should never have allowed Ioane to leave school in Australia and come back here. He wanted to follow his older brother; now look what's happened."

The old man looked at the ground, conflicted. Sharing his thoughts seemed to help.

"You know, he heard about this work with the Chinese from friends on Facebook. They called him, lured him back to the island with easy money. He was supposed to join the Australian Navy next year. Top student my boy was. One of the lucky ones that got outta here. He tell you that?"

"I'm so sorry. I didn't know," Leilani said.

"I know he was proud to be contributing to the family," she continued. "That meant a lot to him."

The white-haired man bristled, looking down at the sand beneath his sandals. *Had she said the wrong thing?*

"He didn't need to contribute. We are not a poor family. He thought he was going tuna fishing. An adventure. That's why he joined. That and the money."

His expression changed from sadness to resolve.

"Leilani. You and I are going to end the shark finning business. I am ashamed of what this village has become. Watching our culture disappear in the face of easy money. It should not have taken Ioane's passing, but I have the people behind me now, even the council. They respect you. You listen; you care. Most foreigners don't."

"Not exactly a foreigner," Leilani said, allowing herself half a smile, despite the circumstances that led to their impromptu meeting.

"*Sa'o lelei*," the chief murmured. *You're right.*

"On that note, before we talk war, let's talk family. Follow me, young lady."

He stood up, rubbed his lower back, then extended a hand to pull Leilani to her feet off the sand. She took it, surprised at his strength.

They walked side by side along a coastal track, overgrown with beach morning glory, bedazzled with purple flowers. Lizards darted off into the undergrowth as they approached. A solid feral pig with sought-after curved tusks, targeted for ceremonial necklaces, watched the pair walk by with beady black eyes, his heavy bristled head raised to full alert, flared nostrils inhaling their scent. The chief took Leilani's arm protectively.

"That one we call Puka. Don't make eye contact with him; he's not your friend," he whispered calmly, increasing the pace of their steps until the boar grunted and returned to rooting in the dirt.

The chief focused on the route for a while without speaking. He snapped off a dry branch and used it as a walking stick, favoring his right leg. It was a hazardous path; tree roots jutted out at all angles. The way forward was getting more and more difficult to distinguish.

"This village – it's everything to me," he said after contemplation."Even my wife's gone. She says she cannot live here without our youngest. Sione drove her to the airport last night. She's going to Australia, stay with her sister. But you, Leilani, you have family here."

Leilani hadn't expected such candor. The last time they spoke, he'd warned her to stay out of his business, a threat more than a warning. Now, there was no pretense, just the reality of a man who had lost someone that he loved. His voice held firm until he talked about his wife leaving Samoa. It seemed her move had caught him off guard.

"Family? I feel connected, but that's a story from the past. All I know is my dad." Leilani changed the topic.

"I haven't been honest with you," the chief said. "But you are a daughter of Samoa. That's why I came to find you. Sione told me everything you've been doing to save the village. He said I would find you by the ocean."

Leilani stayed silent. Maybe Sione knew her better than she realized. She wondered how he was coping with the murder of his brother.

They reached the western edge of the village, where the baked ground gave way to sand covered in shrub and a mangrove-choked river bled into the ocean. An estuary of sorts. The river mouth was knee-deep, stained tea-brown from tannins, leached into the water by a thick layer of fallen leaves. Whitened clam shells and coral fragments stuck out of the black sand that surrounded the riverbed on both sides. A plastic 2-liter bottle of Coca-Cola spun around in the gentle eddies of the water. The boat the Agency had chartered for her was hidden near here.

Leilani had never explored this side of the estuary, assuming the land was too unstable to build on. It was only when the chief pointed towards their destination, she realized she'd seen the lone house before. To reach the other side, they had to wade through the water.

The brackish mixture of salt and fresh water felt cool against her legs. She was thankful for the saltiness. Farther up the river, there were leeches.

Looking at the shack, it seemed to be held together by nails. Sheets of timber and rusted iron hammered down at odd angles. The roof was branches and thatch. Rat-chewed mats lined the floor. Thick poles elevated the hut off the ground, but rodents had found their way in, regardless. Maybe the design had been made with king tides in mind.

It would've failed every building code in New Zealand, Leilani thought. There were no signs of plumbing. No electricity. No cellphone signal.

Out back, what might once have been a vegetable garden was now overtaken by bush. A few scrawny chickens picked at the sand, their feathers dull. The only sounds were the slow wash of swell on the shore, and the constant pulse of cicadas.

Leilani followed the chief's lead as he parted curtains at the entrance to the shack. He announced their presence with a loud cough. There was no response, so they entered.

Inside was spacious, swept and dim. Furniture was limited to a bed and one table with a chair. A Samoan Bible with a navy cover lay open on the table, lit by the tropical sun that made its way through gaps in the walls. There was only one occupant of the home, lying on a simple wood frame that had been built by an unskilled carpenter, the lengths of timber nailed together inaccurately. On top of this, her mattress was thin and needed replacing.

Petite and frail, the old woman sat propped up on her bed with coffee-colored pillows and a sheet covering her chest. The chief helped her to rise, taking her arm in his firm but gentle way. With strong features and wiry grey hair, she would have been a classic South Pacific beauty in her youth. Under the sheet, Leilani guessed both legs had been amputated at the knee. Likely from diabetes complications, as with most amputees on the island.

In a dark corner of the fale, an outdated wheelchair was collapsed, lying on its side. Tires bare, the metal rim within showing from wear and tear, its functionality questionable. The woman's skin appeared jaundiced, yellowish beneath brown, maybe from poor blood sugar management. When she looked towards Leilani and the chief, they could see the centers of her black-brown eyes were milky, like those of Zhang. Leilani was confused.

Who was this old woman? Why was she living alone, so far away from a village full of caring people who would have looked after her?

"After your grandfather passed away, Tulua lived here. To be closer to God," the Chief said, observing Leilani as the information sunk in.

The old woman was aware she had visitors, but her sight worked against her. She spoke quietly in Samoan.

Although Leilani could not understand the words, she recognized the cadence of the formal language. The language of respect. Different from the everyday Samoan used by untitled villagers. A sign of respect between those with a deep understanding of ancient traditions. She knew the chief by the sound of his voice.

"She says to come closer. Don't be afraid," the chief translated.

The old woman beckoned to Leilani to come and sit beside her on the edge of the bed. She obliged, feeling tears forming in the corners of her eyes.

Her grandmother's firm hands caressed her face, neck and strong shoulders, as the blind often do to create a mental image. Helping the elderly woman to visualize her granddaughter better. The cataracts in her eyes created a shroud of darkness around her.

"Asu?" the woman asked, at last recalling the name of her daughter. Leilani felt her heart race, holding back her tears in front of the chief.

"Leai. Leilani," she whispered. "Asu was my mother."

"Leilani". The woman spoke her name out loud, as if trying to place it within a lifetime of memories, like the missing piece of a jigsaw puzzle. Memories that were becoming fuzzier with each year that passed. She took Leilani's hand and placed it on her chest. Through paper-thin skin, she could feel the old woman's heart beating slowly, warm to the touch.

"Tulua," the woman said, introducing herself. They had never met until now.

With Asu being banished from the village for her teen pregnancy, her parents had never met their grandchild. Leilani had been born in Auckland, New Zealand.

They embraced for a long time, her grandmother understanding the connection. Tears flowed freely as they held each other. After the moment passed, Leilani slipped a $100 tala note into her shaking hands, then gently closed her fingers around the note.

There was a rustle as a handful of blinds were pulled back and tied, letting daylight in. A stocky man in his forties was standing outside, wearing All Blacks rugby shorts. He carried a bag full of pineapple, taro, breadfruit and reef fish, which he put down on the deck. His t-shirt was tied around his head to keep the sweat out of his eyes. Traditional tattoos that wrapped around his waist and back were faded, matching those of the chief.

The chief and Leilani's grandmother began a conversation with the man. They spoke loudly, too fast for Leilani to follow – but she understood the topic - the loss of the chief's son. A son of the village. The two men embraced for a long time in silence.

The man glanced over at Leilani, curious. He looked at her as if he knew her from somewhere.

Prioritizing the chief, the man burned a small coconut husk fire behind the hut, placing a rusted grill over the flames. He located a stainless-steel teapot and put it on the heat. Soon the aroma of koko Samoa filled the fale, homegrown hot chocolate Leilani craved. Next, he placed a freshly caught *lupo* – a large bluefin trevally – onto the grill.

Cup in hand, both men and Leilani sat on the floor, cross-legged. Tulua stayed in her bed, upright and alert.

"Asu is my sister," the shirtless man finally said deadpan.

Stunned, Leilani didn't know how to respond. *Why had her father never taken her here before to meet family?*

"I'm Lani. Asu was my mother. Jake is my father."

"Was?" The man raised his eyebrows and burst out laughing, nearly spilling his koko. Tulua and the chief laughed as well.

"Call me Uncle Mose. Maybe you are a silly girl, ay, just like your bloody mother. Fa'asu is not dead; she lives in the mountains behind the village. The council did not let her live down here when she return from New Zealand. She remarried a taro farmer. They have, ah, maybe three or four children, your half sisters," her uncle explained.

Leilani sipped her drink, thinking she needed alcohol for this conversation. This was too much. *Her mother was alive*? Why had she not come down from the mountains to see her own daughter? Surely, she would have heard by now. News travels fast in quiet villages.

"I know what you are thinking," the white-haired chief spoke up, as if reading her mind. "Why hasn't your mother come to see you?"

Leilani nodded, still processing.

"She wants to. I sent word to her when you first arrived, weeks ago. But her family has no money. Even the bus stop is too far to walk. Only her husband comes down to the village once a month to sell his taro. When he comes next week, you will return with him to visit your mother."

Leilani felt overwhelmed. She hadn't seen her mother since her eighth birthday. Nearly 20 years ago. The resentment she felt towards her would not disappear overnight, but some happy memories were still there beneath the surface.

She felt a vibration in her pocket, a text from Sione. Time had slipped by faster than she had realized. They'd spent the entire afternoon at her grandmother's house. She needed to get back in the water and check in with the Agency. And her father.

Visiting her mother's mountainside home would have to wait. She wasn't yet convinced time would heal the decades of abandonment she still held onto.

line came in this morning. again Thursday night. Trust me Lani, please. for Ioane.

Sione must have been given his phone back. The Chinese appeared unfazed, still allowing him to crew, mistakenly assuming he was a simpleminded farmhand, not a threat. They'd overstepped the mark with a murder, and they knew it, but they were not running. It was business as usual.

<h1 style="text-align:center">Chapter 13</h1>

All accommodation should have a side entrance, Leilani thought, as she slipped inside her room without being seen. Through a narrow gap, she saw women still gathered in the church. Ioane's mother knelt among them, white hat pulled low over her face. Sione stood back, silent and respectful. A framed photo had been added to the shrine—Ioane in his high school uniform, handsome and full of hope.

She watched for a while, curious about death rites for a culture only half of her belonged to.

Another family of six entered the church, dressed formally. A strong wind chased behind, blowing flower arrangements to the ground. The door slammed shut by itself. Ioane's mother stood to greet the visitors, friends of hers. She took a minute to get up off the polished floor, obesity taking its toll on arthritic knees. Women embraced for an uncomfortable duration, then the husband handed over a bag of yams. An offering from his plantation, simple but appreciated.

Leilani locked the door. Enough distractions for one afternoon. She needed to be alert, focused. The next raid on the Chinese fishing vessels was on standby, weather dependent. Through the window, she was astonished to see lights on inside and the door wide open to the red store. They were trading as usual, despite being prime suspects in a village murder. She watched a middle-aged Asian woman she'd never seen before stack a bare shelf with cans of mackerel from within a cardboard box. *Must be Zhang's wife,* Leilani thought.

A weather alert pinged, making her glance at her phone. The forecast app confirmed what everyone suspected—the imminent cyclone season was arriving early this year. She'd try to charge the battery before power to the village was cut off. Already, the ceiling fan was nonfunctional. Warnings on the screen flashed in red. Torrential rain was predicted during the night. The winds were strong, even now. They expected a Category 3 cyclone, with gusts of 100mph. Outside the room, palms flexed under the fast-moving force of the storm. A stray green coconut, ripped from above, smashed into the concrete church like a hand grenade, followed by a skull-cracking sound as the hard shell fractured, missing the glass windows of Leilani's small room by inches. After a second one shattered on the wall outside, she took the bedsheet and slept on the bathroom floor, amongst cockroaches.

There was no way anyone was going fishing during a cyclone.

* * *

By morning, the ocean seemed calm again. Leilani wondered if they were in the storm's eye, or if it had passed. She had no idea – this being her first tropical cyclone. Alerts were still coming in hot on the phone. Maybe this was not over. The Agency had emailed, advising her to stay indoors for now. At headquarters, weather teams tracked the storm systems in real time, swathes of green, yellow and red pulsing across the wall of monitors like a gaping wound that's had its stitches pulled out one by one.

With nothing to do until the storm passed and the shark fishing vessels returned to work, she considered taking advantage of the brief weather window to go for a dive. By the time Cyclone Rose moved on to the next island, the underwater world wouldn't look the same again. This could be her last opportunity.

Too late, Leilani realized that diving into the eye of a cyclone was a naïve mistake. The hours she'd expected had been cut short by the weather gods. She'd never known the ocean to feel this still, never felt unsafe in the water, not even hurling herself off the high boards in competition, but now an edge of doubt crept in. Maybe she'd overestimated her abilities.

The water was unnervingly still, a silence that made your ears ring. Not a flicker of movement, not even the brush of a current against her skin. She hovered in the dirty water, suspended in a world that felt like it was dying. Visibility was so low she couldn't even make out the reef. Then, almost imperceptibly, the ocean stirred. Strands of silt lifted from the seafloor. A low groan rolled through the depths, and a pulse of current pressed at her side. In the space of minutes, the calm fractured, eddies spun hard, tearing at her mask strap as the first deep-water surge from the eye wall reached her.

Thirty feet down, she'd imagined the seafloor to be a refuge, calm, an oasis insulated from chaos above. In her experience, it was. Cold, choppy days were still good for crayfish diving back home. Category 3 Cyclone Rose was different; she had broken that boundary and entered the sanctuary below. Even within the eye, the subsurface surge strengthened. Swirling currents and water patterns confused the water column in fast, rolling pulses, shifting mountains of sand and mud beneath, unsettling everything. The storm had not spared the depths; it had returned.

In the hour since she'd decided to go for a last dive, Leilani felt as if she'd entered a wartime underwater sandstorm. The reef structure itself felt as if it was about to be ripped from its ancient limestone base, vibrating with tension and stress. Shells and coral shards spiraled within the murkiness, cutting into the inches of exposed ankle between wetsuit and long fins.

Fish had deserted the area in advance, and visibility was heading towards zero. After only two minutes, there was still air in her lungs, but she needed to surface. Being out here was more than foolish. Without the weight belt around her waist and years of experience, the violent surge would have won, pulling her up into the maelstrom. The shadow of a palm tree hurled past in front of the glass of her dive mask, a warning shot across the bows of the debris to come.

She'd seen photos of the tsunami aftermath that had ravaged the islands. Bloated corpses of livestock had contaminated the lagoon and devastated coastlines for weeks afterwards, tall palms stripped bare of their crowns of fronds. *Was Cyclone Rose destined to reach that level of fury?*

Most resorts along the South Coast had not survived, physically or financially – one reason she was staying in the guest room of a hundred-year-old Mormon church. That, and the fact the Agency never put agents up in hotels. Their long-term presence attracted attention.

As she tried to propel herself towards the weak light of the surface, Leilani thought of her grandmother, vulnerable in that driftwood cabin by the water. She prayed this storm would go around her. Silent prayer was interrupted by nature when she was thrown headfirst into red coral by confused underwater currents. Overpowered by force and pressure, it felt as if she'd been spear tackled from behind by an All Blacks prop. Live coral sliced her cheeks and chin, stinging back thousands of times in defense, like a hot poker searing into the backside of cattle. The collision pushed her dive mask up, chipping the tempered glass. The diamond-like shards floated around inside, threatening to cut into her eyes. Her neck and head throbbed from the impact, as if she'd been in a car accident. Before she could pull her mask back down into place, a rush of warm water and particles obscured her vision as headed on the path towards blackout.

Lightheaded and confused, her face burned beyond any heat she'd known; like dozens of tattoo gun needles piercing virgin skin for the first time. *It has to be fire* coral, she thought. In the murkiness, it was difficult to tell, but what else could it be? Her hands tingled as if electricity was running inside of them, from where she'd pushed herself off the bones of the reef. She could feel venom working its way deeper within her cheeks. She visualized the page in a heavy marine biology college textbook; fire coral (*Millepora spp.*) – lipophilic venom. Fat loving. Where contact had occurred, the skin twitched at will, nerve endings firing at pace. She needed to get out of the water now - before she passed out for the last time.

Avoiding the pier, cyclone damaged and now a navigational hazard, Leilani broke the surface and swam back to shore through whitewater. With shifting columns of acorn barnacles present on both sides, she swam diagonally to avoid being pulled into the broken structure. Even her neoprene wetsuit would be cut open if she rubbed against the smashed pier by accident. With both hands, she secured her dive mask, wincing as silicone made contact with her envenomated face. It failed to seal; the fit was too tight.

Damn it, my face is swelling already, she thought.

It was hard to focus on anything other than the passage of water in front of her eyes. The beach was less than 100 feet away, but it was challenging to make progress in the swell. With wind screaming underneath the pier at a volume that hurt her ears, she wondered if she'd ever make it home.

Feeling sand under her feet brought consciousness back to her body. She rested for a moment to catch her breath, noticing beige foam scum now decorated the beach. A nearby crack of thunder pushed her out of the water, across the wet sand and crawling for cover under the church roof. Underneath wasn't much better; cascades of cool rainwater ran down the sides of the building, off gutters like waterfalls. Coconuts and plant matter ripped by the wind lay scattered around the landscaped church grounds like garbage from an upturned bin.

The village was deserted, most fales locked down as best they could, emergency solar lights switched on. Some families had lashed blue tarpaulins, plastic sheets and torn rice sacks across the open sides of their homes, tying them down with rope and rocks, anything heavy enough to hold against the wind. The possibility of national evacuation to higher ground was real. Older villagers would have remembered the last time they'd run, September 2009, when a tsunami struck ten minutes after an offshore quake. It had killed hundreds, water tearing through coastal villages like a demon. Leilani's family village had been tested, but survived.

She weighed up using the old Pajero, parked inches deep in mud near the back of the church. The Agency had sent it across island the moment cyclone warnings came through, a last-minute lifeline. The manual vehicle had seen better days, but again, in line with operational policy, they weren't about to rent an attention-grabbing new Land Rover. An expat, one of the director's poker debtors, had driven it down to the South Coast, ditched it by the church and caught the last bus back to the city before the weather closed in. There hadn't even been time to offer the man a beer.

Leilani had declined the Agency's earlier offers of a vehicle. With the ocean on her doorstep and the work site a short walk away, it had seemed unnecessary. In the village, cars were a luxury anyway, used sparingly on the narrow, potholed roads dotted with wandering pigs, chickens, and barefoot kids. It was only when dogs chased her she regretted the decision.

The medical clinic in Poutasi was under half an hour away, supposedly open 24 hours a day, but the roads would be flooded. She decided against traveling. Diving into the eye of a cyclone had already been a major mistake.

Objectively, Leilani knew fire coral venom was not a death sentence; even parrotfish could handle the venom. A storm-thrown coconut through the windscreen while driving at night was usually fatal. Nurses at the clinic would give her an ibuprofen and an icepack, anyway. After checking in previously to get a pus-filled mosquito bite treated, Leilani had been told upfront - 'most days there is no doctor on call'. The reality of life on a South Pacific island was sinking in.

She fantasized about driving into the lush mountains to find her mother and sisters she'd never met, to protect them in some way from the storm, but getting lost was the most likely scenario. No signs, no functional GPS, no roadside service. A punctured tire or empty fuel tank could turn into something worse. Petrol stations, rarer than gold in the first place, would be shut, thanks to the cyclone. The island still had attendants filling up cars and taking cash, no automated, unmanned stations in sight.

According to locals, Leilani's mother and family lived inland, deep in the hills. She was no meteorologist, but it sounded safer there. Uncle Mose was probably still at the estuary house, looking after her grandmother. That thought alone gave her some comfort. If the tough woman had survived a tsunami, she could handle annual storms.

There was still no cellphone signal. Maybe later she'd try the satellite phone; a cyclone surely qualified as a legitimate reason to use the expensive connection. She wondered if it was up to the task. Starlink was consistent if you could afford it, but in a cyclone? Back in New Zealand, an hour ahead, her dad would be glued to the 85-inch TV in the lounge, Lion Red in hand. Tropical storms always made the evening news.

* * *

With Cyclone Rose moving on to other island groups and the tide at full ebb, there was no hiding from the harsh truth. One of the Chinese longliners -*Hai Yuan 607*, the larger of the two shark finning vessels anchored beyond the reef, was gone. As were the four men who'd been stationed aboard her.

Records showed the cyclone had torn through at 160 miles an hour, whipping the ocean into massive gullies and stiff peaks. Concrete pilings had broken like wood. The two support boats used to transport crew offshore were both crippled. One lay wedged sideways atop an exposed sandbank, hull caved in like a tin can. The other had smashed broadside into the remnants of the pier's solid base, timbers washing up on the seaweed and coral-strewn shore.

But major loss lay beyond the lagoon, where the outer reef's jagged edge cradled the visible wreck of the *607*. Her stern had gone down first, and the forward cabin now protruded awkwardly from the reef like a broken jawbone. The storm had finished what age and corrosion had started. The boat was now unsalvageable *and* uninsured.

When time zones aligned, someone would have to call China and provide answers. Orders had already been placed, shipments of dried shark fin pre-sold to buyers in Guangzhou and Shenzhen. Containers booked. Reefer vessel refueled and on its way back to the South

Pacific. Documents forged, bribes paid. Once underway, the well-greased export network was hard to stop.

Now the Samoa operation had nothing to offer Asia. No shark fins, no barrels of squalene oil, no tuna in the freezer, no cash. Only wreckage, leaking fuel into the pristine marine environment.

Captain Zhang spent the early hours of the day deep in thought, ash-faced and soaked in diesel-stained rain. He didn't sleep, inhaling strongly from his glass pipe to calm the nerves. Reality gnawed at him like rust eating at steel. Losing men was of no concern to China. Losing a ship, that was a different story.

None of the fleet was insured, and with valid reasoning – insurance invited scrutiny. Coverage meant underwriting, and underwriting meant compliance: agents boarding for audits, inspection of the hold, logbook checks, maintenance of safety gear, engine hours and servicing, and documented port visits.

No insurer would underwrite a vessel running illegal shark fin bycatch through falsified manifests and nighttime offloads to ships on the boundary between Samoa's EEZ and international waters. Even tuna licenses wouldn't save them if a fisheries observer was placed onboard or if a marine surveyor noticed that the refrigerated hold was partitioned to hide unregulated product. Insurance companies demanded documentation: crew lists, gear specs, AIS records, and satellite logs. Information neither captain wanted to provide.

For the crime lords who dominated the industry in the southern hemisphere, silence was worth more than coverage. If a boat went down, so be it. Easier to write off and ghost the registry than risk legal exposure.

Salvaging the wreck would be as poor a decision as a confession. Not to mention the paper trail and the number of unknown factors involved in a third-world country. Additional visibility would lead to exposure, so by lunchtime, the legitimate owners of the *607* erased her existence from the South Pacific.

The loss was to be absorbed, and Zhang would take the fall. Cyclone or not, as captain, he had been accountable for that vessel. Right now, he felt grateful an ocean separated him from the rage of those in charge. It wouldn't stop them forever, though. If the old man didn't move fast, they would catch him. Having already been saved once by China, he was out of second chances.

Leilani stood on the rock wall above the sea. From this angle, she could still see the name on the wreckage, half obscured by coral and shadow. She sent out the compact drone she'd brought with her from NZ. It rose on four spinning blades, humming through the cloudless sky as if it were a seabird. Below, the longliner's remains stretched across the reef, twisted and split open like a pig before roasting, its ribs visible. She guided the drone around with a small joystick, capturing wide-angle shots of the damage, the never to recover scar in the coral, and the oil slick trail drifting into deeper water. The images and GPS coordinates would go to the Agency, documented as evidence for a future court date. She wondered if the hold had been full of fins at the time the ship went down. The saltwater was clear even offshore, but it concealed answers she wanted.

She imagined the long-distance call that would unfold, the silence on the other end as the news sunk in. Then the shouting, swearing and threats. Men like Zhang were not forgiven for losing half a million dollar boats. Not through cyclone, fire or act of God. Not when the money belonged to someone higher up the food chain. Someone hiding far away, but still able to reach him on the island.

She wondered what would happen to the old captain. He'd be lucky if he were demoted to officer. Exiled to some mosquito-riddled, flooded atoll in Tuvalu. She felt almost sympathetic towards his situation. The Chinese Communist Party did not have a reputation for leniency.

"One down," she murmured, uploading photos she'd taken of the wreck to an encrypted agency app. "One to go. Guess I have to thank you for winning this round," she said, talking to the ocean.

Turning around to face the village, she saw the captain sitting on the steps outside his trade store, a bottle of whiskey already in hand at 9am. The expression on his tired face was one Leilani had seen before. It was hard to forget. A man with nothing to lose and running out of time. Those kinds of men, experience had taught her, were the most dangerous.

Chapter 14

"CNN says Cyclone Leilani is heading north towards Fiji now, so I reckon you're in the clear," Jake said deadpan over the phone from New Zealand, changing the name of the storm on purpose. Weather tracking app data disagreed. Following the digital tracks, Leilani was certain the village had been hit directly when she'd been in the water. Signal was still nonexistent, so she'd broken policy and called home via satellite courtesy of the Agency for the first time in over a week. The ever-dependable bedside radio said Digicel was offering free calls to family and friends overseas in the disaster's wake, but she had yet to see evidence of that promise being actionable.

"No way they'd name that cyclone after me; I'm *at least* a Category 5," she teased, lying on her back on clean sheets the minister's wife had left out, at ease for the first time in a while. A shower had washed the night's salt and dirt from her hair, and the sun was shining again. The storm had passed, this time for real.

"Are you doing all right without me? Tell me the truth, Dad," she demanded.

"Mate, I managed alright when you went to Alaska for six months to save those beavers, didn't I?" he countered.

"Otters, Dad. Sea otters." Leilani shook her head at his lame attempt at a joke. He read the brief of every assignment she considered, sometimes even before she did. Out of pride, but also out of fatherly concern.

"Promise me you'll call Fisheries if you see anything shady from the deck, ok?"

"Will do, Lani. Although you've probably scared off all the bloody poachers here over the years anyway,"

"I wish, more that there's nothing left to take. Won't stop them trying though; they'll eat anything. Look after yourself, please. Love you; don't forget to walk the beach every morning."

"Can't forget. Remember who started the tradition? Anyway, love you too, darling. Take care over there," he said and ended the call.

With no one else in the village able to establish a phone connection and the weather coming right, the line had been clear. Hearing her dad's voice gave her morale a lift. She worried about whether he was taking his medication. A high rugby tackle during a club game in his twenties had come close to paralyzing him. The old injury still played up, giving him back pain and a limp. Better than a spinal cord injury, he often said to people, dismissing the conversation.

Leilani had consciously left out of her update the information that her mother was living in the mountains with a new man. He didn't need to hear it, not while he was alone. They'd have that talk later, face to face. Leilani hadn't even met her mother herself since being in Samoa. Their reunification was scheduled to happen later in the week, but with the village in a state of disrepair, it wouldn't be a surprise if the husband delayed his trip to the coastal village. She wondered whether the inland villages had been spared by the cyclone.

By midmorning, the village was a hive of activity. Every able-bodied resident of the community was outside, helping with post-cyclone cleanup. Ankle deep, muddy brown water still flooded sections of gravel road and low-lying land. Several backyard plantations were ruined, crops set to rot. Unsupervised children, barefoot and sun-kissed, played in brackish water without fear of disease, collecting fallen palm fronds, rubbish, and storm-tossed coconuts into woven baskets. Middle-aged women, wrapped in faded lavalava's and old t-shirts, swept wind-blown seaweed, leaves and sand from doorsteps with brooms made from natural plant fibers, one hand behind their back as they'd been instructed by the more traditional generation before them.

Where the cyclone had ravaged the surrounding rainforest, men in fluoro vests without shirts underneath and wraparound eyeglasses, hacked up fallen trees. The *whap* of steel machetes at work mixed with the buzz of chainsaws biting through thick limbs blocking the road. Men worked and moved as well-rehearsed road crews, clearing room for the village to breathe again. Older villagers sat in the shade, offering advice, working away on mats to sell at markets.

Leilani was moved by the community spirit of the cleanup. No resentment, even from teenagers. An unspoken understanding that village life by the sea meant dealing with whatever challenge God tested them with, together.

She joined the women collecting debris on the beach. It was mostly plastic bottles, nylon fishing nets embedded in wet sand, cheap jandals and clothes ripped from washing lines. She photographed serial numbers on orange long-line floats, high and dry. Smashed glass was left in situ; time and waves would convert it to smooth-edged sea glass that children loved to collect. The women chatted as they worked, speaking too fast in their language for Leilani to understand. She returned friendly smiles but focused on the task. It felt refreshing to be working among people who seemed to care about the natural environment. Either that, or as the realist within her was inclined to believe, they'd been ordered to clean up the village by village leaders.

As the sun moved overhead, bringing with it the hottest time of the day, people dropped off from the working bee, returning home. A few men remained behind to repair damaged outrigger canoes thrown onto beachside scrub by the wind.

"Lani!" Sione called out, getting her attention. He was on his knees in the sand, hammer in hand, out of sight behind an upturned canoe hull. He wore a basketball singlet, long hair tied back for work. The "ama" support of the canoe in front of him was snapped. Others looked like driftwood.. He gestured for her to come over.

"Malo uso," Leilani said, keeping her voice low. She stepped closer, out of earshot of the others. It had been a while, but his intel had always come through. He earned every dollar.

"Not all the men agree with your plans, Lani. There's a handful still holding out. They don't want to go back to selling fish and taro. We make a lot more money now."

"I know, let me talk to them this week. There's a way forward. Set up a meeting. The Agency backs me on this, trust me. It's worked elsewhere."

"Alright," Sione seemed intrigued. " How'd you get on last night? I wasn't expecting a cyclone to arrive so early this year."

"Honestly, I was scared; it was different from what I expected," Leilani said, direct as always. "That was my first."

"Wish I could say they get better. Last time, we lost some of our old people. Taken away by floodwaters."

"Damn, that's awful. Hey, I'm really sorry to hear about your brother, Sione," she added, not wanting to avoid the topic forever.

"Thanks. Me too; he was a good brother. You know, I never saw them throw him over the side. They stripped and OD'd him in front of the crew, then forced us back to work. When I came back, he was gone, never saw him again."

Leilani nodded, unsure what to say next. Other crew had told her what they'd seen, but she kept the stories to herself. Maybe it was better he hadn't had to watch his brother drown. She changed the topic. The professional relationship they had was valuable.

On paper, she was still undercover, but Sione knew the truth. Despite being against Agency code of conduct, confiding in him had been necessary to gain access to insider village channels. As far as she was aware, no one else knew that she was an Ocean Enforcement Agent.

Without a stable internet connection, she guessed most locals had never heard of the Agency. Still, Leilani suspected they'd worked out she wasn't a coral researcher. She made a mental note. Next assignment, keep the cover tighter. If this week didn't go to plan, the Agency could still pull her from active duty. It had happened before. She'd read about it on the group chat girls from the Academy used to stay connected. Two accounts had gone silent after being benched, too embarrassed to even tell their partners. When Sione told her most people assumed she was Navy or Police, it was almost a relief. A close guess, but not damaging. He had the good sense to shift the topic of conversation whenever it was brought up.

* * *

Leilani hadn't seen a single villager step inside the red store since the night young Ioane disappeared. Word had spread fast. Old and young alike whispered variations of the grim account. The fishermen on board that night swore they saw it happen. Ioane had ended up on the wrong side of the captain.

Drugged and cast overboard, he'd had no chance of survival. Weak, confused, and in shock, those who'd observed said the dark ocean claimed him within minutes.

Allegedly, an earlier incident during the shift involving a sea turtle had been at the center of Zhang's overreaction.

Not just any turtle. An albino olive ridley, still alive. An anomaly in the Pacific long-lining industry. Most turtles caught as bycatch on the line were dead by the time the winch hauled them aboard, their lifeless bodies tangled in the nylon. Somehow, this one had survived the soak.

Under normal circumstances, upon finding a turtle alive, crew would check if their supervisors were watching, then prize the J hook from its beak and toss the distressed animal unceremoniously overboard. This time, Zhang had noticed the turtle lying on the blood-stained deck, its pale flippers flailing in the air, confused. Its white shell reflected the gleam of the vessel's deck lights. Amazed at the discovery, he'd stopped all operations and asked everyone to come over and have a look.

The captain had been captivated by the beauty of the turtle, his eyes fixed on the priceless shell. But to the men's surprise, Zhang's next move had been to declare the turtle a sign of divine intervention.

Experienced officers had stared in admiration, disbelief showing on their weathered faces, as if they'd hauled in a statue from the lost city of Atlantis.

As the story went, Ioane had stepped forward to rip the turtle from Zhang's grip as he'd lifted it towards the sky, hands pressed against both sides of the shell, murmuring a prayer in Mandarin. The rest of the deckhands had watched on, unwilling to intervene. To the Chinese, the turtle's arrival meant good fortune, that their venture would be profitable.

With Ioane's confidence amplified by methamphetamine in his system, he'd believed his actions to be just, protecting an animal his parents taught him was sacred, regardless of his own personal safety.

He'd moved fast, pulling the turtle free and throwing it overboard to freedom. It had disappeared beneath the surface in seconds, never looking back.

As former soldiers, Zhang's men were always one step ahead. An officer had tackled Ioane around the waist, crashing him down onto the deck. His knee had dug into Ioane's back, pinning him among dozens of fresh shark fins. Then came the boot pressed against his neck, harder and harder, crushing his windpipe with intention. They'd rolled him over and pummeled him with punches, then forced the men back to work.

Later in the day, when he'd spoken back to Zhang in front of officers, the man had reached his limit. Ioane had left the vessel, but not in the way he'd planned. Work boots he'd saved up for would have taken him to the seafloor.

Had they wanted to risk being shot whilst staging a rescue, most of his peers admitted in confidence they could not swim in deep water. Spearfishing in the shallow, clear lagoon was different. After describing the scenario that led to Ioane's death and the beauty of the albino turtle, the fisherman who'd recounted the story to Leilani made the sign of a cross on his chest.

After hearing the story for the first time, she felt physically ill. At least the boy's death had not been in vain. He'd seen in that one in a million white turtle what she saw in all ocean species. Without a doubt, Zhang would have cut the shell from the animal while it was still alive and mounted it inside his cabin, beside the yellowing great white shark jaws on the wall.

Reflecting on the boy's ultimate sacrifice, Leilani realized she'd always felt righteous about protecting the ocean, right from the time she'd watched a pilot whale slaughter in the Faroe Islands on YouTube on her dad's unattended laptop. She'd known she wanted to protect the ocean, but becoming an Ocean Enforcement Agent had seemed out of reach. The agency didn't exactly advertise; the average person didn't even know it existed. When she stopped to think deeply, something she tried to do more these days, guided by the principles of *Ikigai*, she reminded herself that every deployment was more than she'd ever imagined. Any day in the field could be her last, and she meant to make the most of it.

Local men were angry at the horror-movie scenes they'd been forced to watch play out onboard, trapped at sea. They looked as if they had seen a massacre. Their grandparents had eaten turtles, hunting them from canoes, stealing the eggs from mothers that came back to the same beach every year, digging their nests throughout the night. It was rumored that poorer villages along the coastline of Savai'i still took a turtle from time to time, but in this district the younger generations had grown up respecting the sacred residents of their fishing grounds.

A teenage fisherman confided his dream to Leilani. Marine science, university, a future beyond the lagoon. But no student loans meant no chance. Still, he spoke of preventing corruption, of a cousin who worked in enforcement, of laws and village bylaws protecting turtles. Leilani had read the regulations, but hearing it roll off his tongue told her all she needed: he was one to watch.

It was easy to remember the boy's name. Israel from the Bible. He'd be a good leader in the next phase of her assignment. Left alone, she doubted former shark fishermen would return to subsistence agriculture. She would present the next step soon to the community. They needed hope. Fast money has a way of corrupting decent people, she'd learned.

The village rumor mill claimed Zhang had disappeared. Too many of the Samoan crew had seen him order the death of one of their own. The officer responsible had also gone into hiding.

With three police officers allocated to the entire district of eight villages, and every household owning machetes and perhaps an unregistered rifle for shooting flying foxes or dispatching pigs and cattle, chances of vigilantism were higher than ever.

Leilani could feel the new layers of tension as she went about her day, killing time until the next raid on the one remaining long liner. She talked to as many fishermen as she could, approaching them on the beach, outside their homes, after church. Building trust and relationships day by day. They said new support boats were being brought in from Apia. That was all the new captain had been waiting for.

Zhang had been wise to move on after losing his ship, even if he had arrogantly opened his store the day of Ioane's funeral. Village justice was commonplace in the region; in fact, it was even endorsed. A few nights ago, a hard to watch violent beating had unfolded outside the general store owned by a local family. Leilani had been waiting in line, behind schoolchildren, to buy instant coffee. When she'd asked what was going on, an older spectator told her the victim had made sexual advances towards his own niece that night. Rather than reporting his actions to the under-resourced police station, the family had chosen the punishment – to be meted out by three brothers of the innocent girl. No one had intervened, not even when the overweight predator had been knocked out cold, spitting teeth onto the dusty road under the lights of the store.

Wives of the shark finning crew still expected weekly pay and were not afraid to voice their concerns to the remaining Chinese. With one captain and one vessel left, competition for crew selection was high. The new leader did not know or trust the Samoan men who'd worked under Zhang and was cautious. The remaining boat would continue to head out twice a week as usual, but under his command they'd set twice as many lines, to account for the missing productivity. That way he could take more deckhands too and avoid a mutiny. Whether that was practical remained to be seen, Leilani mused, after hearing of his strategy second hand via a text from her informant.

Seeking to assert dominance and instill fear in the village, the brazen captain ordered deckhands to work on the long lines outside the store, in public. Chinese officers patrolled the area, firearms at their sides. At a distance, remaining hidden amongst banana trees, Leilani photographed the scene, hooks and line spread out on the ground blocking the main road. The arrogance was astonishing, in open view of a community in mourning, ready to act in retaliation.

Steel leaders were checked to ensure captured sharks could not bite their way to freedom; hooks were attached or cut off if found to be damaged, and replaced. Both the length of the longline and style of hooks used contravened Samoan law. But checking the gear failed to interest police, who turned their trucks around upon encountering the scene. It was too messy. The deckhands were men they'd grown up with, working to provide for their children.

Over the course of a week, the working party unraveled hundreds of feet of line, section by section, for inspection. After approval, the mainline would be coiled and taken inside at the end of the day and doors locked. GPS buoys were checked, as were branch lines and nylon strength. This captain was a man possessed, impatient, intent on ensuring the gear was ready whenever the weather aligned for overnight shark finning.

Zhang was nowhere to be seen during these days of hard labor. Checking in, Leilani felt like the local men were reaching their limit. Tension simmered below the surface, the men ashamed and angry at having to work in sweltering midday heat in front of their community, for bosses who treated them one step up from slaves. Even building crews were given water breaks and a lunchtime rest. The men knew they needed to get out, but the fate of Ioane and the semiautomatic guns that the officers carried were strong reasons not to break rank. As far as they could tell, there was no way out. From what Leilani had seen, their pay, although decent by comparison to others, was only enough to buy food for their family's dinner, with a few notes put to the side each week for church tithing and savings.

Leilani walked past the minister's house, careful not to wake the pack of dogs that slept by the gate. She scanned the roadside shrubs for a flower to tuck behind her ear, a style she admired on local girls. A few golden-skinned teenagers walked past her, flashing perfect teeth, heading toward the seawall, thick, long black hair swaying down to wider hips. No wonder half the British Navy never came home from,

she thought. Her own father hadn't wanted to either. Having given
up on finding the flower she'd wanted, she picked a frangipani from
a tree instead. Classic white, with a yellow center. As she adjusted
it into place, she noticed the minister watching her from his porch.
Embarrassed, she gave him a polite wave and kept walking.

"Leilani. Good to see you again," he called out, stopping her.
"Please come inside for some tea. We have a guest my wife and I
would like you to meet," he said.

"Sure, OK." She walked over towards the large house,
overthinking his invitation. *What could he want from her? Was this a
social visit?*

Leilani had only been invited inside the minister's home beside the
church once, for dinner when she'd first arrived. Over a glass of New
Zealand wine, they'd enjoyed a plate full of taro doused in coconut
cream and an umu-baked pig's head.

The interior was modern by Samoan design standards. In a rural
village, it stood out. White-tiled floor, Ikea furniture, TV, and ensuite
bedrooms. In the corner of the kitchen was one of only a few chest
freezers in the village. An air-conditioning unit kept the house cool.
Technically, the LDS church owned the building, but the minister plus
family were considered tenants, paying rent via their service to God
and the people. A tenancy had the potential to last a lifetime if the
community connected to their minister and subsidised him financially,
as well as spiritually.

On the sofa, sinking into the cushions whilst simultaneously
taking up half the space, lay the minister's wife, coffee mug in hand.
She did not rise when Leilani entered, but turned to face her, faking a
smile, which emphasized the fatness of her cheeks. Her dress looked
as if it had been custom-made to accommodate her size. The sight
of her elephant-sized feet was not a sight any visitor would have
enjoyed. Although she'd been kind, Leilani felt nervous around the
imposing woman.

That the minister's wife had grown up in New Zealand around
Māori gangs was clear. The woman could see straight through a
lie and spoke as straight as an arrow. Most local people chose not
to, preferring to say 'maybe' instead of 'no'. Having never spoken
to her about the shark fin trade, she did not know the woman's
position or loyalties. Fear of being exposed to the Chinese for
payment was real.

Quiet, sitting unhappily in the leftover space on the sofa, was a plain Asian woman in a housewife style dress. She still had her shoes on, unfamiliar with the customs of the country she was in. Leilani wondered if she'd left China of her own free will or been trafficked. She had layers of white makeup caked on, like a concubine from the days of Genghis Khan. None of the Asian women Leilani met appeared interested in the fishing industry at all, not that they spoke to her much. They spent most of their time stocking the store, cleaning and cooking for the officers of the long lining boats. They were involved in a minimal capacity in breaking the law, accessories to a crime, but given the lawless nature of their husbands and overseers, Leilani couldn't help but sympathise with their lack of autonomy and safety.

"Lani, meet Mi-Hong, Captain Zhang's wife," the big woman said.

"Actually, I'm his mistress," Mi-Hong corrected her. "His wife live in the countryside, China, raise a son, mmm single mother, he send money, lot of money to her," she said with contempt.

Leilani wasn't sure if being a shark finning captain's mistress was better or worse than being an impoverished single mother in rural China. She doubted the man actually wired money back to the mainland. He seemed like a cash-only kind of guy.

"Nice to meet you. Does your ah, partner, know you're here with us? I don't want any issues."

"Nobody see him for so many day now, that's why I take chance to come here," Mi-Hong said, looking down at her tiny feet. Leilani wondered why she hadn't taken the shoes off.

"Ah, can we speak in private?" She asked the minister and his wife, who reluctantly agreed, going back onto the front veranda to smoke.

"The reason I come, I want to help you. Zhang talk about you, so I know everything. Long time I know these men doing so bad things, is not right. But if I say, they shoot me, replace me with new girl. Please, I not go back inside there, when the captain go, they rape me again," her eyes moved towards the direction of the red store. She looked terrified. Leilani could hear oriental music, men drinking, shouting and gambling.

"I can organize protection for you here in Apia or arrange your return to China, if you agree to be a witness in court against the shark finning officers and Zhang. You'll get immunity. Who hurt you before?" Leilani asked.

"Thank you. It was men in Apia who run factory. They not value life, human or animal. I wish they fall into machine that cut up tuna."

Leilani's mind went into overdrive as she listened. She'd long been trying to pin down how the Chinese processed the shark liver oil for export. Other than the celebration night with Sione, she'd never seen the vehicles outside the red store move. Maybe they waited until she was not around. She hadn't seen her minder for a while either; maybe he'd been reassigned to this factory Mi-Hong was talking about.

A seafood facility in Apia with a legitimate front made sense, economically and practically. Oil needed to be purified, and tuna needed to be processed. Fins needed somewhere to go when the reefer ship was unloading in Asia. Mixing the legal with the illegal was not a surprise to Leilani. It was a tried-and-true business strategy in the world of wildlife trafficking. If the trade was to be shut down in Samoa, she needed to visit the onshore heart of the operation, as did Police and Fisheries working alongside her.

"You have an address for this factory?" Leilani asked, the conversational tone of her voice belying the investigative breakthrough against the trade this woman had contributed towards.

Their private conversation over, she waved the minister and his wife back in. The glow from their cigarettes had long disappeared.

"I don't know the address, but I go inside. You take me to city, I show you where is it," the petite Chinese woman replied.

Chapter 15

Leilani parked a mile from the factory, on the side of a quiet road. Zhang's mistress remained inside the vehicle. The woman was too nervous to be of more use. Together, they had made a slow pass down the street. With shaking hands, Mi-Hong had pointed out the entrance, hiding in plain sight.

As she got out of the driver's side, a police officer on e-bike patrol approached, insisting she could not leave the vehicle parked as it was. He also wanted to see her temporary license. Rather than move the car or flash the OEA badge, Leilani smiled and palmed him a 50 tala note. He nodded in thanks, then cycled toward the nearest store to buy cigarettes, unconcerned with her intentions or parking.

Two fisheries officers in navy uniforms were waiting outside the front gate of the seafood factory, as they'd agreed over the phone. Leilani was ten minutes late. Their government-branded truck sat in the guest carpark—directly under several security cameras, in a space reserved for visiting buyers. Monthly inspections were not unusual for Apia's export factories, but Leilani prayed this one would catch the staff off guard.

The police captain had vouched for her officers. Clean records, disciplined and committed to the cause.

"We move on your call, Agent," said the bulkier of the two officers accompanying Leilani. His name badge identified him as Moresi. He towered over his partner; the dome of his shaved head was damp with perspiration already.

"Let's go. Officer Toilolo, you ready to enter?"

She looked at the younger officer, who seemed nervous but gave a hesitant nod. On the phone earlier, he'd admitted that he'd been on marina duty for the past year. Volunteering that information made Leilani trust him more. He was ready to see action.

A tall steel gate blocked their entrance, securing the perimeter of the grey concrete industrial facility. The signage was in English and Mandarin.

SAMOA MARINE EXPORTS LTD.

Beneath it, the lines of Chinese characters. A convincing front for behind-the-scenes operations, Leilani thought.

Moresi stepped forward, pressing the red button on the intercom.

"Department of Fisheries and Agriculture. Open up." He then repeated the request in Samoan.

A light blinked red, then green. The gates slid open, metal scraping against metal, inch by inch.

Inside, a fleet of white refrigerated trucks sat parked in neat rows. Designed to move seafood across the island, or straight from fishing boats to the factory floor. Leilani had seen the name on the side before, back in the village.

Local workers in aprons and knee-high rubber boots were unloading one of the trucks, faces slick with sweat, following the daily routine. The back roller door of a truck was lifted, revealing dozens of plastic crates, stacked high. A brand-new forklift was waiting.

Inside, legal cargo gleamed black and wet. Sea cucumbers, marketed as bêche-de-mer once processed and dried, to sound more sophisticated in the culinary scene. Hundreds of them, each one painstakingly hand-gathered by free divers on one breath. There were no ethical motives to the practice; it came down to the fact that metal dredges were unsuitable, slicing target species into seafood salad or becoming lodged in coral, not cost-effective or practical.

Moresi and Toilolo walked toward the driver of an overflowing truck, iPads and logbooks in hand like idealistic Mormon missionaries wandering around. Leilani followed, her gold-plated Agency badge now on a chain around her neck, as if it were an Olympic medal. A clear message that she wasn't here as an observer.

A thin Chinese man emerged from his office to meet them, pink-cheeked and out of breath, his polo shirt soaked through. With thinning black hair combed to the side, he looked like a middle-aged accountant. Not a heartless wildlife trafficker, rumored to be a member of the Triads.

He offered his hand without introduction."

"Come, come in. We not expecting anyone today."

"That's the point of an inspection," Moresi muttered under his breath, grinning as he walked inside.

The leased industrial space was massive, its air thick with the smell of fish. The receiving area had been sectioned with efficiency in mind, one side lined with work benches, the other stacked high with crates of seafood. Workers moved between stations, sorting wet creatures by size and species. At the tables, others gutted, rinsed, and salted product with mechanical repetition.

The rest of the floor was dedicated to drying.

Row upon row of wooden racks, laden with sliced-open sea cucumbers, lay beneath industrial-strength fans and heat lamps, churning recycled air throughout the space. The drying process, the man explained, could take days. There was no market for fresh sea cucumbers, only dried.

The concrete floor was sticky with white mucus. Every few hours, a worker blasted it down with a fire hose, washing away the stench and the slime. Live sea cucumbers were not fond of being handled.

Near the far side of the facility, a Chinese foreman watched the officers and Leilani, scowling. His displeasure at the presence of law enforcement was clear, even from a distance.

As they were given the approved tour, Leilani noticed security guards around the facility, larger in build than the supervisors and managers on site. They touched no seafood, employed to ensure no theft or disorder occurred in the building. Their presence was discreet, but hard to miss amongst the employees hard at work.

Toilolo nudged Leilani, indicating with his eyebrows towards a door guarded by two burly guards in black t-shirts and dark jeans , leaning against the wall. They seemed uninterested, chatting to each other, killing time until their shift ended.

"I'd like to see inside there," Leilani asked directly, pointing to the steel door.

The man looked irritated, then re-gained his composure, ever the businessman.

"No, no, ahh, under construction now. Not safe. Not good. Cold storage, but the machine does not work properly."

Moresi ignored the owners' excuses and moved to open the door. Blueprints they'd obtained through Agency intel showed there were hundreds of square feet of the site they'd not been shown. The guards stepped in front, then looked to their boss.

He played it cool. "We move on now? We have a staff restaurant out back. My chef makes very good fish and chip. You gonna try." Leilani could only imagine what type of seafood they used in the underpaid workers' lunches.

"Appreciate the offer, sir, but under the UN Convention of the Sea and local regulations, all export facilities are subject to inspection by authorities at any time. Failure to comply with site inspection is grounds for suspension of business. Do you want that?" she interjected, tiring of his act.

Moresi and Toilolo stood their ground, muscular arms folded, looking down.

Leilani could see the owner was thinking on his feet. A criminal himself, he was not intimidated but was calculating the risk. Suspension was a legitimate move, not a threat. The OEA had shut down dozens of foreign operators before. Successful assignments were shared far and wide online once completed, to send a message that trafficking in wildlife would not be tolerated. This was not Shanghai, where he could disappear into the crowd.

"Alright. You go inside, but I tell you, not safe."

With reluctance, the security moved aside, eyeballing Leilani and Moresi. Toilolo remained outside. Someone needed to monitor the man, in case he made a run for freedom.

The storage room hummed with the low, steady drone of freezer units. There was very little light, and the temperature inside was not as cold as it should have been. The boss had been telling the truth. Without fans working, the air carried a pungent mix of expired seafood, oil and grease. Moresi and Leilani each lifted a lid on the scratched chest freezers. They were packed full of frozen, locally caught tuna. It looked like yellowfin and skipjack. The heads were used to bait longlines.

"My nineteen-year-old cousin in Savai'i is married to a Chinaman," Moresi made conversation as they worked. "She'll regret it. After doing this job for so many years, I could never trust any of them."

"My mum was only 17 when she married Dad. A palagi man in his thirties," Leilani replied.

"Not the same though. Palagi are good people. Smart, honest, rich. I wouldn't mind if my daughter married a Kiwi or an Aussie," Moresi said.

Along another wall, blue plastic barrels were stacked two or three high, each labeled with faded black marker in Chinese characters. The rest of the floor space was taken up by empty barrels, ready to be filled with dried sea cucumbers. Shark fins could layer the bottom, hidden under legal cargo.

Moresi prized one of the sealed barrels open with a crowbar he removed from his work belt, breaking the locking ring. Inside were two raw tiger shark livers, their bulk filling the entire volume of each container, inches deep in thick, bright oil that resembled golden syrup. Some barrels had greasy smears down the sides, where valuable squalene oil had leaked during handling.

He wiped his slippery hands on canvas pants. His fingers still felt unclean, as if he'd handled freshly shorn sheep's wool, the lanolin refusing to come off. Several barrels were already strapped onto wooden shipping pallets, ready to be loaded onto the next container ship heading to Asia.

Neither Leilani nor Moresi were surprised to come across shark fins inside large, woven plastic sacks, the kind used for bulk rice or grain shipments. Not all of the fins they harvested could be taken to the reefer vessel. Leilani picked a smaller fin up from an untied bag that had hundreds spilling out. The coloration gave it away. Blacktip reef shark, a dorsal fin, common in the South Pacific, yet essential to the reef ecosystem. The fin was dry, its edges brittle, the skin sandpaper-rough to the touch. Whilst some had been trimmed and cleaned, other fins still had scrapings of dried meat attached. Leilani remembered finding dozens laid out to dry, spread out on the roof of the village church, above where she slept, an image that never left her.

A stainless steel worktable was illuminated by a single fluorescent light, with a white plastic chair behind it. Long, curved knives and hand saws, crusted with dried blood and flakes of skin, lay beside buckets filled with unwanted fin trimmings. A clipboard with shipping manifests lay on the table, naming Hong Kong, Guangzhou, and Taipei as destinations. Leilani photographed it with her phone. Most shipments seemed to be marked under false labels: *dried seafood mix, fish maw, cat food, frozen yellowfin tuna/byproduct and sea cucumber/ marine offcuts,* generic terms meant to avoid the attention of customs inspectors or a signal for those on the trafficker's payroll.

A drain ran along the center of the floor, clogged with sludgy blood residue from the constant processing of seafood.

At the back of cold storage, another roller door led to the loading dock. The final stage, where shipments were transferred to shipping containers, ready to be smuggled out of Samoa under false documentation. Leilani remembered the layout of the facility; she'd studied the blueprints for hours.

"I've seen enough; we could have this goddamn place shut down today," she said to Moresi, her temper rising.

"Mmm," he grunted. "After hours of admin."

Leilani looked at him, raising her eyebrows. "Let me handle that."

The big man didn't challenge her, still looking through every sack of fins he could find. The last thing she needed was bureaucracy affecting the investigation. It was better she oversaw the paperwork anyway.

The factory boss, his guards and Toilolo watched in uncomfortable silence as the duo gathered incriminating evidence inside the storage room. Only the background noise of machines, men and vehicles reversing could be heard. A landmark wildlife trafficking case for the country was on the cards. With irrefutable evidence, jail was almost a certainty at this point for the owner.

He tapped his foot, thinking, while his security guards paced like a rabid dog that fears it will be put down. He patted his shirt pockets, searching for a cigarette. His employees would probably be let off, acting in ignorance or under duress, rather than complicity.

As Leilani and Moresi made to exit the room, satisfied with the results of their inspection, Li stopped tapping his foot, making an executive decision to protect the business. Before Toilolo realized it, the owner slammed the entry door shut without a word.

Metal on metal, hard and final. Then the overhead light cut out, pitching the room into total darkness. Sounds of a struggle could be heard outside the room. The guards were subduing Toilolo, two on one.

A chemical aroma Leilani recognized from years working inside the marine biology lab at university hit the air, formaldehyde.

She could hear the fisheries officer fighting back, boots scuffing, muffled screams against a soaked cloth. Once he was restrained in a chokehold, the fumes would enter his lungs.

"Stay strong, uso!!" Moresi yelled to his partner through the wall. "You'll go inside for this one, *saina*"

He slammed an enormous fist against the door, in vain. Even a man of his size had no chance of forcing it open.

"Open up, you bloody dog-eating bastard."

"*Kefe*," he swore again in Samoan as he banged into something solid in the dark, catching his elbow.

Leilani stayed quiet, thinking of their next move.

Toilolo's breathing was audible, weak, but there. Maybe they'd left him on the floor after he'd passed out and made a run for it.

Now she knew how Sione felt about losing his brother, the weight of responsibility on her shoulders. The officer was young, barely out of training college. She second-guessed herself. Maybe he shouldn't have been involved in an assignment of this nature, not this early in his career. If he died, it was on her.

Composing herself, she tried to focus on the blueprints for the facility in her mind – every door, every air duct, every weak point. The plan had been to gain entry without permission, had they not been welcomed in the front door. Now, she needed a way out.

Moresi's hand touched her shoulder in the dark. She flinched before catching herself.

"Relax, just me," he said, his deep voice steady now.

She breathed out, reassessing where she was in the room.

"You alright?" he asked. "We can get out of here. I know this place well."

"I know, me too. Wait a minute."

The cold air penetrated through her linen shirt, not cold enough to freeze her to death, but uncomfortable. It was an unusual feeling to be trapped in cold storage after being in the humid tropics for so long. The hum of freezer units droned in the background, broken by random drips of condensation hitting the floor.

Then something shifted. It didn't sound like a person or an animal.

Initially, it gurgled like a stomach that hasn't eaten, or a growing sourdough starter. Then it rumbled at a low frequency, like the beginning of a volcanic eruption.

Leilani turned toward the racks, relying on her hearing and sense of smell. It had to be the barrels. Another sound, a dull, wet plop to the ground.

Moresi tensed up. "What the hell was that?"

Leilani was already backing away from the sound when her boot slipped, nearly throwing her off balance. She reached down to the floor to check what she'd come across, dipping a finger into a thick, oily substance with a vile urea odor. Rubbing her finger on her pants made no difference; the heavy coating remained, like diesel on her skin. At least it was not blood, which she'd seen enough of to last a lifetime.

If it wasn't blood or fuel, then she guessed it could be shark liver oil. Crude squalene, raw, fishy and contaminated. Moresi must have knocked a barrel over in the dark.

Leilani tried to make out the shape in front of her, eyes adjusting. A barrel lay on its side, lid ajar, the contents moving, shifting, pushing against the sides as if it were living. She could hear a hissing noise as the toxic gases of anaerobic decomposition escaped from confinement, like air rushing out of a deflating bicycle tyre.

With her eyes accustomed to the darkness, she could now make out a river of dark viscous fluid sliding out of the barrel, pooling onto the floor like spilled motor oil. It kept coming and coming.

Moresi took a step back as his eyes also adjusted. "Jesus. What the f …"

Gas hit them next. Leilani felt lightheaded in the confined space, nearly losing consciousness.

It was more than the rankness of harvested shark organs; this was stronger, more rancid. Fermentation and decay mixed, with notes of ammonia and sulfuric acid.

Factory staff had figured out how to extract squalene from the livers and purify it. After that, they'd stored the barrels without another thought, never looking further into precedent. Without being aware, the factory had now kept crude squalene far past its use-by date. Familiar with storing contraband, ignorance of how to store the new valuable product would cost them.

Trapped inside sealed barrels, the oil had deteriorated. Knocking one over had been the tipping point.

"It's gone off," Leilani said, covering her mouth with her shirt. "Been here too long. We've got about five minutes left, I reckon."

Appreciating the gravity of the situation, Moresi covered his mouth and nose as she had. Her eyes honed in on the glistening, growing pool of oil underneath his steel-capped boots.

Aware of the liquid under his feet, he spoke, but the words were too muffled. There was no way either of them wanted to remove the shirts from their mouths.

They moved in darkness, shoulders brushing. Leilani cursed as her foot caught on a pallet. Pain shot up her ankle, but it held. Then they heard three quiet knocks on the roller door they knew was at the back.

At first, neither responded, assuming there were factory workers outside, carrying out routine tasks. Then the knocking came again, this time in a pattern.

"Morse code," Moresi said to Leilani, resting his hand on her back after she stood up.

"Trust in God, and he will deliver."

Hand in hand, not risking being separated, they walked towards where they guessed the door must be, prepared for anything on the other side.

Metal groaning broke the silence within as a wide sliver of light appeared as the roller door lifted, the padlock smashed off.

Outside were Zhang's mistress and a bearded Samoan factory worker, seafood apron, hairnet and gloves still on, sledgehammer in hand. He seemed to know Moresi, embracing the officer as the big man walked into the daylight. Leilani hugged Mi-Hong, grateful for her help. After being trapped inside with noxious gas leaking from the barrels, the fish-scented air outside felt as pure as the first breath after a deep dive. There seemed to be no one waiting to capture them, all employees working inside or at the front of the lot.

"My nephew, Petelo," Moresi said, introducing the worker to Leilani. "The man who first tipped off your agency. He found shark fins beneath sea cucumbers here and came to talk to Fisheries."

"Thank you, good to have you with us, Petelo," Leilani said, shaking his hand. "Now we need to get the hell outta here. Which is the best way?"

"Alleyway over there," he said, pointing to the rear of the property. After a promise to catch up soon, he went back inside the factory. The trio took his advice and ran towards a thin, overgrown gap of green between two warehouses leading out to a road.

'I stay long time in car, very hot, but you not come, so I look for you. Your nephew, he see me, he say he know Zhang from before" Mi-Hong said, short of breath from the dash across the gravel yard in the heat. She was unfit. Moresi grabbed her by the arm and pulled her along to keep up.

"How about we review what went wrong once we're out of here?" he said. She didn't seem to understand, but was thrilled with her unexpected role in the operation.

Back in the truck's safety, they realized no one from law enforcement would've come looking until later in the evening, when Moresi failed to return to the office for night shift.

A top student of chemistry and mathematics, Leilani was certain they would not have survived till then. She'd done the calculations in her head even before the door had been opened. With hydrogen sulfide, ammonia and carbon dioxide in a confined space of that size, they would've blacked out faster than in a garage filled with carbon monoxide.

Officer Toilolo had been left behind, but not left their minds. Li was unlikely to risk a murder charge in a country with a friendly relationship to China. But they could not go back inside the factory at this point. Not only would their actions compromise the entire investigation, but they would likely all be captured again. His rescue needed to be an organized affair.

Supported by the Fisheries division and Leilani's evidential photos of falsified records and tons of illegal product being kept on site, they hoped the judge on duty would grant an arrest warrant and shut down notice for the factory, effective immediately. If all went to plan, they would have a team of armed police inside the factory within an hour. There was a good chance workers would be ordered to destroy all evidence, while high-level staff tried to flee the island.

The imposing Chinese Communist Party headquarters (or Embassy, as they maintained) in Apia's middle-class city center reportedly had a helipad on the roof. Urged on by the myth, Leilani had spoken to residents, who allegedly watched the helicopter come and go daily behind towering, barbed-wire adorned walls. They were more than happy to talk about it, but no one had shown her conclusive photographs or video from their phones.

Moresi prepared Leilani for what to expect next on the drive over from the port to the grand Apia courthouse - ironically built with funds provided by China as a loan.

Judge Penamina took his time reviewing the evidence, but was ultimately satisfied with the incriminating documents and photographs presented to him. Sitting in his chambers alone at 4pm, wearing a green shirt and the red ula fala necklace begetting his authority, the white-haired man approved the shutdown, extraction of Officer Toilolo, and arrest warrants for the owner and supervisors. He praised the pairs timing and investigative work, noting that collaboration between domestic and international agencies was pleasing to see.

In another thirty minutes, he cautioned, he would have been at home having a cup of tea, out of reach. A phone call to the Chief of Police sent an armed enforcement unit on its way to the seafood factory, sirens turned off as they swerved through the tight corners of Apia's industrial zone.

As the convoy of trucks raced along quiet roads, past the cathedral and over the bridge, men, women and children stopped to watch. They would be disappointed if they planned to watch the 6pm news. Until the assignment was complete, and the poachers detained or killed, standard Ocean Enforcement Agency media injunctions would remain in place.

Chapter 16

After returning to the village, Leilani's first move was to check on her grandmother. She left the truck outside the church and took the walk in alone. The directions were seared into her memory. Her decision to walk proved correct, the sand track to the beachfront shack being unsuitable for the vehicle, narrow, overgrown, and soft underfoot from last week's rain.

Dogs chose not to get up. They growled from under the shade where they slept, used to her by now. A group of school children with backpacks slung over their shoulders waved as she passed, still half-asleep. Women were hanging their washing on outdoor lines. The air was warm and heavy. Village life went on as usual.

Granddaughter and grandmother sat together on mats, drinking sweet tea her uncle prepared before he went back to work on the taro plantation. Tulua had been reading the Bible when Leilani arrived. The 88-year-old woman listened as Leilani shared her stories, starting at the beginning. How much she understood was hard to tell, but there were tears in her milky eyes. Eyes that had seen it all. Leilani's spoken Samoan had improved during her time on the island, but progress had stalled at a conversational level. As an academic, not being fluent grated on her. She made a promise to herself that she'd fix that.

Her grandmother reached out a hand, the lines and crosses of the traditional *malu* tattoo faded over the years. She placed it softly over Leilani's own. Their skin color was similar, Leilani a shade lighter. The woman's arms were thin, muscle atrophied with age. Their heads rested close together. The old woman's soft white hair smelled of soap and saltwater.

"The village talks," Tulua said. "At church, women are worried. What will happen to our fishermen?"

Leilani nodded, understanding. Without knowing all the pieces, the puzzle felt incomplete. She saw sadness in the old woman's eyes, embarrassment at what their community had become complicit in. Among many of the elders, she'd heard the men labelled as sell-outs. Trading traditions for cash. Some on the village council wanted to banish the fishermen from the village along with the Chinese, to start again fresh.

"I remember," her grandmother reflected, "when the reef was enough. Our ancestors took only what they needed. The ocean cared for us because we cared for her. Nobody went hungry here when I was a girl. We had more seafood than you can imagine. Not like these days."

A sea breeze drifted through the open-sided fale, ruffling strands of white hair that fell across Tulua's caramel-lined skin. Outside, a light sun-shower peppered the surface of a rippling ocean. As the tide came in, Leilani watched the water level in the tannin-stained estuary rise, hour by hour, to an unnerving level. Wood rot on the foundational supports of the hut marked the level king tides had reached during the aftermath of Cyclone Rose. Despite ocean views, this was not a safe place for a home.

Leilani watched her uncle at the back of the property, hands on head as salt water trickled amongst his taro seedlings, ruining the new crop. Climate change lectures she hadn't quite believed in at the time came forefront of her mind. She felt the weight of responsibility settle on her, her resolve to protect her community from environmental and social collapse deepening with every quiet word her grandmother said.

"E le sua se lolo i se popo e tasi," Tulua recited from memory. *You can't make coconut oil from only one coconut.* Leilani understood the message behind the proverb her grandmother shared. To end shark finning on the island, she'd need the village on her side. A goal that had not escaped her mind.

"Things will get better," she promised, meeting her grandmother's cloudy eyes. "Trust me. I'll find a way."

Her grandmother smiled, squeezing Leilani's hand in silent trust before shuffling to her mattress, lying down for a nap. She looked as if she wanted to talk more, then dozed off. Leilani walked over, pulled a sheet over her, then kissed her on the forehead before leaving.

"Alofa ia te oe, grandma," she whispered. *Love you.* There was no resentment in her heart toward the old woman, just unconditional love. The estrangement between her grandmother and her mother had occurred in a different era. Understanding the complex dynamics of an isolated village rooted in thousands of years of tradition could not be achieved over the duration of a three-month visit.

* * *

Officer Moresi of the Department of Fisheries & Agriculture called in the morning. To Leilani's relief, Samoa Marine Exports Ltd was no more. With business permits and work visas canceled, the facility was shut down. Even the permit to export sea cucumbers and tuna had been revoked as a result of their actions.

Officer Toilolo had been rescued during a risky extraction and transported to Apia General Hospital via ambulance, where doctors awaited the return of chest x-rays. Medics, who had waited outside the factory alongside police units, suspected broken ribs and internal lung damage. Non-fatal, but painful. He would be on unpaid medical leave for a long time.

The owner of the seafood factory, Li, was being held on remand at Tafa'igata Prison, confined to a holding cell while investigation deepened around him. His senior staff had already been arrested and charged as accessories to illegal wildlife trafficking, their roles in the processing and export of protected species clearly documented. From what Leilani had been told, prosecutors expected these trials to proceed without complication.

Captain Sina was holding back dfurther charges against Li. She wanted to see how the Friday night sting would unfold, whether the last remaining longliner would be caught in the act, whether fresh evidence would link Li to operations at sea. If so, his existing charges would multiply.

Back in the village trade store, Zhang's replacement would have heard by now. News travelled fast. The collapse of the factory, the arrest of its owner, radio silence from the city, none of it would be missed. And if he had half the ambition of his predecessor, he'd already be calculating the additional risk. And enjoying every second of Zhang's downfall.

Mi-Hong hadn't returned to the coast with Leilani. She'd accepted a casual role as an informant in Apia, along with a signed agreement trading prosecution for intel on the illegal fishing network. Her contribution was less operational and more background, solidifying the case, connecting the dots, naming key people. She remained undeniably an accessory to the now-missing Captain Zhang, whose name had gone public and was tied to murder, meth distribution, fraud, illegal fishing, and wildlife trafficking. A warrant had been issued, with his image everywhere, courtesy of the Samoan police's Facebook page. A $10,000 tala reward had been posted, no small incentive in a country with minimum wage sitting at $1.50 US an hour.

The deal Zhang's mistress signed had an end date. After the next sting, successful or not, Mi-Hong would be extradited to China, as she'd requested. Police had valid concerns about her safety, but returning was her decision. She confirmed what Leilani had guessed: none of the Asian women involved in the trade had come to Samoa voluntarily and were not paid. That added human trafficking to Zhang's rap sheet. Another decade in prison if he was captured.

For these women, there had never been a choice. Until the day they arrived, they had never heard of Samoa. They worked without pay, passports taken on arrival, trapped in the compound under the promise of a genuine job that never existed. By day, they scrubbed blood from the trade store floor, cleaned fish guts from the back of refrigerated trucks, and laundered the crew's salt-stained overalls, heavy with the odor of fuel and fish oil. They dried fins in the sun at the back of the building, packed them for export, and swept sand from outside the store before it opened to customers early in the morning. At night, they cooked for the men, massaged their tired bodies and prepared multi-day fishing trip crews with lunchboxes of rice and dried fish. No one outside the crew ever saw them for more than a minute.

They were ghost workers, hidden, silent, and expendable. Listed as cleaners or shop assistants on forged customs paperwork, treated as property behind closed doors. According to Mi-Hong, some women were forced into sexual slavery at gunpoint. Most were too afraid to speak, too far from home to run, with a language barrier in the way. No medical care, no wages, no contact with family. Just the threat of deportation or death. If any of them had tried to leave, there was no question where she'd end up. Zhang made people disappear. The women knew it, and so did the men.

When asked why she hadn't sought help from the Chinese Embassy whilst in Apia, she said there had always been a minder, the same man who'd watched Leilani, following in the distance. Even if they had made it inside the building and sought asylum, she claimed the staff were all on the payroll and she'd be handed over, never to be seen again.

* * *

A call came in from a US number as Leilani walked back to her accommodation. She was surprised the reception was good enough, given the persistent rain over the last week. It was Director Ventura, her boss, checking in.

"Agent Brown, I'd like to congratulate you personally on the factory shutdown and the arrest; that city has been on our radar for too long," he said.

"It's been quiet on our end; I apologize for that. We've had complications with the whale shark project in the Philippines; agents were arrested, and we've been in damage control, to put it lightly. So I'm glad to hear your assignment in the South Pacific is on track. Only a few weeks left before we see you back here." Leilani nodded; she'd been hoping for this call. Words of affirmation from the top meant a lot to a rookie agent.

"For a first solo mission, your achievements are setting the bar high for this year's Academy intake, I'll say that much."

Leilani felt a sense of relief. Not one to care what others thought of her, his words still gave her a dopamine rush. "Thank you, sir. I'm ready for whatever comes next."

"As always," Ventura said, then moved onto business as usual.

"I've read the strategic plan for Friday night and spoken at length with Captain Sina in Apia. You have our full support. I wish you luck. If you need additional resources or men on the ground, reach out. We've got people in Australia who can be there in 3 hours if necessary."

Leilani felt her confidence rising, ready to finish what she'd started. Re-connecting with the Agency, even over a call, made solo fieldwork feel more manageable.

Despite a full night's sleep, there was one feeling she could not push aside after the factory takedown. She worried about the seafood factory employees, men and a handful of women, who had been terminated without compensation, ordered to return home, many on the bus. Police hadn't even taken down their names. They were small fish, unimportant.

The degree to which they understood the illegality of their employment varied from being completely in the dark to naively optimistic about the prospect of bonuses. In any scenario, their testimonies were ruled inadmissible to the court, compromised by their involvement in facilitating the shark fin trade.

In the end, it was their families who would pay. No food on the table. No money to send the kids to school. After two months in the village, Leilani had seen firsthand what the face of poverty looked like in the Pacific islands. The struggles low-income families faced back in Northland didn't come close.

Apia's fishing industry could absorb eighty new workers, but there was no guarantee. Most would try their luck with Starkist in American Samoa, earning US $5.56 an hour on the cannery floor, if they could find the money for an overnight ferry trip, work permit and a bunk in the overcrowded accommodation the tuna factory provided for foreign employees. Others might fight for coveted hospitality jobs in coastal resorts. Either way, hard times were coming.

Officer Moresi and Leilani kept in touch over the following days by text. He was sharp, reliable, and knew the area. Experienced at sea and a part-time lecturer in law at the University, he was the natural choice to lead the Friday night patrol. She'd asked him to take the port-side approach around the reef, one half of a coordinated pincer movement designed to catch the longliner red-handed in the act of shark finning.

He'd earned the leadership role. Inside the factory, under pressure, he'd stayed the course and got results. Now, he'd get the chance to do it again, this time offshore.

Captain Sina would lead the starboard arm of the pincer approach. She knew the coastline better than anyone on the team and had run enough offshore operations to anticipate escape strategies. They planned for the possibility that the longliner crew might run. Cut the lines, kill the lights, and head for international waters. It would be a rash decision. The odds weren't in their favor. If they ran, they'd run out of diesel long before the ex-New Zealand police launches did.

The rusted hulls and patched fuel systems on the Chinese vessels were built for days at sea, not for high-speed showdowns. If it came to a chase, Sina would back Samoa every day of the year.

Another text buzzed on Leilani's phone. It was Sione this time, sending an update from behind enemy lines.

Forecast good for Friday. It's all on. LETS do this.

The weather gods were blessing the operation. Calm conditions gave the patrol boats an edge, less risk of capsize, more pace on the approach. Sione had briefed the few deckhands he could trust with his life. Men he'd grown up alongside, played rugby with. Police and Fisheries had their launches fueled, waiting at the water's edge. Leilani would be onboard to oversee the operation, upholding the international mandate of the Oceanic Enforcement Agency.

The last captain remained determined to bring in an illegal catch. He'd lost only one distribution channel. The reefer ship still lurked unseen near international waters, the vast hold empty again after a return trip from Asia. Leilani had eyes on the elusive man at all times. He wore the same blood-stained flannel shirt nearly every day. None of the locals or crew knew his name, but Mi-Hong had identified the man as the ringleader in her attack, a cold operative with no family back home and no heart.

Chapter 17

Crowded around a small box TV at the back of their store on a rainy evening, following the local election coverage while eating noodles, the Chinese fishermen doubled over in laughter when Captain Zhang's face appeared on the screen, followed by a safety warning and reward offer. They would have traded him in for the money in a heartbeat if anyone knew where he was, Mi-Hong told Leilani. The wanted captain's former partner was still in communication with other women trapped inside, working daily with Samoa Victim Support on a plan to get them safely off the island.

Captain Sina had rung during the night: two more factories operated by **SAMOA MARINE EXPORTS LTD** had been shut down after raids uncovered barrels packed with shark fins. Hours later, arson had destroyed an industrial building—rented to the same company.

Police arrived to find the offices gutted, with the stench of petrol still hanging in the air. Photos emailed to Leilani showed a scorched interior: walls blackened; evidence turned to ash. This wasn't about protecting the industry; it was a message, a warning. So far, there had been no further arrests. Just court-ordered shutdowns and canceled visas. The trafficking ring was damaged but not broken. They were fighting back.

Two more seafood factories closed meant 100 local staff on a small island left without an income, in a country with no social welfare. Returning to fishing and farming was possible, but Leilani needed an opportunity to talk first. She felt her hand was being forced, trying to uphold the law at the same time as saving a community. With the village in a state of confusion and resentment, she asked the council to arrange a meeting, where she intended to address the situation before chaos took over.

Men who had continued to head out every morning in their wooden, hand-carved canoes for the past few months shared their stories with the unemployed who returned home. The ocean was providing more than enough, as it once had. Maybe removing the sharks had been a blessing in disguise. Scientists don't understand the ways of our people, they said.

She tried to understand their short-term thinking but struggled. These men needed to consider what they were saying. Not only was talking about abundance naïve, it was also not a savvy business move. More canoes returning to the water would further dilute sales.

As Leilani had witnessed over regular dives since arrival, the entire southern coastline of Upolu was undergoing a silent change, a biological shift. She'd seen no sharks at all on her last few dives, even at dawn and dusk. Only juvenile blacktip reef sharks swimming along the shoreline in inches of clear water, their fins too small for even the most ruthless poacher to target.

As she explained in layman's terms to any man, woman or child who would listen, the reef was dying. But they couldn't see it. They didn't want to. Most women had never entered the water past waist-deep, and their husbands were coming back with more fish than before.

It pained Leilani to allow the sole longliner to continue setting its miles of line every night outside the fringing reef, knowing locals were conflicted. Everyone needed to be patient. In two days' time, the bloody trade on the island would take a knock down they would not get back up from again.

The foreign-flagged tuna vessel she could see operating in the distance had been forward-thinking enough to register independently. On paper, this crew had no association with the illicit activities going on in Apia. Footage of Li's trucks parked outside the trade store provided by Leilani was not considered sufficient evidence of association, the police had informed her.

With so many men out of work, the 6am bus to Apia had spare benches available for the first time. There was no longer a need to stand in the aisle, or for students to sit on each other's laps. The driver, who had once given her a hand onboard, ignored her.

She was tired of eating chicken and tired in general. She needed iron in her diet, and taro leaves were not cutting it. To buy red meat, a trip to the city was required. The big man behind the wheel of the bus had looked at Leilani, waiting under the roadside ramshackle shelter, shook his head and kept on driving.

In New Zealand, the driver would've received a warning from his boss, but here, his bus was his business; he could drive past her every day if he chose to. Denied boarding, there was no choice but to use the Pajero.

Taking the bus had been her preferred, safer choice. That someone could've messed around with brake lines or the fuel tank of the truck played on her mind. The journey across the island was dangerous enough, with flooding, potholes and wandering cattle. She knew the men in the village could cripple a vehicle and make it look like an accident if they wanted to. Taking apart old cars was more than a hobby here. Shirtless, they worked under the hoods until it got too dark to see.

Confessing she was an agent on assignment hadn't gone down well with everyone in the community. Some families she knew well and enjoyed meals with were angry, feeling like their secrets had been used against them. Now these families had nothing, and they couldn't understand why. The village seemed to have moved on from the death of Ioane, the young fisherman and son of a high chief, pushed overboard to his death by foreigners.

As Leilani walked down the dirt road towards the ocean for a dawn swim, a ritual to keep her sane, men working nearby in the plantations ignored her. There were none of the friendly waves she'd come to expect in the Pacific islands. Women cooking breakfast in open-sided fales didn't look up, no smiles, no eye contact. As far as most people were concerned, their families had lost steady income, their place of work shut down while a foreign shark finning vessel still worked the coastline untouched, setting lines of death wherever they liked. Local men who still crewed on that boat were so lucky, they said.

Down at the water's edge, out of sight from the village below volcanic black rock walls and palms, two men were waiting. Instinctively, her hand went to her gun, but the pockets of her rugby shorts were empty. Of course, her gun was in the room, taped to the underside of the bed. The men sat on a huge, waterlogged tree trunk that had washed ashore after the last cyclone. She realized it was Sione and his father, the chief, then relaxed. There was no need for a confrontation.

Coral fragments crunched under her jandals as she made her way over. This conversation needed to happen. Sione shielded his eyes from the rising sun with his hand to confirm it was Leilani approaching, then stood to give her a hug. His father shook her hand.

"Is this some kind of ambush?" she joked. Only Sione knew where she liked to swim. There were miles of uninhabited beach, yet here they were.

"Sorry, Leilani, but the village talks; we had to get you alone. The Apia situation has not gone unnoticed by our council," the chief said.

"We … they, support you. You cut the head off the dragon. If God wills it, the tail will be destroyed this week." He then turned to his son and spoke in quick-fire Samoan, frustrated.

Sione took over, translating. "My father is ashamed to tell you, Lani, but many families here don't understand what has happened. Women of the village are angry with you. Their husbands thought they were signing up for tuna fishing, a good career. As far as families are concerned, the men lost a good job because of you. At home, I know they continued the lie about tuna fishing. People don't know why we are talking about sharks."

"You're right," admitted Leilani, casting her eyes to the sand.

She felt uncomfortable, wishing there were a senior agent on the island to seek guidance from. This turn of events was unexpected. She'd assumed the village would view her as a hero, taking down the first barrier in the fight against illegal fishing that was killing their coast.

"I've asked the council to organize a meeting. I want a chance to explain everything. Please, we're close now."

"So we heard, we'll be there. Ah, something else Sione and I talked about, Lani. We want you to come and stay with us. No one can touch you there," the chief offered.

His offer surprised Leilani. A move would be taken as a serious sign of disrespect to the minister and his wife, who rented the accommodation to the Agency at a fair price.

As if reading her mind, he continued.

"The minister cannot protect you. That is a fact. They don't even live in the same building. Besides, the man is a pacifist. His family is not from here."

"We have dogs," Leilani said, then realized how weak her argument sounded. The mixed-breed canines the Minister kept had a bark worse than their bite, malnourished and lacking the energy to subdue an adult.

"The men see the big picture. They understand from talking with the deckies. It's the women I'm worried about. Some didn't finish high school because they were pregnant. Most have never left the island. They're an unknown factor, and they have more influence over the men than they should."

Sione scrolled through his iPhone and showed her a few photos. They showed his face, hardly recognizable behind bruises, a black eye and purple lacerations.

"I was not the best husband, but I didn't deserve this," he confessed.

Leilani looked away. Growing up in Northland, she'd seen her fair share of domestic abuse up close, but the photos were intense.

"Women on the island are different, Lani. Where you're from, they live off a benefit in a government house, or work for good pay. Here, they can have a job and still their children go to bed hungry. It breaks them inside. Trust me, women here are capable of anything. Dad and I are worried they will direct their anger towards you now their husbands have no work, your room is an easy target."

"I'll think about it. But right now, I need to get into the water and clear my head," Leilani said, looking towards the ocean, ending the conversation.

The chief nodded. "Thank you. That's all we can ask for, your consideration."

She thanked them again for the warning and made a mental note to lock the door to her room. Adapting to the trusting island way had become second nature. She'd become complacent, even leaving keys in the car.

Rubbing around inside the tempered glass of her dive mask with her finger, she spat inside, dunked it in the saltwater, then adjusted the rubber strap over messy hair and corrected the mask on her face. Firm to prevent leaks, but not so tight as to dig into the skin under eyes and cheeks. She moved stray strands of hair out of the way. The snorkel mouthpiece between her lips tasted salty - thanks to forgetting the freshwater rinse after using it last time. As she took the plunge, the visibility astonished her, no matter how many times she'd seen it before. Even with the rain the south coast had been experiencing, it felt surreal, like diving into an aquarium.

Sione watched her go under, then took his dad's arm for support, helping the old man safely traverse the beach and back through the palms.

Underwater was Leilani's time to think. Freediving was supposed to relax her mind, but for the first time in years, Leilani had started having tension headaches. Throbbing pain behind the eyes, into the back of the skull and neck, that Panadol and Ibuprofen from the medical kit had no effect on. It was reaching the point where she was considering asking a woman in the village to treat her the traditional way, with strong massage using homemade coconut oil. The power in the woman's hands and arms made her hesitate. She was not experiencing dehydration; she was not tired; she was eating well, so the cause could only be anxiety.

With projects for NGO's under her belt before joining the OEA as an agent for the ocean, she understood the root causes of poaching and wildlife trafficking, but there needed to be separation, in the same way police try to disassociate from what they see at work. Her clients were the ocean and its inhabitants. But having caused distress to so many ocean-dependent families as a step in the investigation, shutting down the factory, remained hard to live with. This was not a fly-in, fly-out contract.

As Leilani watched a cow-tailed ray shuffle on the sandy seafloor ten feet below her, clouds of sediment rising as it ruffled its wings, her distracted mind returned to the chief's warning. *Was she actually in danger from people she'd set out to help?*

As she glided under the surface, hair tied into a protective, water-resistant bun, her first thought was that the cyclone had killed more coral than expected. With the prevailing wind and swell, there hadn't been a chance to dive this end of the beach until now. The northern end, where she'd entered the water, had fared better.

But something felt off; the section of reef she was looking at wasn't smashed. The wide table corals were still intact, as were the acres of staghorn that dominated the seascape out to the fringing reef. Every branch, every tower, perfect in structure, was bone white. Not temporarily bleached or broken, totally dead.

It was a ghost city of coral, abandoned, algae the only tenants. She tried to swear underwater; the words garbled in her snorkel.

As she kicked her fins high above swathes of brilliant white skeletons, she found those responsible for the chaos below. A loose arrowhead of hundreds of dinner-plate-sized, spiky discs, marching with intent across the reef.

Unmistakably, crown-of-thorns starfish. Her favorite marine science lecturer had labeled them "terrorists of the ocean".

They would've arrived at night, drawn by the scent of a reef in collapse. Now they were feeding in daylight, which meant one thing: they were desperate and starving. She watched as a slow-moving purple starfish climbed over another in its way, like a bully pushing a younger boy aside in the cafeteria line. Their urge to feast was primal.

Even without brains, they always seemed to know where to go when an ecosystem was dying. Following the scent of coral like a shark detecting swirls of blood in the water. They devoured soft coral tissue, digesting it right off the skeleton with their eviscerated, acidic stomachs, leaving trails of chalky ruin behind.

With shark numbers down, middle of the food chain hunters like grouper and snapper had exploded in number, a population boom the reef wasn't prepared for. She wished she had her spear gun, there were plenty of them out, chasing down smaller fish. If only they ate crown of thorns starfish, almost nothing here did. This was a reef undergoing change at a dangerous rate.

As Leilani observed and photographed the invasion below, she thought more about what to say at the community meeting. The men and women of the village needed to understand what was going on beneath the surface of their ancestral fishing grounds.

These predatory species she was seeing everywhere needed to be speared, taken on the handline or rod. They were wiping out herbivores. Parrotfish, damselfish, the ones that scraped algae off the coral and kept the system in balance. Looking around, it felt like the reef was nearing collapse. Crown of thorns were only the executioners, moving in to finish the job. Once they moved on to fresher pastures, opportunistic algal mats would suffocate the bones of the reef in a never-ending blanket of wispy green and brown. The coral tableau below her was trapped in a death spiral she had no confidence it could get out of.

Her fingers shook as she photographed the starfish invasion. This was textbook **Phase 3**, as marine biologists knew it. Collapse in motion. On the road towards a coral graveyard. Even with extensive human intervention, it would take decades to reestablish decent coral coverage along this section of the reef.

Checking her phone after drying off from the swim, Leilani saw one of the older Agents online on the work group chat, with whom she had a good professional relationship. They messaged about the guilt she felt inside. A fatherly man, he reminded her this was only her first mission, that conflicting emotions would fade over years ahead. *Was that a good thing?*

She was thankful when he steered her back on track, reminding her that her focus had to be on the ocean and the wildlife if she were to be successful as an agent. Their mandate was as an environmental agency, not a humanitarian agency. A positive overall result for local communities was secondary, the final stages of an assignment.

There was a well-known, unofficial story told to every student coming through the Academy that her mentor brought up. Years ago, an American agent working in the Gulf of Mexico had been murdered by artisanal fishermen in a poor fishing village, after they'd freed one of the last remaining vaquita from a fishing net straining with fish, losing the men their entire week's salary. She could only imagine the PTSD her partner officer had. It was a grim story, but a necessary reminder that the focus was on saving sharks.

She imagined she'd feel better once the final stage of the assignment could be implemented. Ecotourism. She planned to introduce the concept at the village meeting, promote it as an alternative to shark finning. The OEA had never taken a mission in the Pacific Islands until now, but the strategy had worked well in Honduras, Guatemala and Mexico – all developing nations – so why not in Samoa?

Chapter 18

'*Unknown number*' appeared on Leilani's cellphone during an online team meeting. It was her mother's husband, at last down from the mountains to sell his taro. He was ready to return, now or never, her window of opportunity closing by the minute.

Ending the pixelated video call to Apia police station as fast as she could without being rude, Leilani packed a change of clothes, her gun and underwear into a dry bag. She checked the church room was locked for a second time, then jogged to the rendezvous point.

An old Toyota Rav 4 was waiting as promised, engine idling. It stuttered every minute or so. She guessed the front right tire had fallen victim to a pothole, as a smaller spare replaced it. Mud and layers of dust coated the lower half of the vehicle. Gravel roads had chipped the silver paint. In the passenger seat, she reached for a seatbelt, then realized there wasn't one.

Behind the wheel, her mother's second husband wore his lavalava, cracked rubber jandals that needed replacing and no shirt. The driver's seat also appeared to have no belt. His upper body wiry, hard muscle built from working the land, his brown skin darkened by the sun. His tightly curled black hair had been buzzed into a flat top.

"You must be Aiono, nice to meet you," Leilani said with a smile. The passenger door did not seal all the way. Aiono shook her extended hand and grinned, revealing a gold-plated tooth.

"I'm not speaking too much English," he said with a glint in his almond eyes, then began driving back towards the mountainous interior of Upolu, one hand on the wheel. He drove at speed, avoiding potholes like a pro, with auto-tuned music blaring too loud for conversation. An expensive stereo, complete with iPhone charging port, replaced the original Japanese edition. Momentarily, the connection would cut out as they drove further away from the coast, leaving an awkward silence, then it would come back on.

He sang along where he knew the lyrics, unashamed, pleased to have finished work. A half-finished 750ml bottle of warm Taula rested in the cup-holder compartment between them, beer sloshing around, threatening to spill whenever the car hit a bump. From time to time, he would take a swig with his free left hand. Leilani felt uncomfortable, holding on tight, but at least he wasn't drunk.

Before the ascent onto the cooler roads of the interior, they passed a 2 pump petrol station. Aiono slowed down and pulled alongside one of the rusted pumps. A man in floppy bucket hat, t-shirt and shorts, leaned against a wall in a plastic chair straining under his weight. Surprised by the revving of the engine, he arose from his sleep to come over and serve his customers. He raised a hand in greeting, then the middle-aged man stood patiently outside the vehicle, hand on pump, as if waiting for something.

"Fifty," Aiono said to Leilani. "For *penesine*". Over his shoulder, she could see the orange petrol warning light. She wondered how long they'd been traveling on fumes. Petrol stations were scarce once you left the city.

Unsurprised, Leilani handed over a crumpled blue note, which Aiono duly passed out the window to the service station attendant. The man nodded, pocketed the cash, then filled the Rav 4 up while the engine continued running. As the meter ran up, Aiono tried to light a cigarette inside the vehicle. Leilani took the lighter out of his hand, leaving a dry cigarette in the corner of his mouth. He removed it, embarrassed.

"Air?" the attendant asked, kicking the rear tires. He eyed up Leilani, then looked back down at the wheels, walking around the back.

'*Leai, fa'afetai uso*," Aiono replied. No thank you, brother.

As they drove off, Leilani looked at the dash. The gauge showed the tank 3/4 full, for the equivalent of 35 NZ dollars. At home, the needle on her Subaru Outback wouldn't show halfway for that price.

The steep road had no metal guardrails and crumbled at the edges. She wondered whether Aiono had a driver's license. Not that she cared, but it was obvious he had no warrant and no registration. If the police pulled him over, she wasn't about to pay the fine or a bribe.

When her dad drove on road trips, she always slept. Not this time. Focused on the sheer cliff edge that descended to a Jurassic park type canyon below, there was no chance of switching off. The bus had taken this route before. Driving to Apia herself, she usually chose the longer coastal road, winding through palm-fringed villages along the water. It was slower, but better than risking these mountain passes or cattle that stepped out of the bush without warning. Aiono's home was in the mountain valleys, so there was no other way than this.

Panoramic views of endless rainforest-clad valleys, thousands of feet below, pinned with homesteads every few miles, took her breath away. Spray drifted in through the open roll-down windows when the car's side faced the right angle. When the true wet season rain arrived, there was no way she'd travel on this road. Mudslides, rockfalls and river breaches were common; she'd seen the YouTube videos. Overcrowded buses disappeared too, swept away by floodwaters when crossing bridges. Fortunately, the Agency planned to have her back in New Zealand before the heavy rains came. The assignment could not go on forever; funds were not unlimited.

More than once, the Rav 4 lost traction, skidding on the wet road as if it were black ice. Leilani felt nauseous, questioning her decision to travel with a man she didn't know. All her Academy training and parental advice over the years cautioned against it. Aiono noticed her nervousness, guaranteeing everything would be alright. Her hand gripped the vibrating door handle to steady herself. Once in a while, he would completely take his eyes off the road, enjoying playing tour guide, pointing out the cascades of freshwater that ran down sheer walls in the rainforest. His old-school flip-top cellphone rang twice, which he checked both times, eyes off the road again.

Every time the small 4WD spun around, Leilani heard heavy objects shifting in the trunk. Eventually, curiosity got the better of her and she twisted around to see what was going on back there.

Aiono glanced at her.

"*Pua'a*" he said, looking pleased with himself.

Sure enough, alongside taro and a stalk of green bananas he'd been unable to sell during the day, was an adult pig. It lay on its side, pale-skinned with coarse hair. A blow to the skull had killed it, judging by the head wound, saving a hard-to-find bullet. No doubt Aiono was happy because his children would have full stomachs for the coming days. In the cooler, elevated climate, fresh meat lasted longer than on the coast without refrigeration too.

He pulled off the single road that transected the island, the location of the unmarked turnoff memorized by repetition. The truck bounced up and down as they drove upwards towards the family's shack, set deep within a rugged Jurassic landscape. From a distance, Leilani saw young girls standing outside, waiting for their father to return home. Behind them, the descending sun lay low in an orange, hazy sky.

His children wore oversized shirts and NZ rugby shorts. There were no neighboring properties or power lines. No signal on the satellite phone. The dominant feature was a huge concrete water tank, blanketed in vines. Barking dogs ran toward the moving vehicle. A stack of scrap metal, tires and broken car doors lay beside the house. At the back of the cleared land, there was a plantation, taro thriving in rich volcanic soil. The acrid scent of melting plastic hung in the air, with no breeze to disperse the toxic smoke. Someone was burning rubbish.

As the vehicle came to a stop outside the house, Leilani's heart raced for a different reason. She'd mentally rehearsed the words she wanted to say to her mother since the woman had walked out after her eighth birthday. After a nerve-wracking hour in the car without conversation, she was ready to talk.

* * *

"I don't know why you come here, Leilani," her mother said when she first saw her daughter approach. She'd recognized her firstborn child within seconds. She appeared embarrassed about the state of her house and land.

'There's nothing here for you. It's better live your life in New Zealand. Stay there. More opportunity."

Those were not the words Leilani had been hoping to hear. Then again, she wasn't sure why she had expected anything from a woman who had not tried to contact her daughter for twenty years. Yet here they were. Aiono took the overweight woman aside for a word.

Asu seemed preoccupied with the idea that people were following her daughter, trying to kill her. It seemed secondhand accounts of her agency work had been blown out of proportion; the stories travelling far around the island. But to date, there had been no reason to suspect the Chinese knew she had family here.

After her second sugary cup of tea, the woman relaxed, forgetting for a while the curse she believed was following Leilani. She still resembled the old photographs, but life had taken its toll on her beauty. Mother and daughter sat in front of the house on a rectangular tombstone, overlooking the expansive valley. The rain had stopped; a vivid rainbow crossing the gap. Chickens pecked at the dirt around their feet.

"Marrying your father was seen as a blessing by everyone in the village, you know. They so jealous. Jake, he successful, tall, a white man. But I was just a schoolgirl. Didn't know anything," Asu shared, staring out into the distance.

"Every day away, I miss my brothers and sisters. My parents. I'm not liking New Zealand. We live in Wellington at first, worse than Auckland. So cold and lonely. New Zealand is different back then, there was not many of us - islanders. My only regret - that I leave you there. I didn't have a heart to take you away from your future. And now, from what I hear from the village, I was right. Although, you're braver than I was. Fighting to protect our way of life. No one has done that here before." She wiped away tears from the corners of her eyes with her sarong.

"I know you don't know me or remember much, Leilani, but you were the most beautiful, amazing young girl that a mother can ask God for. You so smart, even from a young age. To be honest, I wasn't ready to be a mother. Too young, you know. But I loved you. I still do. That's why I leave you there with Jake, without fighting for you, without disturb you. I never thought I will see you again."

They sat in contemplative silence for a while, watching distant silhouettes of fruit bats emerging from the trees against a sunset.

"I remember you," Leilani said, tearing up. She couldn't bring herself to use the word *Mum*. She didn't want to, it had been too long. "And I forgive you."

Aiono gave them privacy, going out back to process the pig before it was too dark. His three daughters observed the butchery from a safe distance, with a curious mix of shock and awe. Despite being raised Seventh-Day Adventist, their father wasn't above admitting that life was too hard in the mountains to turn down meat of any kind.

Leilani wasn't sure what to make of the situation. There were confessions, questions and crying on both sides, but none of the magic she'd imagined would still be there 20 years later. Her mother had moved on, forgotten about her past life and family. It took her a while to find English words for what she wanted to say, having only lived in New Zealand for 8 years, decades ago. Her sentence structure was irregular, skipping words here and there or changing them to suit as she pleased. They hadn't spoken English much at home either, when she was little. A fast learner, Jake had been fluent in Samoan by the time he'd met Asu. She guessed that had been part of the attraction, as well as his money.

It was good not to have her father on the island for this reunion. It would've broken his heart to see the mother of his only child living in poverty, banished to a few acres in the island's interior, owned by an effeminate uncle who'd passed on without successors. He was buried directly beneath where mother and daughter now sat and talked. They couldn't afford a headstone.

She wasn't sure how to, or if she should keep the meeting a secret. For an honest woman, it would be hard to stop the truth of the night from coming out once she returned home. With her dad, Leilani shared every secret. He was a best friend and a father. Their close relationship was something a lot of her friends back home had been jealous of, not having stable parents in their lives.

Talking to her mother brought up too many emotions. The compassionate side of her brain wanted to hug Asu, hold her and tell her that everything would be alright. The analytical side reasoned that the family was doing fine comparatively. Living life on their own terms, no rent, no mortgage, no rates. Aiono had elderly parents who lived in a modern village on the outskirts of Apia. They could move there if they chose to. The old couple loved it when their grandchildren came to visit.

Regardless of the complex feelings Leilani felt towards her mother, her half-sisters were innocent. The girls were gorgeous, seemingly happy and thriving with their isolated upbringing. The oldest of the trio, Ana, even spoke good English. They were thrilled to have a big sister from New Zealand. Leilani promised to stay in touch, although she wasn't sure how to do that. She wished she'd brought more in her backpack to give them than lollies and muesli bars, there just hadn't been enough warning.. She'd make sure there was another chance to come back before leaving the island, after the mission to eliminate the shark fin trade was complete.

Dinner was served as darkness descended on the valley. A generator hummed in the background. Rooftop solar panels distributed by an NGO with good intentions were not functioning again. Aiono led the family in brief prayer, then the group ate warm pork and smoky taro with their hands, sitting on the floor in relative silence, disturbed only by the wingbeats of moths fluttering around the light.

After dinner, Leilani announced she'd head back to the village in the morning. There was still work to be done. Her sisters tried to get her to change her mind. Together, the girls settled for the night on their mats, whispering and laughing until midnight. Leilani showed them her phone, underwater photos of sharks, turtles, and explained why she was in Samoa. Their eyes were fixed on the screen, only pretending to sleep when she appeared from the dark, lavalava held to her chest, belt loose in her hand. Her voice carried into the next valley when she yelled at the children. She told Leilani goodnight, then crossed to her husband's side of the room. Moments later, the room was silent except for the man's snoring.

Instead of dreaming about her family, Leilani rolled as negative thoughts tormented her for the first time in months. She had visions of 12-foot pythons, no doubt roaming the undergrowth of surrounding forest. A dog-eared guidebook she'd purchased in an Apia tourist store, sitting alongside shell necklaces and flowers made from polystyrene, alleged there were snakes on the island. *Far from urban environments, inland* – the book stated. *Exactly where she was now.*

She could swim into dense schools of barracouta and spearfish above sharks, freedive deeper than most men would dare to go on scuba, but snakes were still her kryptonite. An aunt in Queensland had made jokes for a week upon discovering this weakness when Leilani had visited the rural family home surrounded by eucalyptus bush.

Her thoughts drifted to her half-sisters—Fa'amanuia, Ana, and Losa—as she lay on the mat beside their sleeping bodies, all three under a single sheet. She'd only learned of them weeks ago, yet the love Leilani had imagined she would still have for her mother had shifted to them. Bright girls with few opportunities ahead. Seven-year-old Losa wasn't even in school. She lived with constant ear pain and needed a complex operation they couldn't afford. The local two-teacher school had sent her home after learning she struggled to hear.

Self-aware enough to realize her blossoming career as an Ocean Enforcement Agent wasn't in alignment with the reality of parenting, Leilani allowed herself to entertain a small hope of adopting her sisters one day, bringing them to live in New Zealand. She could teach them to dive and surf, ride horses across the sand dunes and eat seafood straight from the ocean. Maybe they'd end up playing rugby for the Black Ferns, as she had once dreamed of, before the pull of the ocean, academia and diving competed for attention. At least she had the funds. Her agency role offered more than sufficient income to buy her own place by the beach back home *and* to hire a top immigration lawyer. Other Polynesian families did it all the time. Maybe it could be more than a dream. But for now, the dozens of photos all the sisters had taken together would have to suffice.

* * *

Waiting in light rain for a ride back to the coast with Aiono once he got his act together, Leilani noticed someone had been throwing cigarettes into the bush. The heel of a boot had pressed them deeper. Littering was nothing unusual, nor was smoking; her mother's husband never seemed to stop. But he smoked hand-rolled, using plain paper wrapped around fragrant tobacco he grew himself, sometimes with a little marijuana mixed in. He'd offered her one last night after dinner.

These butts, buried in mud near dense wild grass at the edge of the property, had red and gold filters. Not a local brand. Theories rushed into her mind.

Never one to overlook evidence, she crouched and scooped the dirt with bare hands. She brushed away soil clumps with care, trying not to tear the waterlogged paper of the cigarettes. Part of their brand name was still legible, but she couldn't read it. The word was written in Chinese characters.

Chapter 19

The phone rang as soon as the truck descended from the mountain range towards the coast, reception kicking in.

"Lani, we can't text. You know why. Only call me on WhatsApp," Sione said.

"Understood," she said, not wanting Aiono in the driver's seat to translate the conversation. English ability in the rural areas varied so much. There was no way of knowing how much he knew or understood. Men on the island pretending to be uneducated was a common ploy when they wanted to listen in.

"Everything on track?" she asked.

"Village council has called the *fono* you asked for. The meeting you wanted, it's happening tonight. You ready?"

"Okay, thanks. 7PM, I'll be there," Leilani replied and hung up. She'd rehearsed her speech to the community a dozen times. Direct and to the point, without complicating the science that backed her message. The intention was to clear the air and get the unconverted on board with ending shark finning in Samoan waters.

Butterflies fluttered in her stomach, but not from the sudden change in altitude. It was the cultural protocol for the evening she worried about. Where to enter the meeting house, where to exit, how to stand, who to make eye contact with, who to address first. Did she need to bring gifts? No one had ever taught her, leaving her unprepared. It was not a feeling that sat well with her.

* * *

By age 12, Leilani could name every species of dolphin found in the South Pacific, but when it came to cars, she would walk away before the bonnet was up.

Her father and grandfather, all capable men on the tools, had tried over the years to teach her the inner workings of a truck, but vehicle maintenance was one skill Leilani had no patience for.

By necessity, the exception was boat engines. As a trainee at the Academy, she'd forced herself to understand them inside and out. Theory exams had been challenging, but she'd passed. Practical had been less of a challenge. Being adrift at sea during a solo mission was a death sentence she had not signed up for.

Now, she resented not having taken those early mechanic lessons on board. It didn't take a professional to work out that the Rav 4 she sat inside was dying with every minute they drove. At least they'd left the mountains of the interior behind, with the home stretch to the coast ahead.

As she'd guessed, the engine coughed like an old man with lung cancer, then conked out. Aiono steered the vehicle, still in forward motion, to the grass verge on the side of the road, where it came to a standstill. He seemed unconcerned, like this had happened before on taro runs.

Leilani made to get out of the car, undoing the jammed seatbelt, but was waved back.

"Please stay in the car. Samoa driver, no good, no license," he laughed, unintentionally ironic.

A man of action, not words, he gathered an old toolbox from the boot.

Leilani felt paranoid, thinking about the red cigarettes. She placed her hand on the gun inside her jacket. The Chinese had been in the village. Last night or the week before, it was hard to tell, but they knew her family were there and they would exploit that. The vehicle breaking down out here didn't seem like a coincidence.

Even diving in murky waters where she knew great white sharks swam didn't bring on a feeling like this. Sitting alone inside the car, broken down on the side of the road, she felt like a target at a gun range. For a moment she entertained the notion that Aiono was working for the Chinese and had lured her inside their web. She was a trapped, struggling fly, feeling vibrations of a spider coming to consume it.

Looking in the rearview mirror, Leilani saw a car approach from a distance, its lights still on despite the sun having risen above the mountain range. The road was standard width, yet the black Land Rover came in at speed, close enough to scratch the paint. Tinted windows hid the identity of its occupants. She waited for the nozzle of a semi-automatic to be pushed out a slit of opened window and bullets to spray across the gap, but it never came.

Aiono coughed as dust clouds came his way, his head and upper body deep inside under the hood, his hands streaked black with grease.

He swore at the vehicle that passed, then spat on the ground in their direction.

Ready to take charge if needed, Leilani kept her head down and removed her gun from the internal pocket. Tourists and locals would never have driven past a broken-down vehicle without offering to help. She stayed down until Aiono mocked her in Samoan and told her to get up. They were not coming back. Ten minutes later, she conceded he was right.

After a while, emerging with a dipstick in his hand, he rubbed its length along his singlet. Only a faint smudge of oil showed up against the fabric.

"No oil," he said, embarrassed. For a local man who restored tires for a living, it seemed an out-of-character mistake to make. Even Leilani knew that older vehicles required oil top-ups to run smoothly.

They were about to walk towards the next village to ask for help when a family Nissan van appeared on the horizon. Despite the familiar model of vehicle, Leilani still ducked down as they approached. This time, there was no rush of hot air as they drove past.

When she rose to look out the window, she could see they'd pulled over, sliding doors wide open, revealing a horde of shirtless children in the back. Their mother, an older woman with a potbelly, no bra or shoes, stood with her back against the vehicle, as her husband spoke to Aiono.

"Lani, it's okay now to come out. This is my cousins. They take you to the village. Tavita come back with a oil."

Hiding place revealed, Leilani brushed her clothes off and climbed into the back of the van with the children, who smiled and laughed at her. They were eating homemade taro chips, which they offered to share. She accepted, wishing she knew where to buy the salty snack; they were addictive.

Aiono pressed cash he'd made from selling taro into the husband's big hand, then waved to Leilani as the family van sped off, leaving him alone with his damaged vehicle in the middle of nowhere.

It was only when the whitewashed triangular roof of the church with its wooden cross came into view that Leilani felt able to breathe freely again. She'd made it back without being shot at or kidnapped.

* * *

With her first village meeting only hours away, Leilani would soon stand before chiefs and a packed crowd, every word judged. She needed a crash course in cultural protocol—what to say, what not to say, and how to respond to those who called her out. This was a different ballgame from a Department of Conservation meeting back home.

She found the minister's wife on the balcony, folding sun-dried laundry in the late afternoon heat. The big woman didn't pause when Leilani asked for her help, just waved her to a seat and rolled her eyes. Her expression clarified that this would take a while.

Choosing an outfit to wear to the *fono* in the evening was a task she was more comfortable with. There were three choices inside the wardrobe. Colorful women's formal wear, traditional and expected. There wasn't much room for hanging clothes up, as the Mormon missionaries who usually occupied the room wore the same uniform every day for the duration of their Christian missions.

The first top and skirt combination, a figure-hugging number, Leilani had found in a store in South Auckland, before leaving New Zealand. Given that there are more Samoans in Auckland than in Samoa, she'd had options.

The second one, a patriotic blue design, she'd discovered amongst the thousands of dresses hanging up for sale in the Apia markets. The price had been better than in NZ; the hand-printed cotton material higher quality too.

The third and final choice, pink with fake pearls attached, had been a rushed purchase her first day in Apia. She'd wanted one dress, as she wasn't sure when the next chance would be. The silky material felt cheap, like a dress from SHEIN, but it hadn't been cheap either. She planned to leave all dresses behind for her sisters when she left the island.

She decided on the blue option, showing national pride couldn't hurt.

* * *

"Talofa lava. Fa'afetai tele lava mo le avanoa ou te tautala ai i luma o outou i lenei taeao.

"I will begin by acknowledging the matai, the women's committee, the church leaders, and every family represented here tonight. Thank you for welcoming me into your village."

She looked around the open-sided building to make sure no one in attendance shouldn't have been there. There was no issue; fishermen acting as security guards had taken care of that.

"My name is Leilani Sapunaoa Brown. Many of you know my family. My mother and grandmother are from here, but I was born and raised in NZ, so I speak today neither as a stranger nor as a local. I come with respect for your land, your ocean, and your ways."

"I work in ocean protection. I'm here because I believe that the people who live closest to the sea know it best. I'm here to share what I've seen, what I know, but also to listen."

"You may have heard me say this, but I want to repeat it. Sharks are more than predators. They're guardians of the ocean, as your ancestors knew. When sharks are taken, the balance breaks, reefs start to die. Over time, the entire ocean system can collapse. What's happening out there will affect your fishing and everything your community relies on for a long time."

Leilani looked around; she had their attention.

"At night, those boats you think catch tuna have been targeting sharks. Cutting the fins off and dumping the bodies back into the sea, still alive. Their operation runs from here all the way to Apia. Last month we saw what these men are capable of with the tragic death of Ioane.

"If you don't believe me, see for yourself." She pushed play on the portable projector connected to her laptop. The display on the pull-down screen set up earlier looked even better at night.

The video ran for around five minutes, a compilation she'd cut together from the violence, brutality, and horror she'd witnessed onshore and offshore. There was no censorship; the footage was raw, graphic and unflinching. Thousands of shark fins stacked in the factory, barrels of fermenting livers, a discarded tiger shark corpse, finless and rotting on the sand. Finning at sea, blood-soaked decks, underwater chaos and devastation on the reef.

Officers were identifiable, cigarettes in their mouths, shouting orders and abuse as local fishermen retrieved the long-lines. Sharks of every kind came aboard, thrashing. Machetes were waiting.

Long-range footage showed turtles and rays surfacing on the lines as bycatch, overturned and drowned. It was a hard watch.

Some in the audience looked down in shame; others shook their heads in anger, murmuring discontent. They wanted blood for the schoolboy who had drowned. Most women looked shocked. *Isn't ignorance* bliss? Leilani thought.

With the video finished, she continued her speech.

"This week, with support from the Samoan Police and Fisheries, we'll be carrying out a coordinated operation to end the shark fin trade. I can't share details. I wanted to speak with you first, out of respect," she said.

"What happens next affects your families. You deserve to know what's coming, and that it's being done to protect you and the ocean."

For the first time, Leilani noticed there were dozens of local men and women standing outside the building, listening in the dark. It was a full house. She caught Sione's eye in the crowd. He nodded in approval and gave her a thumbs up; she was connecting.

"After this is over, the next phase can begin. A better future for all of you, a stable income. The resorts are on board; they've agreed to help develop reef tours. Diving, snorkeling, and outrigger excursions, guided by men and women from this village."

"I know you don't have any reason to believe me, but in other parts of the Pacific, we've done it; we've proven that a shark is worth more alive than dead to a community. We'll also look at creating a new marine protected area if the village votes in favor. That means you'll earn at least as much as you're getting now. I'm pleased to announce the Ocean Enforcement Agency will subsidize the start of this project too, but it will belong to you. Your reef, your future."

"Fa'afetai lava. Soifua."

There was a long pause as the village absorbed what they had seen and heard. Then a standing ovation, clapping, cheering and banging on the floor like drums. The people were behind her.

Leilani took this as her cue. With head lowered in respect, she passed in front of the chief's table and placed individual envelopes of cash in front of all the leaders. They nodded in gratitude. The minister's wife had done right by her.

Eventually, a white-bearded chief in an alo'a shirt leaned forward from his seat behind the table, his carved walking stick taking most of his weight. Once standing upright, he addressed the crowd, a respected orator. Silence settled once again. Sione's father, the head chief, sat beside him. He nodded imperceptibly to Leilani when they made eye contact.

"Fa'afetai lava, Agent Brown. Thank you; your evidence speaks for itself. What is happening in our waters is not the way of our people. On behalf of the village council, I apologize to all of you here tonight for our role in enabling these men. Leilani, we will support you in whatever comes next. This village stands with you."

With that said, he sat down and waved the masses away. There was a smattering of polite applause. She knew she'd broken through the barrier, but the admission of culpability surprised her. This was now a community united in what they wanted.

In typical island fashion, everyone took their time to move off, except for a group of middle-aged and older women, who remained sitting on the floor, cross-legged in their lavalavas and t-shirts, gossiping. Two or three men remained behind as well. Some of the remaining group had money and papers at their feet on the concrete. A young girl emerged from the main house, carrying steaming mugs of coffee. After handing these over, she went back to get more. Instant mix from the sachet, loaded with sugar, a local favorite.

Leilani waited until the *matai* had left, then whispered to the woman beside her.

"What are they waiting for?" She hoped they were not expecting an encore; there was nothing else to say. The projector screen had already come down.

The woman smiled at her innocence. "Bingo," she said, producing four papers from her handbag, printed with squares containing numbers. "You want to play? You have this one."

Wanting to get the women of the village on her side, Leilani agreed, sitting down beside her new acquaintances. Surely her understanding of Samoan numbers was good enough for a game. At least they repeated each number twice. Only when the caller was ready to start, using a cellphone to generate random numbers, did the woman beside Leilani produce two of the colorful, essential to the game, ink-filled dabbers and ask her to pay both their entry fees.

Chapter 20

The shark fin nailed to the door was fresh. Watery blood seeped out of the puncture wound where the nail had penetrated, streaking the white-painted wood below. They'd hammered it in without waking Leilani.

The message was clear. Poachers wanted her off the island and saw her as a threat. She texted to make sure her sisters were safe in the mountains. Operatives had been up there, and somehow they'd found her Achilles' heel. With no reception at higher altitudes, Aiono would only get the message if he was down on the main road.

Provoking wildlife traffickers to this point was what Leilani lived for. The Academy drilled it in early. When the enemy lost control, it wasn't bravado. It was the first sign they knew the game was over.

She photographed the fin nailed to the door and sent it to the police captain. 12 hours out from the sting, they needed to remain vigilant. All signs pointed to the longliners being prepared to fight. A minute later, her phone chimed with a reply message from Sina, with a new photo attached.

Expecting the worst, she opened the file and instantly looked away. It was hard to take in, though the sweep of colonial architecture in the background gave away the location, central Apia.

Strung up on a flagpole, the same one police raised the Samoan flag up after daily prayers, were two working dogs, 30 feet in the air, hanging from their back legs, tongues lolling out, eyes rolled backwards. Leilani saved the image for evidence, examining the scene no longer than professional consideration required. With no blood or visible injury to the beautiful German Shepherds, she guessed they'd been killed by strangulation or poisoning. No doubt a necropsy in Apia would confirm it, though toxicology results would take longer. *Sadistic bastards*, she thought.

The two women needed to talk. This conversation was not one to be had over text, both players in an upcoming operation being targeted needed consideration. The captain picked up on the first ring.

"Looks like the Chinese are on the offensive." Leilani said, shaken. "Please send my condolences to the K-9 Unit."

There was a pause at the other end.

"Those dogs were like family," Sina said after a while. "Our trainers spent years working with them, getting them to the level they needed to be at. Still remember the day they arrived like it was yesterday, first time in police history on the island. No animal deserves to end up like that, especially those that serve our country."

Leilani hesitated, hearing the strain in her colleague's voice. "I'm so sorry."

Sina was holding back tears. "Thanks Lani. This was a message, you were meant to see it, and so was I. We all were."

"Been on this job fifteen years," she continued, "never seen anything like this. Some of the public stopped on their way to work, so I know photos will do the rounds on social media soon. Trainers haven't even arrived yet; poor guys don't know what they're walking into. And to be honest, a new canine unit isn't in the budget. We have only 3 dogs on the island." She stopped, then corrected herself. "Had three." The last words came quieter. "It's going to hit the unit hard,."

Wanting to move on, she changed the topic. "What about you, how you feeling? A shark fin nailed to the door, that's mafia-level tactics."

"I've lived through worse," Leilani played it down, not wanting to accept what had happened. Her head had been resting on a pillow, less than six feet from where the men had been standing outside. They could've easily forced the door open, shot her at point blank while she slept.

Another text came through whilst she was still on the line. Aiono, replying with a thumbs-up emoji, confirmed the family was safe. Relief flooded through her body.

"Alright, see you soon. Counting down the hours," Leilani said, ending her call with the police captain. There was no need to discuss strategy; the operation was planned down to the last second.

She went outside and looked at the curved, grey fin that remained pinned to the door. Ironically, all that was needed was a hammer to remove it, using the claw on the back of the head.

5 32am. She needed sleep, but villagers seeing the fin on their way to the bus stop would only cause drama. With reluctance, Leilani realized her only viable option. Waking the minister or his wife was a risk not worth taking. They'd probably ring Director Ventura and try to convince the Agency to recall her. Plus, a man of God probably didn't even own a hammer.

Twenty minutes later, Sione arrived in his father's car, blurry-eyed. He came prepared, tools in hand. A wooden *kilikiti* bat, for village cricket tournaments, lay on the white leather of the passenger seat.

He was annoyed and amused equally when he saw why he'd been called out early in the morning. Without knowing the full story behind the threat, it looked like a prank between fishermen.

"Come on, Lani, that's a blacktip fin. What are you worried about? You could've done this."

Leilani rolled her eyes. "Trust me, if I had a hammer, you wouldn't be here. So, if you're not gonna do this, can you just give it to me?"

She was becoming impatient, standing outside for so long, in lavalava and an oversized sleeping t-shirt. It wasn't cold, but at this time of the morning it wasn't warm outside either when the wind blew.

The shirt was a Flipper the Dolphin number her father had given her when she was younger, before he realized her activist stance against keeping marine mammals in captivity. She hadn't had the heart to throw it out. If she was honest with herself, Jake had done an amazing job as a solo father, finding every ocean-themed gift in hotel shops when he was away for work.

Sione had the fin off the door in under a minute, his hands red as if he'd been painting. She looked at the door. It needed a wash down, or there'd still be questions.

"Sure you wanna go ahead with tonight?" he asked, concerned. Getting blood on his hands seemed to have adjusted his attitude. "Remember what they did to my brother Lani; don't underestimate them."

"I know. Don't think about me; just stick to the plan. We need you at your best tonight," she said. As an informant, he was not someone she should be confiding in. Even their friendship broke policy. And with the end in sight, she was already in full operation mode.

"Alright," Sione shrugged, sensing there was no more headway to be made. "You want this?" he asked, offering the rubbery fin as a memento.

"I'll pass," Leilani replied with a hint of a smile. She twisted around to check whether anyone had been watching them. Her phone showed it was past six, yet the sliding doors of the red store remained padlocked, well past opening time. Students often stopped in for two-minute noodle bowls before catching the bus. A trio of girls in uniform arrived, knocked on the locked door, then moved on when no one answered, with no time to spare before the bus left. There were no lights on or movement inside the property either. When the silence continued, Sione muttered he had somewhere to be and drove off with a quick wave, leaving Leilani standing in the street, staring at the unopened store, wondering what was going on inside and who was still in there.

By now, there was no doubt the poachers and their offshore bosses knew her name, why she was on the island and where she was living. They also knew she'd kneecapped their illicit business in Apia, orchestrating the shutdown of the processing factory and arrests. Reflecting, Leilani conceded some of the high chief's safety concerns for her had been valid. For the first time since becoming an Oceanic Enforcement Agent, she felt exposed. Part of her wished she'd been able to maintain her undercover status as a coral researcher.

If the sting worked, Samoa's shark finning operations would be finished within twelve hours. The plan was solid, but both maritime police and the OEA kept constant watch on the island and from afar, knowing their opponent could change the rules of the game at any minute.

At around 10 AM, the police captain rang for the second time in the morning. Leilani locked the door to her room and sat down on the edge of the bed to take the unexpected call. A cockroach ambled across the white-tiled floor under her bare feet. She kicked it away; they were so hard to kill. Crescents of dark sand lodged in cracks along the base of the wall. The minister's wife had taken her broom back, apparently the only one in circulation. The missionaries never went down to the beach and barely ate, Leilani had been told, when the woman came by to inspect the accommodation unannounced.

"Captain? Everything okay?" Leilani answered.

"Officer Moresi hasn't shown up for work. His family said he left home this morning as usual. Walked to work."

"Any chance he's running late?" It was a genuine question. In her experience, Pacific Island men were not known for their awareness of time.

"Doubt it; nothing is open around here before 9. Not answering his phone either. My officers never miss roll call, not without calling. He has a wife and kids; he'd never risk losing his position."

"Alright, appreciate you letting me know. Can we operate tonight without Moresi? I have him down as leading the port side approach."

"Yeah, I'll bring in someone else until we find him. I trust these guys with my life, Agent Brown." She ended the call, clearly concerned for the safety of her team. Leilani was too; the big man's instincts had kept them safe during the operation inside the seafood factory. Moresi was a valuable asset to the force.

The implications of his disappearance were unspoken. Trafficking money ran deep in the South Pacific, with Leilani's calculations estimating the fin and liver trade generated more each month than the casino on the Apia waterfront. Restaurants and hotels, export firms with forged paperwork and hidden freezers, laundromats doubling as fronts, any could've taken a hit when the factory shut down, and any could have people inside willing to protect the industry.

The absence of a senior, essential government employee the day before the sting showed how far the network could reach beyond the coast. Zhang, the former long-lining captain with blood on his hands, was potentially still on the island too, operating in the shadows. The question on Leilani's mind was whether Moresi had been compromised or had been taken as a hostage. Given what she'd been through with the man, the first option seemed unlikely.

A skin and bones cat with matted brown, striped fur caught her attention, breaking the train of thought. Cats were not native to the island, and far less common than dogs. Stowaways from England hundreds of years ago, they'd feasted on rats in dark ships' holds. Finding an abundance of tropical birds upon arrival, they'd survived and established feral populations in the bush. Kittens captured by children came and went as they pleased.

This cat had something large in its mouth that, from a quarter mile away, looked like an oversized pigeon. Its muzzle was wet with water and blood. Leilani hoped it was not a beloved *manumea*, the critically endangered tooth-billed pigeon featured on the blue Samoan fifty-dollar note. The animal labored under the weight of its catch, struggling to drag the body over sand and dirt. Invasive myna birds, black with yellow beaks, hopped closer, unafraid of the feline. Curious, Leilani walked with caution towards the scene. The cat hissed and bared its short fangs as she came closer, its thin tail erect, claws unsheathed and back arched. It fixed its unwavering gaze on her, weighing up whether to abandon the prize or attack. Reluctantly, as her tall shadow intimated the cat, it gave up and raced to safety behind the warm concrete of the red store, continuing to snarl at Leilani.

The abandoned catch was not a bird of any kind. Up close, she could see it had once been a six-foot shark, half-eaten. A blacktip reef, the kind Leilani watched in the shallows on her morning walks.

Remains of the body were missing dorsal, pectoral, pelvic and caudal fins. The men who'd nailed the fin to her door must've thrown the body into the bush, where the cat had come across it. The gray body was dull; the eyes glassy. Leilani estimated it had been dead for more than a few hours, but not days. Maybe the fishing crews had been out last night as well, without her knowing. Not wanting to waste any of their catch, the men would've kept the other fins cut from the small body, adding them to the stack. On a shark that size, she estimated the other fins would span only the width of her hand, or a little more.

Despite chasing wildlife traffickers for a career, Leilani struggled to get inside the heads of the men she hunted, to understand the mentality. *Why kill even the smallest of sharks?* These men working at the middle-and upper levels weren't desperate fathers, working to feed their children. They were part of a multi-billion-dollar criminal industry. It was impossible to understand the inner workings of people who valued a dollar more than the life of a juvenile shark. She guessed the allure of wealth was their only guiding star.

Fishing down to the last shark before moving on to a new area was a cold-blooded business strategy, used all over the world. The same approach had been used in New Zealand at the intertidal zone, rockpools stripped bare, down to the last periwinkle, barnacle and starfish. Groups moved across the zone, some with balaclavas against the wind and spray, scraping the rocks clean with piano wire, filling their buckets with anything edible. A mottled octopus hidden beneath platforms would trigger shouting in Mandarin, wives hurrying from the waterline where they were gathering sea biscuits, faces shaded under sun visors. Public pressure had finally forced the Ministry of Fisheries to update laws that had never expected this kind of rape. Confiscating gear hadn't worked, but fines and warning signs in their language at the walkway entrance seemed to make a difference.

Leaving the feral cat to tear at the shark carcass, Leilani went back to her room and powered up her laptop. The strategy document opened in seconds, the plan she and the Samoan police had built over months staring back at her. Headquarters had signed off days ago; now it was down to execution. The satellite Wi-Fi held steady, no small advantage in a place where the network could vanish with a rain squall, as she scrolled through each phase of the operation. Patrol patterns, interception points, and arrest procedures were locked in. Hundreds of hours had gone into preparing the takedown, every move cross-checked against the terrain, tides, and habits of the fishing crew they were targeting.

In her gut, she knew it would work. The last longliner still in play had been sighted nightly, its deck lights a telltale glow against the black horizon as it worked the edge of the drop-off, setting miles of baited line for sharks. Operating undisturbed for now, that would change in hours. With an officer missing, police dogs executed, and an explicit warning nailed to her door, the cost of failure wouldn't be just the loss of a case. Lives were at risk here.

In her inbox was an email from her father, which she left. Staying in the zone psychologically for the night ahead was essential. Below an email from Auckland University, subject line - *Research Grant Application 2026*, was an unopened message. Marked with a red exclamation mark by the Agency's antivirus, it caught her eye for the wrong reasons. She was surprised, and a little impressed at whoever had sent it, spam messages not usually making it to the inbox, culled by different software long before seeing the light of day. It seemed to originate from an encrypted email account with no identifiers. Hesitantly, she clicked open, worst-case scenario being a hostile takeover that the IT team sitting in the dark in Honolulu would take down. They'd probably even enjoy the challenge, she thought.

It was not a scam, ad or virus; it was a legitimate email, and Agent Brown was the intended recipient. Toying with a salt-dreaded lock of long hair that got in the way, she stared at the screen for a long time, re-reading the message again and again. Tech classes at the Academy had prepared her, but she'd never expected it to occur on her first solo assignment. This was the stuff of movies, surely.

It was not a death threat, as she'd been expecting from the shark finning industry. It was an invitation. Intimidation had failed; now they were trying seduction.

The anonymous message gave a time and place. Apia Marina, 1:30 p.m. She checked her watch. It was nearly midday. Enough time to cross the island, but the question was whether she should. If intimidation had failed, what could they hope to achieve in the open, in front of security cameras, where visiting yachts moored before making the long run east across the South Pacific to French Polynesia? Maybe they'd offer her cash. She'd be able to identify the men, but at what cost? Killing an international agent was a line even they might not want to cross, not in a public setting, with the risk of an international incident.

Still, she knew how things worked here on the island. Security cameras existed, but the feeds were watched by underpaid guards in a hot oceanfront office. The men watched movies on their phones and often left their posts to make coffee. If they'd already been bought, they wouldn't see what they didn't want to see. A "public location" in Samoa could be as private as the traffickers needed it to be.

As a new agent, still green in dealing with organizations with money to burn, it took Leilani a moment to grasp the letter's real purpose. The closing line read: *We appreciate your dedication to ending ocean crime in the Pacific and would like to recognize your work with a donation.* So it was not an invitation or another threat, it was a bribe.

Chapter 21

Weeks out from peak cyclone season in Samoa, Apia Marina felt abandoned. The outer mooring buoys sat empty, and the inner berths hosted only a scattering of boats, mostly older yachts and weather-stalled liveaboards riding out the incoming storms. Leilani recognized the lone sportfishing launch by its deep-v hull, triple-tier flybridge, and the teak-floored aft deck where a fighting chair was bolted to the deck like a throne. Game fishing stirred conflicting emotions within her ocean loving self. She loved the dopamine hit of a fair battle with a billfish, but in contrast to many of her male colleagues in academia, had never been enthused by the standard practice of catch and release. Growing up by the sea, her grandfather had taught her better. Eat what you catch, catch what you eat, had been his mantra.

She walked the cracked concrete pontoons, past rust-stained cleats and sun-faded utility boxes. This wasn't the original version of Apia Marina she was looking at, but it failed to compare to tourism hotspots like Fiji or Tahiti. There was only one fuel pump. Paint peeled from pylons in vertical streaks, underneath layers of guano. Most of the yachts that remained in the flat-water berths were owned by a handful of older expats who remained on the island after the copra industry had shut down in the early 2000s.

At a loss for how to find the undisclosed meeting point, she walked the piers without purpose until she came across what was undoubtedly a research vessel. She'd been on enough of them to recognize the shape. Workboat lines, a flush deck, the utilitarian design. Sixty feet, maybe more. Grey aluminum hull, low freeboard. Twin radar domes sat above the enclosed bridge, flanking a mast that doubled as a satellite tower. Leilani's eyes caught the remotely operated machinery on the stern deck, useful for launching a dive tender or recovering oceanographic equipment. This boat was not a showpiece, she was built for range and function.

A flag fluttered off the mast, unfamiliar. East Timor or Nauru, maybe. She couldn't say for sure, so snapped a quick photo. Two men moved about the deck in overalls, checking systems. The exhaust vents were still warm, with clouds of smoke puffing out.

One man noticed her checking out the boat. His straight black hair was slicked back with too much pomade, and he wore chrome aviator sunglasses with reflective lenses.

"Agent Brown. I wasn't sure you were coming!" he called out across the water, in a Chinese-American accent she recognized but couldn't place. Over-friendly to someone he wanted to blackmail, the man beckoned her to come on board, showing the stepladder at the stern. Thick mooring ropes secured the boat to solid concrete poles. The second man on board turned around and bowed in greeting. He was older, with a Confucius style, wispy goatee.

Against better judgement, Leilani boarded the vessel, looking around first to check if the marina cameras were still where they'd been last time she was here. They were. Surely diners on the deck of the marina restaurant could also see and hear her, if they looked up from their fish and chips, through the sparse forest of masts.

"Call me Li. Not sure if we have met officially," he said, with an amused expression, extending his hand. Leilani recalled his name on the side of the white vans that loaded product from the village. *The shark liver dealer. Was he really mocking her right now? Had he known she'd been watching from inside the store the whole time?*

" My colleague here is Captain Xu. Best fishing captain in South China. We flew him in last week after the terrible tragedy that befell Zhang. May he rest in peace. Would you like some green tea?"

"I heard nothing about that," Leilani said, declining a drink. The man in front of her was indirectly confessing to murder. Or at least ordering the hit. She felt sorry for Zhang's mistress, still working in co-operation with the police for her freedom. She felt even more sorry for the man's children, abandoned back on the mainland and now with no source of income being wired across oceans. At least they would never be drawn into his trade.

"We sent a press release to the Samoa Observer, but they never printed it. All they do is share those posters with the reward for his capture," Li said. "I was told he drowned, but we never found his body."

Not wanting to become an accessory to a complex crime, Leilani shifted the subject. As usual, she chose a direct approach.

"Why am I here? What do you want?"

"Mmm, a woman who knows how to hold her own, love that. We could use you in our organization, you know. The pay is not bad, more than what you're getting."

Leilani ignored his attempt to wind her up. Knowing her opposition's abilities, he probably knew her salary. He was a charmer with a black heart.

"Straight to the point? Ok, as you wish," he said, as she felt Xu grab her from behind. He was so light on his feet that she hadn't heard him move. His bony, wiry arms were vice-like, from a lifetime of illegal fishing. Overpowering her, the two men pushed Leilani's head down and forced her inside the cabin, out of sight of tourists and dock workers.

Inside, the combined scent of oil, coffee, and stale cigarettes overpowered her, standard issue for any foreign oceanic research vessel. The interior was steel and composite, painted grey and white with non-slip flooring and stainless grab rails. The main operational area housed a navigation station, a compact galley, and a long bench bolted to the bulkhead, with tie-downs beneath for gear. A sonar monitor blinked beside the comms panel. She could see the AIS data cable was unplugged.

Four pairs of shoes on a rack indicated there were more people on board than just the two men holding her hostage.

Li patted her down like a customs officer. He started at her shoulders, down her arms, across her sides. When he reached her lower back, his hand paused. Her gun came free in one motion, which he passed to Xu without a word. There was no attempt to restrain her, not yet, but Xu blocked the stepladder leading back up to the deck, making it clear she wasn't free to leave.

"You belong in a lab, Agent. Not out here, looking into things that don't concern you," Li said to her. "I used to work in fisheries biology, if you can believe it. Never published as many papers as you have, though," Leilani stood her ground; she was used to dangerous men trying to assert authority.

"It's a risky life you've chosen, Leilani Brown. All we ask is that you suspend your current inquiries. There are bigger causes worth your energy, and we're offering you freedom to pursue them. This vessel is yours if you want it, Agent," Li said with a straight face, emphasizing the last word. "In fact, we took the liberty of registering it under your name. I understand you already have your skipper's license?

Captain Xu is a talented hacker, but you made it easy for him. He does passports too. Expensive, but worth it."

The old man smiled at the backhanded compliment.

Li came closer to her face, close enough to smell the sashimi he'd eaten for lunch.

"The esteemed captain here is a close associate of a top bank in Hong Kong," he said. "Fifty thousand US is waiting for you there, under your name. In the Pearl River district, past where tourists wait for boats to see the pink dolphins." Li's tone was casual, as if the money were pocket change. He deliberately left out the name of the bank. If she wanted the cash, she'd have to follow the trail herself.

The old man blocking her way didn't flinch. His face was gaunt, like a prisoner of war. *Where the hell had they found him*? The only color on his thin body was the red and yellow dragons winding around his forearms, traditional Chinese style. Leilani wasn't sure he even understood English, but there was no mistaking that he was a man who would do whatever was needed of him.

She wasn't sure if she was being bribed or blackmailed. It seemed like both. Trying to work through the scenario in her mind, it seemed clear the shark fin bosses would try to frame her if she didn't accept the boat. Claims would be made that she'd been corrupted and worked as a double agent the whole time. She wouldn't be the first Agent to do so. Two that she knew of, through word of mouth, were now before the courts in The Hague.

"And what if I want to remain an Agent?" Leilani asked, her heart pounding with adrenaline, not fear. She'd read Li's known criminal record and profile on the Agency database after the first day she'd become aware of him. Interpol often shared intel on environmental criminals with the OEA. His background story had surprised no one on the team. University graduate, senior fisheries analyst turned CITES officer in Shanghai, fired and imprisoned for taking bribes to facilitate the shark finning trade. No doubt he'd risen within the secretive ranks of the organization after being recruited to the industry upon his release by experienced players. She wondered if he'd somehow been connected strategically to Zhang whilst in prison. As for the older man Xu, she'd never heard of him. Another operative working in the dark. There was a good chance he was the mastermind behind the entire South Pacific longlining enterprise.

Li remained calm in the face of rejection. "You leave me no choice, Agent. We will have to supply Interpol with these documents we've put together on your behalf. Bank account in Hong Kong with 50 grand in it, registered owner of a million-dollar research vessel moored in Samoa, CCTV footage of you meeting with us towards the end of your assignment? Even for a woman as gifted as you, Agent Brown, this will take some explaining."

"I'll take my chances," Leilani replied, defiant. Her employers would see straight through the ruse. Whether Interpol would, could be a different story. The last thing she needed was a Red Notice on her CV. Director Ventura would need to come to her defense in court. The two men looked at each other, surprised at her choice.

In a move she would never have expected, Li seemed to respect her stance. He nodded, then pushed Xu out of the way of the exit, gesturing for her to leave.

Once Leilani was back on the relative safety of the concrete platforms, Li leaned on the starboard gunwale of the boat, staring at her.

"It's a shame that we couldn't come to an agreement, Agent Brown. My men were not planning on driving back to the mountains. Not much to do up there. The altitude affects their lungs; you know us smokers, we prefer the coast, and the casino. But I guess your mother and sisters don't have any choice, do they?"

Leilani fought to control the rage within her at his threat. Marina staff sweeping the area watched the exchange with interest. The research ship had overpaid for their two-night stay in US dollars, readily accepted in place of tala.

Security cameras caught the exchange in grainy 720p, maybe even recorded Li's words. From the right angle, the footage would be enough to identify the men, but even with a subpoena, she knew the footage would never see the light of day. The drives were in a locked cabinet in the marina's security office, and the men watching those feeds had been bought. It could even be used against her in court, providing the time and date she met with known criminals to discuss a bribe.

Choosing not to take the bait, as she'd been trained, Leilani turned her back on the vessel and began jogging toward the Jeep. Even they would not risk shooting an Agent in the back on camera. Marina security would be forced to intervene.

By the time she reached the vehicle, the bright blue sky was fading towards late afternoon. She'd been aboard longer than she realized. On the fly, she came up with a plan. First, pick up her sisters on the drive through the island's interior. Then, secure them somewhere safe before the operation at sea kicked off. Hopefully, Captain Sina could spare a few armed officers to watch over the girls. She tried to push self-doubt in her abilities as an Agent from her overactive brain. *Maybe Li had been right. Perhaps she was better off as a research scientist. Then, her family wouldn't be at risk. Why hadn't she seen this coming?*

With dark sunglasses on and her humidity-frazzled hair untied, local women with nothing to do other than talk could not recognize her. She backed out of the blistering car park as the research ship's foghorn cut through the heat, warning the marina it was moving out. Leilani figured it was headed south to link up with the last longliner still working the coast. Now that the threat of abduction at sea was gone, it felt right to check in with the Agency. Driving while talking on the phone wasn't her first choice, but the lorry ahead was crawling under thirty with a load of mined coral sand, belching fumes, her heart still racing from the encounter.

* * *

No-one came out to greet her as Leilani found the unmarked road that led up to her mother's house. The front door was open; the grain faded to driftwood silver. She left the engine running and walked around the outside. A rusted pickup truck missing two wheels she'd never seen before sat at an angle, sunken into the damp grass, next to Aiono's outdoor workshop. His bench was littered with tools of the trade, an open pack of chewing gum and a can of pineapple Fanta, as if he'd been working on the vehicle during the afternoon, then been interrupted.

Between the knotted wood poles that kept the corrugated roof aloft, she could see the colorful school bags of her sisters, thrown together on the floor near their sleeping mats, where they completed their homework by candlelight. A long thatch broom lay on the ground in the middle of the room instead of up against the wall.

It was only as she reached the back of the property that Leilani could hear distressed high-pitched squealing, coming from beyond the plantation. *There's no way that was a person. Right? Please don't let that be a person.*

She pushed through rows of banana trees until she found the source of the noise. Splintered wood lay scattered, thick branches with nails jutting from them, broken and leaking sap. Aiono stood in the middle of the scene, oil-stained singlet clinging to him, shorts soaked through, frustration all over his unshaven face. Deep scratches ran across his right shoulder, the skin raw, and a bruise was blooming under his eye. His daughters were over a mile away, rinsing off under a waterfall that descended from a sheer wall of rainforest. Their mother sat on a flat rock nearby, barefoot, smoking, scrolling on her phone. She swayed as she sat, laughing at TikTok videos.

Beyond the thin ripple of the river, were a herd of angry pigs, feasting on taro seedlings. Fat-bottomed, their short bristly fur was wet and caked with mud. Triumphantly, out of reach of the girls and Aiono, they grazed in peace on the hillside, snorting and looking back as they detected another human's arrival.

Leilani had only visited the property once, but she knew the large animals were supposed to be inside their enclosure, now smashed in pieces on the ground before her.

Aiono raised his eyebrows in greeting when he noticed her and pushed his wet hair backwards, still catching his breath. "Gun shot spooked them," he explained. "Broke free, been running wild for 'bout an hour. We try to catch but they so fast. Even the girls too slow. Dogs fear the boars. Must be Tana, on the farm over there." He nodded towards a distant home in the next undulating valley with a few brown cattle wandering the slopes and mimed with two fingers, firing a gunshot to the side of the head.

The shocked expression on Leilani's face made his sun-leathered face crease into a wide smile.

"Ha, not him, girl. One of the bull has been getting out of hand. Dangerous."

"Oh yeah, fair enough," she replied, no stranger to the reality of life on a farm. "You need better dogs."

He smiled at her advice, accepting defeat for the night. If only she knew how much a purebred cost on the island. "Why you come here Lani? You leaving Samoa?"

"Not yet. But I'd like to take the girls with me, just for a few days, to keep them safe. The shark fin traders know where you live. I think they've been here too."

Aiono shrugged, then winced as the pain in his dislocated shoulder caught up with him. "Can't say I'm surprised; the men I play cards with say they see strangers the other night. But your mum makes the calls around here. Better to ask her."

Asu didn't look up as Leilani approached. Their reunification had been underwhelming so far. In contrast, the girls, still in their wet t-shirts and shorts, rushed over to hug their big sister, giggling and smiling. She could see they'd been doing more than swimming. Lying on the smooth stones of the riverbank were a pile of soaked clothes and a bar of soap.

Holding all three sisters close to her body protectively, not concerned about the wet marks spreading on her shirt and pants, Leilani confronted her mother.

"I want to take the girls with me. The shark fishermen know you are here alone, with no one to protect you."

Finally, the dark-skinned woman looked up, irritated, and scoffed at her. "You think my husband cannot protect his own daughters?"

Her breath smelled strongly of local beer. In just a dirty t-shirt and lavalava with no bra on, Leilani was shocked to see how overweight her mother had become. Rolls of fat strained against the fabric. Instagram was open on the glowing phone screen on her lap.

"Please. This will all be over before the end of the week."

"Uh-huh," she said, only half present in the conversation. "50 tala for bingo first, Agent Brown." Reluctantly, sensing the sarcasm and no room for negotiation, Leilani ran back to the Jeep to find cash in the glove box. When she returned, her mother put the cash behind her ear, gesturing to take the girls without so much as a word. The youngest said "bye Mum" as they walked hand in hand with their older sister to the truck, to which Asu raised a hand in a lackluster attempt at goodbye.

Leilani had attended enough shed parties in the Far North back home to recognize a woman who drank too hard. She guessed her mother was at least half a box deep. Her husband seemed to have enough sense not to get in the way. For someone who believed in unconditional love, Leilani was surprised to feel no compassion for the woman who'd given birth to her. That love she reserved only for her sisters. The trio reminded her of herself when she was young, headstrong yet kind and full of energy, embracing nature, unaware of the material poverty that surrounded their family in the mountain valley.

Chapter 22

With the door locked and a painting of a blue-eyed Jesus watching over them, the sisters took selfies together inside the room, moments to treasure and upload later, then settled in to watch a movie on Leilani's laptop.

Technically, the movie was a documentary, great white sharks hunting seals off the South African coast. Leilani had downloaded it a year earlier, before heading offshore on a research trip. When the girls spotted the Netflix logo on her screen, they asked about it, only to be disappointed when she explained it didn't work in the village. Here, getting online was a privilege.

It felt surreal to be on the eve of the most important enforcement operation of her career, yet for the village to be so peaceful, everything so normal and calm. Through white curtains, Leilani could see the enormous shadow of the minister's wife, pegging clothes to the line, wearing one of her potato sack dresses she had custom-sewn. The Minister was in his rocking chair, reading the Bible as he often did on pleasant evenings, pen and paper on the table beside him and a cup of coffee, preparing the next sermon. With the sun still to shine for at least another hour before dark, their clothes would dry fast.

From her position in the room, she could only see half the building, but the red store still looked padlocked. Whether the crews still lived there was anyone's guess. Locally owned stores weren't complaining; their share had grown. The landowners said rent still arrived on time. Off the record, police warned Leilani she'd need a warrant to enter. Without one, they'd have to charge her with breaking and entering. The OEA mandate did not extend to land-based searches without cause.

A call had come in from Apia. Zhang's mistress had disappeared, reneging on the deal she'd made to work as an informant. Leilani spared a thought for the middle-aged woman. Without her help, it could have all ended inside an Apia fish factory. She wondered if the woman's ageing lover had truly fled the island or Li had tracked him down. Only time would tell.

Leilani's three sisters were excited to be visiting the village their mother had been born in. They asked questions constantly. Asu had never taken them to the south coast, focused instead on building a new future inland, away from the trauma of the past. Their father had thought about it during long, solitary taro runs, bringing them to see their frail grandmother by the sea. A family-oriented man, her isolation troubled him. But in the end, he'd decided against it. Provoking Asu's fast-rising temper was a risk he no longer took. When she saw red, she became a demon, capable of anything, guilty of nothing. Her mind left her body, and rage eclipsed reason. Aiono dreamed of leaving her one day in the night, if only to protect his daughters.

He'd confided this duality in his wife to his older brother, working in the coal mines of Australia, over blurry video call. After initially laughing, his brother suggested couples counseling. Then it had been Aiono's turn to laugh. The man had clearly been away from the islands too long, forgotten the pride of his people. He knew his wife better than anyone; Asu would rather die than women in the village find out she was attending therapy. *Palagi life*, she'd said during one of their sober conversations, when alcohol in the village store had sold out and her husband felt safe enough to talk freely.

Using subtle interrogation techniques she'd learned at the Academy to get information out of people without them knowing it, Leilani worked out the girls knew fragments of backstory, but their mother had intentionally left gaps in place. She wasn't sure it was her place to fill in those blanks, having known her younger sisters for less than a week.

Still, the pattern was familiar. A mother who drifted in and out, emotionally and physically, and a dedicated father who stayed, worked hard, and loved unconditionally, suffering in silence.

That part at least, they had in common. And she was eternally grateful for it.

* * *

Shark fishermen and local laborers made their way down to the beach as Leilani watched from behind thin curtains. There, they would wait until nightfall for transport offshore. Several men were already drinking, bottles in hand, cigarettes burning down between their fingers. If boats were late and the weather was cooler, they would sometimes light a coconut-husk fire on the sand.

At all times, two high-ranking Chinese operatives remained aboard the longliner, anchored beyond the reef's outer edge. When at sea, the support skiffs would tie up alongside, rising and falling with the swell.

As sunset transitioned to night, the offshore crew approached, outboard engines running warm. Early on, the boats had kept navigation lights off, but after months without intervention, operational security had relaxed. Now, headlights were on, a sign of growing brazenness.

Onshore, waiting laborers waded out to their knees and boarded the incoming boats, six men each, plus the skipper. No lifejackets, only machetes.

Once all wake disappeared within the coral pass, Leilani lost visual contact. The remaining longliner remained recognizable, its cabin light on the bridge giving it away, the rest of the ship a smudge of gray against a dark horizon.

By ten, the girls were asleep on her mattress, worn out after a game of cards. She'd slipped them coins to play with, something their parents forbade, big sisters being allowed to break a few rules. With the house quiet, she pictured the operation unfolding at sea without her. By now the longlining crew would set baited lines; around two in the morning the winches would start hauling them back, sharks dragged up out of the dark. That was when the vessel would find itself surrounded.

Sione was on board undercover. She'd seen his yellow bandanna in the distance, a way for authorities to identify him if gunfire broke out. She trusted him; he'd already been through hell, losing a brother to the trade. His message later in the early hours of the morning would be the spark to turn surveillance into a takedown.

Over VHF, Leilani listened to the Samoan Maritime Police and Fisheries officers check in, boats staged and ready, miles down the coast, out of sight.

"Alpha One, standing by." "Delta Two, engines live. Awaiting green light."

The OEA tech team had encrypted channel 14 on the radio. In under an hour, she'd be on the water.

As she drove, Leilani checked the rendezvous point again on her phone. The team was holding position under Captain Sina's watch. Their chosen village hadn't been warned. No sirens, no advance notice. The risk was very real. One loose word and the entire operation could fall apart.

As a global enforcement agency, the OEA had unfiltered access to global AIS vessel location via satellite. More detailed, real-time and less restricted than the free service accessible to the public online. Pulling over on the side of the road, she logged in with her agent passcode and waited for a darkened map of the South Pacific to load on her laptop. The screen showed dozens of green dots, cargo ships en route to Pago Pago or Auckland. A handful of blue dots showed legal commercial fishing vessels, mostly Taiwanese and Korean, operating under bilateral agreements. It was the expanse of black space between them that made her uneasy. Somewhere beyond the reef, men were working in silence on 'ghost ships', soon to be finning sharks by moonlight, their vessels broadcasting no signal at all. She wondered whether the research vessel had joined them.

Police were waiting when she arrived, their boat already in the water. At another beach towards the western tip of Upolu, a partner vessel was doing the same, ready for a pincer strike attack. She waded out to her knees, then was hauled onboard by her ballistic vest. She barely recognized the captain, clad from head to toe in camouflage combat gear, as were her men. Fisheries officers Leilani had met after the factory takedown were onboard, in uniform. In neoprene shorts and long-sleeved wetsuit top, she felt as ready for her role as she could hope for.

The agency-issue waterproof pack was heavy, stuffed with mask and snorkel, torch, weight belt, dive knife, a hood to hide her signature curls, and an electric shark prod for emergencies. She was offered a thermos of coffee and steel-dart gun. Underwater, bullets don't work. She took both. After checking the safety, she tucked the waterproof pistol into her waistband.

With GPS and depth sounder glowing on the dash, they had no need for running lights. Standing at the center console, the armed skipper guided the aluminum skiff through coral-dominated water like he'd done it a hundred times before, blindfolded. Even to a marine biologist like Leilani, the reef layout appeared random, like a puzzle. To the police skipper, finding a way through was like reading a novel.

They cruised slowly, around five knots. Less wake, less disturbance. Lower chance of being picked up on radar by the longliner or the research vessel, lurking in deeper water. Having been inside the research ship, Leilani knew it had more navigation tech than both Samoan patrol boats put together. The key question she had was whether it was out there.

As they drew closer, the ocean surface calm; she tried to make out the telltale shape of fishing buoys bobbing in the blackness, holding the baited lines up. Hitting hard plastic with the bow would give away their location on a quiet night, sound travelling further across water than on land. She held her breath involuntarily when they passed over a drifting gill net, unsecured. Fouling the prop with a ghost net could mean calling it a day. Losing the element of surprise would be unforgivable, but she wished there'd been a chance to get it out of the water.

After a while of searching the surface with night-vision binoculars, the team located the long-lines. Set past the reef pass, where clear waters descended steeply towards blue-water, baited hooks suspended in the water column at a depth where sharks hunted. Fortunately, the lines were not set close to the target vessel. A sensible decision from the opposition, strategy-wise, Leilani thought. The shadow of a hull, even at night, often deterred larger predators from taking a bite. Electric pulses from outboard motors in neutral, mimicking active fish, would attract sharks to the stern, away from the J hooks.

"Ready to go?" Sina whispered.

"Now or never," Leilani said and slipped into the water without a ripple as only professional divers can, hood already pulled over her hair. After an intentional surface breath, she was gone from sight, only distorted light from her torch beam below indicating a diver was present. She'd turned the torch to its lowest setting, a necessary risk. If arrests made during the multi-agency sting were to hold, laying eyes on the nylon lines of death first was essential.

She checked her watch underwater, 1:30 a.m. She needed to photograph the line, then get out. The timestamp on the image would be shown in court.

Leilani had freedived the mainline before, as part of her covert surveillance, but every time felt like a punch to the gut. It was like diving into a snuff film behind the scenes. Hundreds of monofilament branch lines drifted out in parallel, ghostly strands of a suspended spider's web. Every baited steel hook a death sentence.

She kicked her fins up and down slowly at 90 feet, conserving oxygen, eyes moving between casualties at regular intervals. A distressed manta flapped its wings, entangled, nylon digging into its flesh. Leilani cut it free carefully, willing the manta to swim away to safety.

Being impartial as possible, she assessed the damage she'd caused. It was okay; two severed side-lines would not raise suspicion when the gear was hauled in. All sea turtles she'd counted so far were dead, as were most of the sharks. Drowned when they became unable to move oxygen over their gills, suffocating. Dozens of others still thrashed, contorted and snapped at the thin lines, refusing to die. Through her camera, Leilani recorded oceanic white-tip, gray reef, scalloped hammerhead, tiger and pelagic thresher. Protected species in Samoan waters; the long-line did not discriminate.

Leilani surfaced, inhaling a deep breath of night air, then looked around for the police boat she'd come out on. It was half a mile away, the current playing its part. With no lit cigarettes or underwater floodlights to give its location away, it was hard to make out. The commercial vessel that still seemed to be anchored in the distance continued to keep its cabin lights on, unaware it had company. Bobbing up and down, she checked her watch. Within minutes, she expected the last longliner would move into action.

Breaststroking across the distance, Leilani was careful to minimize splashing and stay down. Remaining underwater was challenging, after already pushing her lungs' capacity to the limit during the dive to the line.

"Hope your inside man is up to the task," the captain said, as Leilani removed her hood, climbed up the stern dive ladder, shaking out her hair. She strained her eyes, looking at the deck of the illegal vessel. Deckhands were moving around now with purpose, pulling up anchor, but there was no yellow headband to be seen.

Sina held the VHF radio close to her ear and listened. "Second boat in position," she said to the team onboard. "Ready to strike. Waiting on you, Agent Brown."

"Wait," Leilani said, shaking out her mop of hair once more, then tying it back into a salt-matted ponytail. "Sione will text once they start finning. If we go early, we risk not getting the prosecution we want."

The Captain agreed. They'd been over this scenario in the meeting room of the Apia police station, but Leilani saw a shift in the men's eyes, tension rising. If the tuna boat carried mounted guns, the team were nothing more than targets, fish staring down a speargun. No one had been aboard, so its level of firepower was an unknown factor. Fear was justified.

Minute after minute passed in uncomfortable silence, only the faint crackle of the radio breaking the peace. Leilani tried to avoid making eye contact with the anxious crew, instead focusing on the vessel ahead in the dark.

Finally, a text buzzed on her phone. Leilani held her breath as she read the message. There was too much on the line for this to go wrong again.

Lines coming onboard now.

At half throttle, the skipper drove the police launch forward. Officers readied their weapons, aimed at the wheelhouse. Sina turned her loudspeaker on for the official warning as they drew closer.

From her position in the bow, behind a row of firearms, Leilani could see the line hauler retrieving the mainline, its roller belt protesting under strain. Samoan deckhands flanked the line, unclipping hooks and sorting the catch, the rest coiling branch lines into blue plastic barrels, jandal-clad feet sliding on shark blood and seawater. The hauler jerked, dragging the line up slowly. Salt-encrusted monofilament snapped taut, strained like tendons. Diesel fumes rolled across the deck.

Behind the deckhands overseeing line retrieval were a line of finners. Powerful men, muscles trained by backbreaking years on the plantation, ready for action. As sharks were thrown or rolled across the blood-slicked deck, one after another, the drug-fueled fishermen hacked at fins with machetes left, right and center, like a worker on a fast-moving processing line in a meatworks.

Shadow-striped tiger sharks were too heavy for the old gear. As the winch did the lifting, tigers were gaffed mid-body, then muscled aboard by two deckhands guiding the bulk over the rail. They thrashed aggressively, despite exhaustion from hours trapped on the line.

Closer now, Leilani recognized through the binoculars a man she'd seen at church with his family, pinning down a metallic hammerhead in the throes of death with a bare foot, gills heaving and tail slapping like a whip on the wet surface. The black eyes on each side of the broad T-shaped head rolled back in their sockets, a protective mechanism before the impact of attack. Before the shark knew what was coming, the man's machete stuck on dense cartilage at the base of its dorsal fin, then pushed clean through with a rubber band snap. The grey sickle-shaped fin slid to the deck as the shark bled out, where it lay amongst layers of others - all colors and sizes.

On both sides, men followed the same routine, puffing from exertion as orders were shouted at them in Mandarin, then repeated in Samoan. To remove each pectoral fin, he pulled the skin taut to ensure a clean separation from the body. Grabbing the tail around the shaft with both hands, he lifted and used the shark's own weight as momentum to flip it over. Lower value pelvic and anal fins came off next from the exposed pale belly of the shark. Sweat-soaked and shirtless, long hair tied back, the man she watched moved like a serial killer who knew his trade inside out, no pause, no mercy. Blood mixed with streams of seawater spun around the feet of men at work in pink eddies, entrails freed by careless cuts clinging to the metal deck. Ammonia filled the air as if a chemical accident had occurred at sea, and deck drainage failed as it became clogged, regurgitating red water.

Stripped of fins, yet conscious, the hammerhead twitched as a dull blade severed its tail lobes, a sawing motion needed to break the firm layer of skin, muscle and rays of cartilage. Then the body was heaved over the side, sinking to the seafloor, unable to swim but still alive, as it descended past sheer walls of coral and sponges that marked the drop-off. Forgotten as the next sharks were moved in front of the crew. The next one Leilani watched was a juvenile grey reef shark, with the steel long-line hook still embedded in the corner of its mouth, not moving. She felt vomit rise in her throat, along with anger. These sharks had never bothered her when doing research dives in the South Pacific, only checking in like curious Golden Retrievers.

Sharks continued to be hauled onboard, alongside turtles, rays and tuna. Thrown back dead, or kept for eating later. Dead or alive, all shark fins were taken, the procedure the same.

As the police launch drew closer, another ship emerged from behind the rusted bulk of the tuna longliner in the dark. Smaller, with the profile of a research ship, Leilani recognized it immediately from her visit to the marina. Upon realizing the main ship was surrounded, the smaller vessel tried to block the line of sight to the blood-soaked deck, preventing further photographs from being taken. She could see Xu, the old man who'd grabbed her from behind, at the helm. Li stood beside him in wet weather gear, a stern expression on his face.

Any minute now she expected him to order the longliner captain to cut their losses and run to international waters. On the high seas, detaining a foreign-flagged vessel became a lawyer's worst nightmare. If they ran, the video she had was enough to stop them from ever returning. No judge on the islands would even need to deliberate. With witnesses from three law enforcement organizations on board, these shark traffickers were asking for a long stay in an old Samoan prison.

The second police launch, helmed by Moresi's stand-in, blocked the poachers' escape route to the west. The boat Leilani was on blocked their escape to the east. Inshore, the water was too shallow for the larger longlining vessel. If they refused to surrender, they'd be chased down at sea.

"Attention vessel Liao Yuan 18 and associated support craft, this is the Samoan Maritime Police." Captain Sina spoke into the loudspeaker. "We are accompanied by agents from the Oceanic Enforcement Agency and the Ministry of Agriculture and Fisheries. You are operating illegally within the Samoan Exclusive Economic Zone.

We have evidence that your vessel is engaged in the prohibited activity of shark finning. All shark species are protected under the Fisheries Management Act of 2016. You are therefore in direct violation of Samoan law.

We have grounds to suspect breaches of national labor legislation, not limited to unlawful employment and conditions consistent with forced labor.

Liao Yuan 18, prepare to be boarded. All crew must appear on deck immediately with hands visible. You have 60 seconds to comply. Failure to do so may result in the use of force. If you cooperate, you will not be harmed."

The Captain delivered the warning from the bow with her enforcement team at her back, unafraid in front of the intimidating bulk of the ship. She'd tell no one, but Leilani admired the woman. Her leadership was an inspiration, breaking down cultural and gender barriers since graduating as the country's first female police officer. Dozens had come through the program since.

The captain then repeated herself, translating the warning and instruction into Samoan for the confused deckhands, many of whom still had blood on their hands. Finally, Leilani saw Sione in the lineup, floodlights catching his reflective bandana. His eyes gave away his surprise at the scale of the nighttime operation, unsure whether police would keep their end of his deal.

An Asian man in overalls and fogged-up glasses broke rank from the others and sprinted for the hauler. Acting on instinct, he grabbed the mainline above the roller and hacked at it with a military-style knife, sawing hard. The blade bit deep into the thick layers of nylon. Sina raised a hand, signaling her officers to hold fire. A dead man would complicate the court process, even if justified. The fisheries officers and Leilani had seen this before. Cutting the lines, Strategy 101 in the illegal fishing playbook.

The line snapped with a crack, vanishing into the sea in seconds, taking hooks, sharks and bycatch with it. From an evidentiary angle, the team was not overly phased. Half of the line had already been hauled in on camera.

"They're making a run for it," Leilani called out. "North by northeast. Trying to cross into international waters."

Sina didn't hesitate. "Alert the nearest ship. Get Pago's sector traffic on the line."

After checking the move had majority consent, Leilani radioed in. A friendly ship was nearby. Next, she called the second police launch over that had been acting in partnership. "Good work team, appreciate it. Now, I need you to retrieve the line they cut. It'll take a while." Bobbing orange floats gave away the location of the shifting, endless nylon. Not only was it evidence, but there was no way she'd allow that gear to continue entrapping marine life as a ghost line under her watch.

"Leave it. Too much. Waste of time." A police officer said over her shoulder.

Leilani ignored his ill-informed comment and retrained her night-vision binoculars on the fast-moving foreign vessel. They were heading offshore, as expected. So far, there had been no reply to the formal warning.

Minutes later, an American-accented voice crackled over the comms.

"Samoa Police, this is *Southern Voyager*, United States flagged tuna purse-seiner, home port Pago Pago. We have visual on the fleeing vessel. Interception possible in five minutes. Standing by for instructions. Over"

It was the first white man's voice Leilani had heard in a long time, other than her father's during their irregular calls.

Relief showed on Sina's tired face. "That ship has no chance, and they know it," she told Leilani. "She holds more fuel than we do, but she's not designed for racing. Any minute now, Agent." Looking at the unimpressive speed at which the largest ship in the convoy was travelling, Leilani agreed. It was the modern research vessel that was an issue, travelling alongside at a cruising pace by choice. When pressed, the crew would abandon ship and disappear into international waters in the faster research vessel, although she doubted the heartless men would give anyone mercy.

The experienced police skipper pushed the dual Yamaha outboards as hard as he could without overloading. Missing the protection of coral reefs and sand islets, early morning rollers appeared offshore, born deep in the vast South Pacific Ocean. A sliver of orange emerged beneath the horizon as the sun rose, illuminating the telltale M-shaped wingspans of frigatebirds riding thermals. Built for the chase, the fiberglass hull of their launch smashed through, becoming airborne between sets. The chase reminded Leilani of dawn fishing trips off the coast of New Zealand, with her grandfather at the helm. She grinned for the first time since the sting had begun hours ago. With coordinated support from a political ally, American Samoa, there was every chance they would capture and board the illegal fishing vessel.

The race was on.

Chapter 23

As promised, the US-flagged *Northern Light* detoured to assist. With nerves of steel that came from setting tuna purse-seine nets over million-dollar schools of fish, the skipper intercepted the illegal longliner in a game of 'chicken'. The ship veered to port at the last possible moment, to be confronted by a Samoan police launch below, armed officers standing at the bow. The captain gave permission to fire. A warning volley of shots were fired over the bridge.

"Liao Yuan 18, surrender now or we will be forced to sink you." Captain Sina shouted through the loudspeaker.

Realizing their advantage was over and not wishing to engage in an offshore skirmish with trained officers, the vessel cut its engine and came to a slow halt. Men began appearing on deck, hands in the air. A white flag was hoisted up the flagpole, alongside the blue and white of Liberia, another country willing to exchange registration for cash without asking questions.

With the target subdued, the American fishing vessel peeled away with a low blast of its horn. The radio stuttered.

"Samoa Maritime Police, this is Northern Light. Pleasure working with you. Until next time, *manuia lou malaga* and see you in Pago … " the American accented voice said over the airwaves.

"Fa'afetai tele lava, Northern Light. Samoa mo Samoa. Over," Captain Sina replied, taking the VHF out of Leilani's hands.

"One people, different flags," she said, explaining her choice of words to Leilani. Only colonization and imaginary lines divided the people of the two Samoas.

Given the tonnage of the Liao Yuan 18, they were left with two options. Pilot it to shore, or scuttle it.

Evidence orientated by nature, Leilani argued for the legal option. Older and with more court cases under her belt, the captain argued for sinking the Chinese vessel.

"Agent Brown, no disrespect, but you don't know the judicial system here in the islands," she said, eyes still trained on the ship before them. "Our environmental laws are still evolving. Until recently, ocean disputes were handled at the village level."

The captain looked away from the stalled ship to confront Leilani directly.

"On paper, I agree with you. We need evidence to guarantee a win. But in reality, commandeering a ship outside Samoa's EEZ opens us up to a legal nightmare. Not to mention the seafood industry will fly in a legal team in a day. Direct flights come from China now."

Leilani nodded. Sina made a strong case, but all of her training and legal education pulled her in the opposite direction.

"Destruction of the ship will lose us this case, captain. Their defense will argue prosecutorial misconduct. Inspection in port could be the difference between this ship being back on the water in weeks, or never again."

The Captain sighed. The men around the two women were becoming impatient, ready to board their target. Fisheries officers sided with Leilani.

"Agent, listen. We're exposed here. We detained them outside Samoa's EEZ. Yes, we can argue high seas enforcement under regional fisheries agreements, but their lawyers will challenge it, argue we acted beyond our mandate, then claim unlawful arrest."

She raised a finger as Leilani was about to argue back. "The flag state issue's no joke either. This vessel's flagged to Liberia, not China. Their registry is a disgrace, but still sovereign on paper. If their government files for protest, this whole thing turns political."

Another finger. "Then there's chain of custody. Once we move this vessel into port, every item of evidence is open to procedural challenge. One mistake and defense will claim tampering."

She maintained eye contact. "And what about retaliation? The shark fin industry knows how to work the system. We seize this vessel; they'll bury us in injunctions and delay tactics. Even if we win, could take years to work its way through the courts while the same company operates under a different flag on a different island."

The captain paused.

"Sometimes, eliminating the target at sea is the safest choice, Agent. They can't get insurance on those vessels."

Leilani agreed to some extent, but felt annoyed at police trying to take over the case. They had no legal jurisdiction out here; the hierarchy of authority was being disrespected. Her first impulse was to call the Director to restore balance, then she took a deep breath and reconsidered. *No, outside of Samoa's EEZ, this was her case.*

She glanced at the navigation screen. The vessel's position blinked steadily on the digital chart, well beyond the red line marking Samoa's exclusive economic zone. They were firmly in international waters.

"Captain, I'll be straight; we're now outside Samoa's jurisdiction. The Liao Yuan 18, under suspicion of IUU fishing, is being detained under Oceanic Enforcement Agency high seas enforcement authority. As the lead OEA officer present, I am assuming command of this operation. Your objections will be noted in my report, but my decision stands: we will escort the vessel to Apia for inspection."

Leilani turned to a senior officer, waiting for an order, gun in hand. He looked between the two women, unsure of whom he had to listen to.

"Officer, call Apia, inform Fisheries and the Attorney-General's Office that the OEA recommends immediate diversion to port under high seas enforcement authority, citing regional conservation agreements and WCPFC protocols. I'll file an incident report en route."

The man nodded, repeating her message into his VHF.

The police captain watched and shrugged. "As you say, Agent, it's your call. Let's hope you made the right decision."

* * *

On board for the first time, months after laying eyes on the illegal fishing vessel, Leilani was taken aback at the stench. Unrefrigerated barrels of shark livers inches deep in squalene, salt-hardened clothing and stained mattresses, mixed with spilled diesel and thawed bait. The boarding crew spread out, beginning a formal search.

"Over here!" a fisheries officer called out after a while, raising his hand.

Deep within the musty, humid hold, he'd found rice sacks stuffed with fins, edges curled and sun-dried. Next were clear plastic bags full of white crystals found stuffed under cushions in the mess. Ex-Chinese Army rifles were removed from under the narrow bunks. Every room on the ship offered evidence of additional crime.

Even hardened officers paused at this discovery. Sina nodded at Leilani, accepting she'd been wrong to want to sink the vessel. This was more than a fishing violation.

Man after man, captured crew were zip-tied and documented, details recorded on an iPad by police. Samoan deckhands tried to shuffle away from the Chinese officers, distancing themselves from crimes they had no control over. Sione, the Agency informant, was processed in the same manner, the enforcement team careful not to out him. Leilani gave the young man a subtle nod as she passed, for reassurance. He'd been invaluable, trustworthy till the end.

Leilani knew most of the crew hadn't signed on for this. She'd seen them in the village, with their families, in church; some she knew by name. They were not innocent, but they weren't criminals either. They'd signed on for tuna fishing, excited at the prospect of steady wages. Once at sea, the rules had changed. It had been made clear, leaving the shark-fin trade was never an option. Forced into crime under threat of violence, the men existed in a gray zone of human trafficking and forced labor. If the defence could prove coercion, the law would see them as victims and witnesses, testimony traded for freedom. Whether or not they liked it, the deckhands would be compelled to appear in court. Their village needed answers.

She felt sorry for the local men. They'd expected hard day's fishing, regular pay, but came home at night with burns, nightmares, and blood coursing with methamphetamine. Young Ioane had paid the ultimate price. Leilani had watched these men kill sharks, maim them, through her binoculars, but now, looking around the ship, the story was coming together. After the first week, they had no longer been fishermen. They'd been a means to an end.

Leilani's thought process was disturbed again by another officer calling out, raising his hand below deck. Beneath giant spools of line, the men had found more crates of dried shark fin, jammed behind rusted fuel drums.

The boarding team spread out, clearing each compartment as they'd been trained, deliberately, no blind corners. They logged evidence as they went: photographs with scale markers, weights and measures, barcodes on barrels for the chain of custody. Every item was sealed and tagged; the Oceanic Enforcement Agency demanded a watertight evidence trail if this was to stand up in court. Every find was cross-checked against the vessel's paperwork, building a clear picture of fraud layered on top of trafficking.

When they reached the dim engine room, the silence beneath the water level was oppressive, as was the heat radiating off the metal.

Officers swung their torch beams across the machinery, searching for contraband. One man froze, his light focused on a shape crouched low behind the auxiliary generator, attempting to hide. It was the Chinese captain, sweat-slick and cornered, his knuckles white on the grip of a pistol pointing directly at the Samoan officials. He'd waited, gambling on panic and surprise. The confined space magnified the danger. Neither side wanted to fire. One gunshot down here could punch through the thin hull plating and flood the vessel, or rupture a diesel line, engulfing the Liao Yuan 18 in toxic flames.

The captain stayed quiet as he was informed of his rights in English. *"You are being detained for suspected violations of international fisheries law, including unlawful shark finning, possession of controlled substances, and human trafficking offences.* This vessel will be escorted to port for investigation. *You have the right to remain silent. You are entitled to an interpreter. You have the right to contact your consulate and an attorney. Anything you say may be used in proceedings against you.*

Officers in adjoining compartments heard the warnings delivered; the official script always read verbatim on a foreign-flagged vessel.

The words echoed through the passageways of the longliner as more boots came down the ladder. One by one, the boarding team filled the engine space until eight weapons were leveled at the fugitive, an Asian man in a flannel shirt and white singlet, his back pressed against the bulkhead with nowhere left to move. With the headcount above unfinished and the man's identity unknown, it took even Leilani a minute or two to recognise him, his usual arrogance and swagger gone in the face of death.

Outnumbered, he dropped the pistol and raised his hands in defeat. The unit closed in fast, kicking the weapon clear while another pulled him forward by his shirt collar and bound his wrists with steel cuffs. Ziplocks were snapped around his ankles as well, as an extra precaution. This man was essential for a conviction, the link between the blood-soaked deck of the ship and the syndicate's financiers offshore, a man whose testimony could cut both ways, damning himself, or handing his offshore superiors over to courts who would never find them. But they would find the captain. Body-cams recorded the entire sequence as he was searched for hidden weapons, then documented and taken up onto the deck, his cowardice on display for his entire crew.

The Liao Yuan 18 eased through the narrow harbor entrance under escort, flanked on both sides by Samoan police launches. Black smoke drifted from the longliner's funnel, its engines laboring as the foreign officers and deckhands stood assembled on deck, silent but compliant. The low profile of Apia's urban waterfront rose ahead, with moored fishing boats and the faded concrete structure of the fish market. Makeshift stores lining the waterfront sold everything from coffee to fish and chips. Nearby, the colourful buses Leilani had experienced in her first week lined up beside the waterfront park, vendors wandering up and down between vehicles trying to sell fizzy drinks, cold spring water and snacks. Young lovers sat on the seawall, knees touching, facing the ocean, away from the prying eyes of their villages.

Leilani remained in the wheelhouse, overseeing the landing. The Chinese captain remained in her line of sight, restrained. He said nothing, his face emotionless, his eyes dead. No doubt he'd been caught before, even tortured overseas. Docking the fishing vessel was only the beginning of this last step in the operation.

"Harbor master's cleared berth three," a senior police officer informed Leilani via radio. The Samoan skipper, who had assumed command of piloting the large ship back to shore, looked over and nodded at her, acknowledging he'd heard the update.

She took a deep breath of smoky air, at last feeling some of the adrenaline from the sting seeping away.

Both patrol vessels sounded their horns. Line handlers stood ready as the longliner pivoted awkwardly under its own power, mooring ropes thrown forward. Metal groaned as the hull kissed rubber fenders.

Above the floating dock, a convoy of government vehicles was already assembling. Senior fisheries officials, customs agents, police captains, politicians, media. The circus was about to begin; the 'easy' part was over.

Foreign fishing crew were led down a narrow gangway, then transferred to a medium-security prison in white Ford trucks, their fate soon to be in the hands of the court. Local deckhands went to a different prison, a temporary holding facility infamous on Facebook for escaped convicts, until the courts could determine their level of involvement.

Once the deck was clear of officers and crew, uniformed men and women swarmed the vessel like bees in a hive. Despite being exhausted, Sina and Leilani led them to the key sites below deck, revealing the sacks of shark fins, barrels of squalene oil and packets of methamphetamine. The two women watched the process with keen interest. Even onshore, the risk of corruption was possible.

From the deck, Leilani watched police push down the head of the last of the Samoan fishermen, manoeuvring him into the vehicle. She felt conflicted about their arrest, but there had been no choice. Upon release, it would take a while for the local men to reintegrate, transition back to a subsistence lifestyle, after cashing in on shark fins at sea for so long. There was no risk of re-offending, she was certain. Without foreign connections, the infrastructure and shipping channels in place, shark fins were worth less than taro on the small island.

By evening, she'd relaxed a little, walking the track to her uncle's fale. It still felt surreal that the shark finning industry on the island had come to a halt, even if the reefer vessel and the smaller research ship had escaped. Leilani's sisters were waiting outside, sun-browned and barefoot, eating boiled lollies. They bombarded her with questions about the operation before she'd even reached the door. News spread fast in the village.

Unable to sleep, she worked on her Agency report, typing until 3:30am, then uploaded it. 40 pages of detail, not counting exhibits. She laid it out as a prosecution brief – timelines, offender profiles, drone footage of offshore transshipment of fins, lab results she'd received in time, along with high-res nighttime footage and stills of shark finning occurring on deck. The photos were hard to look at after having watched it in person. All of that, plus OEA annexed satellite logs and chain-of-custody documentation, was more than enough to convict.

The faster research vessel would likely arrive in Tonga in around two days, then the men would catch a flight out, abandoning the expensive vessel or selling it for cash. The last time she'd seen it, the smaller boat had disappeared behind the ghostly bulk of its mother-ship, leaving the island far behind. Leilani watched them go, disappointed to have lost Li and his associate Xu, but the operation had been far from a failure. The primary vessel, Liao Yuan 18, was in custody, and with it, the men responsible for killing thousands of sharks. She tried to put it into perspective; that was the win that mattered, for now.

Her last glimpse of the massive refrigerated cargo vessel had seen it fading into the horizon, colossal grey hull, low in the water, name obscured by rust, glare and distance, flying a blue, white and orange flag she'd never seen.

"Marshall Islands, flag of convenience. Allegedly, their registry office is run out of a P.O. box in Virginia. Guarantee you no one onboard's ever been there, shady as hell," a middle-aged police officer onboard had said to Leilani, noticing the direction of her gaze.

She'd checked the screen on the dash. Blank, no AIS return, as expected. But a transponder wasn't needed to recognize the vessel. As the daughter of an architect, outlines never left Leilani's academic mind; once traced, they lived on in her memory. The recognizable profile of that reefer was burned in deep, a last bridge between the South Pacific and the markets of Asia, an artery that carried illicit product north on the high seas. Seeing the ship again was guaranteed if the Agency stationed her again in this part of the world. Wildlife trafficking in the region depended on it. Maybe next time there'd be a way to get onboard.

Captain Sina rang late in the morning after a restless night. "Lani, don't overthink this. I've been where you are. We got the ship, the men, and we found the fins. Worry about the local guys later; today they're still locked up. Justice works slowly here on the island, like everything else. Trust me, this is a win. Take it, okay?"

"You know as well as anyone we can make a case here; the court can't deny us. And forget about that damn reefer; it's not gonna happen. I will *never* allow my men to chase a ghost into open water, and neither should you."

Back on shore, Leilani deferred to the captain. "Alright, let me log it with my team, least we can do is open a file. They made good money here these last few months. She'll be back."

Chapter 24

One month later

Dengue fever had killed six children already, the newspaper said. With relentless mosquitoes beside the estuary, Leilani wondered if she'd made a fatal mistake staying overnight by her grandmother's side. The old woman slept soundly, unfazed by the invisible threat. There were no glowing red coils or fine nets hanging from the ceiling out here. Her repellent was in a toilet bag inside the church bathroom miles away. She slapped at her arm in the dark; the whine returning an instant later, inches away this time. Sleep had nearly arrived when the laptop chimed, a new email, 2:30 a.m. Her pulse jumped; early morning contact was rarely good news. Then she remembered the time zones. It made sense; some of the team thought she was in American Samoa, an entirely different country.

It took minutes for the screen to load, even on the Agency's premium Starlink connection. Once it finally opened, Leilani breathed a sigh of relief: written consent to remain in Samoa had been given, and she remained on the payroll. Better yet, project funding had been granted.

Staying in her grandma's traditional house felt like time traveling back to the days before Europeans arrived in the South Pacific. Sitting on the edge of the deck watching the sunrise, she noticed lizards lying on the volcanic rock nearby, absorbing morning heat. All wind had died away. Beyond the glass surface of the lagoon, she found it hard to believe a thirty-foot longliner had sat anchored there, outside the reef, for months. Without her intervention, they'd still be out there, pretending to catch tuna, finning sharks at night. Throwing drowned turtles, dolphins, and seabirds over the side as they went. For a few moments, Leilani allowed herself to appreciate she'd made a difference. It wasn't a feeling that came naturally to a high-achiever.

Establishing a commercially viable ecotourism venture had been less challenging than expected, with no opposition from village council. Outrigger canoe tours and fishing trips to the reef were selling out, with snorkeling bookings within the now protected shark breeding area coming in faster than website admins back in Honolulu could handle. Former deckhands from the shark finning crews now worked for the village, profit after wages invested back into the community.

Leilani refused payment, even when it was pushed onto her. Transitioning to sustainability was always the final chapter in any assignment; her Academy training had hammered that point home. The Agency had cut off the easy money once made from shark fins, so now it was her job to help replace that income with a setup that could last.

Resorts had been quick to sign on. Promoting conservation while offering cultural and adrenaline-fueled tours on an otherwise sleepy coastline made sense from a business perspective and a social one. Villagers could feed their families, cover school fees, and leave the reef to recover to a point where it could provide for them once again. Led by locals who'd observed a similar set-up in Kiribati during their Mormon missions, a conservation-focused giant clam nursery was also set up, for reef restoration and sustainable harvest. There were even talks of export at a later date.

The ecotourism project ticked all the boxes, yet Leilani took no chances. She ensured snorkeling tours stayed well out on the reef edge, in blue water where depth prevented ignorant tourists from smashing decades of coral growth with rubber fins. Reef-safe sunscreen was mandatory; common brands from Australia and New Zealand carrying chemicals lethal to coral. Village children, eager to be involved, checked pictures and logos on every bottle, confiscating those they learned were a danger to the ocean. Most tourists incorrectly assumed their sunscreen would be returned.

Leilani ran safety like she had in the dive shop: buoyancy aids on every guide and tourist, waivers signed. Sione gave the briefings, still speaking English as if he lived in Australia. No one was drowning, not after what it took to get here. He liked to wear his fluoro headband, a memento from the dark nights he'd worked as a double agent. His work with the Agency had been lucrative; the payout building a concrete-block house on the edge of the village. Across his shoulders, a tattoo burned red with inflammation, his brother's name written in cursive, a memorial to the schoolboy taken by the shark finning trade.

As word of the community tourism initiative spread, the New Zealand High Commission stepped in with a development grant, under the official category of *rural development and sustainable livelihoods*. Thankful, Leilani was cynical. Anything to stabilize a part of Polynesia no one wanted slipping further into the grip of China. The funds allowed the village to increase its canoe fleet, build a proper dive shed with composting toilets, and train more guides. Step by step, the operation was becoming self-sufficient.

As agreed upon at a village meeting, profit after wages and overheads went back into the village. Change was slow, but visible. A filtered rainwater tank was constructed behind the church. Solar panels were added to the roof of a primary school. Damaged canoes were repaired. The 24-hour clinic that six villages in the district shared received a refrigerator for storing vaccines. For the first time in decades, families were earning enough to stay on the island, rather than sending family overseas for work or relying on remittances.

At Leilani's request, fishermen began cutting their dependence on imported gear from the city, turning back to methods their grandparents had used. For the first time in generations, nets and lines were made from hibiscus fiber and coconut husk, strong enough to endure months of use in saltwater. Hooks were carved razor-sharp from pig and cow bone with the edge of a machete. For use on the reef flat, spears and harpoons were shaped from hardwood felled in the forest behind the village, the tips fire-hardened bone.

For offshore fishing, when conditions allowed, lures were hand-fashioned from wood, bone, and mother-of-pearl, the polished surface flashing under sunlight to mimic fleeing baitfish. The craft required patience, but Leilani wasn't surprised to learn the lures outperformed plastic versions everyone relied on back in New Zealand.

A workshop was built back from the beach, hammered together from salvaged timber and leftover roofing iron. It gave the men a place to work while tourists in alo'a shirts and shorts were welcome to sit in the shade, observing a trade that had come within years of disappearing forever. The gear made here was meant for use during the week, tools not props. Most village elders could not carve or fish anymore because of age and health, but they shared their knowledge freely.

Ten generations earlier, the ancestors of these men shaped hooks and canoes with stone adzes and shark-tooth knives, each surface polished with sand and coral, the hulls of their canoes heavy with traditional weapons as they ventured between the two islands for trade. Today, all they needed was fishing gear.

With beer bellies on show beneath unbuttoned shirts, the old men arrived each morning, some leaning on sticks, staggering across the sand, others supported by grandchildren holding their wrists, clearing the way. Without them, there would have been no return to the old ways, no revival. The island way had remained within their collective memories, never written, carried forward one story, one demonstration at a time.

For Leilani, the most satisfying moment of her routine was when she stood on the beach, watching hardened, tattooed men who'd once finned sharks for a living, paddle excited tourists across calm water, teaching them to fish the traditional way. Beneath their fast-moving canoes, coral gardens shimmered, a kaleidoscope of living color.

Brave tourists dived at the drop-off with resident sharks, local guides at their side. The reef ecosystem, once broken, was now beginning to heal. Leilani felt like she was no longer needed, which had always been the goal. Other coasts, other countries, other fights waited. The south coast of Samoa was now on its own journey of recovery.

Chapter 25

New Zealand

The water was colder, but it felt good to be back home. Razor-billed kingfishers sat in manuka trees outside the waterfront property scanning for prey. Herds of cows grazed hillside paddocks beyond the pine forest that grew down to the dunes. Once she had the white sand of Pakiri beach between her toes and a paddleboard under an arm, Leilani felt back in her element. The speargun could wait until the weekend.

Muscle memory brought her rhythm back. Stretching forward, entering the water with the tall paddle, then pulling out as the blade reached her hip, as her dad had taught her, swapping sides every eighth stroke. Standing on the stable board, she turned to look back to shore. Dawn sunlight reflected off the ocean surface, disturbed only by the zigzag ripples of baitfish escaping kingfish on the hunt.

The beach was as majestic as she remembered, an endless crescent of crushed white shell as far as the eye could see, backed by second-growth forest, pockets of native bush, and the dark green wall of commercial pine. At the south end, where she'd stayed overnight with a stranded orca years ago, horses were being exercised along the waterline. Other than them, the entire stretch of sand was empty and silent.

Movement on the bright horizon swung Leilani's attention back to the water. For a moment, she hyped herself up; it might be dolphins. No matter how many times she came across them, the thrill remained. They seemed to come into the bay when no-one was around. Calmer days made it easier to spot the pods, spy-hopping or playing in a gentle, rolling swell.

Repetitive movement and telltale wake gave away the source of the action as they drew closer. They were three outrigger canoe paddlers, training before working on the farm. Local Māori, dreadlocked and tattooed from shoulder to hands, reclaiming their ancestral way of traveling across the ocean. Their fast-moving, narrow canoes were identical in design to those the Agency had commissioned for the ecotourism venture in the village, but different in composition. These canoes, which she'd seen hauled up on grass near the concrete boat ramp, were made from fiberglass instead of wood. A 3000-year-old traditional design, refined by generations of fishermen and navigators of the South Pacific.

Leilani raised a hand in acknowledgement to the paddlers, tightening her core to avoid losing balance on the board. The men waved back, sacrificing a stroke in their powerful, consistent movements to greet her.

Once her back and shoulders ached, she started the return paddle. It required less effort, the streamlined board gliding on incoming swell. As she came closer to shore, from her standing vantage point, she could see through the winter water right down to the seabed, an endless desert of featureless sand. Hoping to spot the dark blanket of a short-tail stingray, she kept her eyes focused on the sea floor. As morning sun backlit the water and warmed her body, her polarized sunglasses eliminated the glare.

Instead of a stingray, she caught sight of dozens of grey shapes darting past in the clear water beneath her. Leilani set her paddle down along the board and sat, legs dangling in the sea, unafraid. More shadows zipped past, but this time her eyes were ready. It was a school of juvenile hammerheads passing by, unfazed by her presence. Their T-shaped bodies flickered into view for only moments before vanishing.

A three-foot individual swam by himself just below the waterline, with only his grey, curved dorsal fin showing above the surface. Moving faster on an incoming tide, Leilani stood up on the board and followed the ripples he made in the water from a respectful distance, until the fin descended slowly back out of sight. Only when the young shark had disappeared, she realized her heart was racing, stiff fingers gripping the handle of her paddle. Seeing these sharks thriving in their natural environment, a commercially targeted species on the black market, put her South Pacific assignment into perspective. Even if the fin trade had ended on just one island, it had been worth it. The industry had received a message it couldn't ignore. Their days of working without consequence were done.

Leilani's father waited on the ocean-facing deck, shirt and board shorts with no shoes, his standard Zoom meeting attire, with his first beer of the day in hand. He waved at his daughter as she walked up the dirt pathway they'd cleared together years ago. Her salt-matted hair hung in dreadlocks from months in the water, bad enough he wondered if a buzzer would be needed. The black wetsuit still dripped, her body shivering beneath it. At this time of year, the weak sun made no difference once you were out of the sea.

"Surprised you fit that suit after all the taro and corned beef you've been eating," her father joked.

Leilani laughed, not offended. Sarcasm had been their default mode of communication for a long time. Almost a platonic love language.

"I wasn't on holiday, you know. Saving sharks is not as stress free as it sounds," she replied.

Six months apart hadn't affected the closeness between them. Jake had taken the news of his ex-wife's new life in the mountains of Upolu well. At least he had closure. After a while, he'd admitted to being happy for her; he'd always known she wasn't built for New Zealand.

Hearing about Leilani's half-sisters had made him emotional. Another part of the family he'd never dreamed she'd have. Not giving her a sibling had been his one regret. Encouraged by his reaction, Leilani still held back from mentioning plans to adopt the girls. The right time would come.

After soaking under hot water for as long as she could handle, Leilani emerged from the house in jean shorts and a hoodie, tying her curly hair back into a ponytail. Jake flipped his iPad over when he saw her coming. She didn't need to know about the guesthouse he was building just yet. She looked relaxed, ready to leave, searching for her favorite trainers.

"I'll do dinner tonight. Call came in while you were out too," he said, nodding at her phone on the kitchen bench inside. It had an expensive, waterproof case, but Leilani usually left it behind. *'Time on the water's only real when nothing gets in the way'*. One of her waterman heroes like Kelly Slater had said that in a surf magazine once.

"Thanks Dad, sure, be back before dark. Wanna get a steak & cheese before Oceanside closes. So hard to find in Samoa, you wouldn't last a week. Bike still in the shed?"

Jake smiled, leaning back in his chair. "Course it is. I couldn't sell that for scrap metal even if I wanted to."

Leilani shook her head at his sense of humor, heading over to the corrugated iron shed where the 'toys' were kept, protected from the elements. Every year, there seemed to be less space inside. The padlock code was the same as she remembered from her childhood.

Only pinpricks of light piercing through tiny holes in the metal allowed her to make out the shapes in front of her. Kayaks, fishing rods for every situation, crayfish pots, handmade flatfish spears and surfboards. Propped up against the side, big hunks of driftwood Jake intended to carve into sculpture when he had time. There was even a damaged dinghy inside the shed that had washed up after a storm, missing its oars. Undisturbed for years, threads of silk now spanned across her splintered hull, invisible trap lines that stretched to the wall.

Given the sandy foundations beneath, there was every chance these silken threads were katipo webs, a New Zealand relative of the deadly black widow. Reversing the bike out with care, Leilani was careful not to set off vibrations on the hair-trigger lines. The nearest hospital was not close, as the last stonefish victim in the bay had found out. Besides, her car would need jumper cables to start unless Jake had remembered to start the engine while she'd been gone.

Out of the dark shed and into the sunshine, Leilani conceded her dad had a point about the bike. The road bicycle had spent almost as much time immersed in sand and saltwater as she had over the years, and it showed. She lay the bike on the ground and crouched to check the rusted chains. The tires were in bad shape. Back in the cluttered shed, she dug for a helmet and a puncture kit among old fishing tackle, half-expecting to come face to face with the spider. A blowout on the way to get her pie felt likely.

Oceanside was a pretentious name for a small cafe built among shifting dunes in the middle of the bay. A new boardwalk ran out to it from the main road, sparing walkers and cyclists from the sand and dotterel nests. The place was open. Two tradies sat inside, coffees in hand, taking their break.

A white Ford Ranger was parked on the beach near the waterline. Leilani recognized the vehicle. Abandoning her plans, she took the sandy track down for the second time that day. The morning calm had given way to a 15-knot breeze, spinifex rolling across the sand like tumbleweed in a desert. Overnight, kelp had washed up in thick swaths. The tangled mats of seaweed were alive with sand hoppers that swarmed through the mass like fleas on a dog.

An old woman passing by paused as her dog sniffed the mountains of kelp.

"We used to use that in the days before foil," she said to Leilani. "Wrap the fish inside and put straight in the fire. Best tasting fish you ever had."

Behind the Fisheries vehicle, a solid man in canvas pants, stab-proof vest and white shirt stood ankle-deep in water, emptying 2L buckets of surf clams back into the wet sand. He finished the job, washed his hands in the ocean, then smiled when he saw Leilani approaching, the fine carved lines of his traditional face tattoo creasing at the corner of his green eyes. They hugged for what felt like a minute, then pressed noses, acknowledging each other in the way of his people. Since Leilani and her dad had moved north twenty years ago, Hone had become family.

"Back from the islands!" He was pleased to see her.

"The Mrs and I been following your work online, when the connection allows, up there in the bush. Shutting down the shark fin factory made the news here. Didn't say it was you, but course we knew. You should be proud; I know your dad is."

"Thanks Hone, appreciate it. Promise I'll tell you everything next time you come round for a feed. Ah, what's with the *tuatua*?" she asked, staring at the layer of shellfish that were now burrowing into the sand, as if grateful for their unexpected release.

With a taste that was hard to forget, Leilani remembered when clams could be dug by the handful in the surf zone, waist-deep in front of the lifeguard tower. Back in those days, a bucket filled in half an hour. At home, the shells would purge in cold water, spitting out sand, before being boiled open and eaten with vinegar. *If only it were still that easy to find the beds, she thought.*

Hone sighed, looking at the patch of sand where he'd emptied his buckets. Only dying clams were still visible, partially dug in.

"City folk, think they drove up from Auckland for the day, took nearly two times the limit, greedy buggers. My people too, should know better, bloody embarrassing the rest of us. More kids than you can feed ain't an excuse to rape the ocean, excuse my language, Lani," he said.

"Please tell me you threw the book at them?" she replied optimistically.

He laughed, shaking his head.

"How long you known me Lani? I ever let them get away with it? Not my style, they just do it again somewhere else. Better to hit them hard."

Descended from the first tribes to move into the area, Hone had been protecting these waters for as long as she could remember. Kaitiaki, guardian, honorary Fisheries Officer, titles never mattered. The government didn't pay him, but everyone knew who held the line here. Long before she wore the OEA badge, he'd shown her what it meant to fight for the ocean with the law on your side.

He paused, thinking about whether to breach contract and tell Leilani about the vehicle, trailer and jet ski he'd confiscated.

"My ancestors caught enough fish here to feed the entire tribe. Same for Nana and Koro. No one can do that these days. No supermarkets or benefits back then, just *Tangaroa* providing for our people. Anyway, we do what we can, ay, where are you off to next, girl?"

"Somewhere in the Pacific. They'll call," Leilani said with a smile. She hadn't expected Hone to open up, and it caught her off guard. Their relationship had shifted. She felt less a mate's daughter to him now and more an equal. Next time, she'd walk him through the shark finning operation step by step. If there was anyone she'd take career advice from, it was the man who protected her home waters.

The radio on his belt crackled into life. Another tip-off from the public was coming through.

"Well, get to it, young lady; the ocean ain't gonna save itself," he said.

Satisfied that the illegally taken shellfish had been returned to the ocean, Hone climbed into the cab of the truck and drove away, leaving tire trails on the pristine sand.

Leilani was left standing alone at the edge of the ocean, water foaming around her bare feet, watching a red-billed gull pecking away at a dead, legal-sized snapper. There were more fish drifting around in the shallows, all around the same length, barely legal. Their silver sides made them easy to spot against the blue-green water. She counted a dozen, guessing they'd been dumped by trawlers to make space for more valuable fish. The veteran fisheries officer had been right. The ocean would not save itself.

The Crime Behind The Fiction

Blue. Thresher. Hammerhead. Mako. Oceanic Whitetip. Tiger.
Every year, an estimated **73 million sharks**, from whale sharks down to blacktip reef sharks, are killed for their fins. **That's over 200,000 sharks every day**. The true number may be far higher.

Composed of cartilage, collagen and connective tissue, most fins will end up in shark fin soup: a status symbol across Asia. The soup is nothing more than a broth flavored with stock and other seafood. Simmered for hours, the fin itself imparts no flavor, only a stringy, gelatinous texture.

Over twenty countries have banned shark finning outright, but enforcement varies. The illegal trade continues, driven by profits that can reach **hundreds of dollars per kilo**.

Why do we need sharks? As apex predators in a reef environment, they maintain balance. Without sharks, mid-level carnivore populations explode, wiping out herbivorous species that reefs depend on. Algae spreads unchecked, coral health declines, and over time, fish stocks dwindle. Coastal communities that rely on these fisheries for food and income are left vulnerable. When sharks disappear, entire ecosystems start to fall apart.

It doesn't have to be this way. Change is possible. Global awareness campaigns have already cut shark fin soup consumption by more than 70% in some cities.

If you were moved by the issues in this book, turn the page to learn how you can join the fight against the shark fin trade.

Clarke, S. C., et al. (2006). Global estimates of shark catches using trade records from commercial markets. *Marine Policy*, 30(3), 396-408.

Protect sharks. Defend the ocean. Start here.

Shark Angels is a global non-profit dedicated to protecting sharks through **education, advocacy, and grassroots action**. They focus on turning fear into fascination, inspiring people, especially youth, to become ocean stewards.

By supporting Shark Angels, you're investing in **education, youth empowerment, and global shark conservation,** helping to secure a future where sharks and our oceans can thrive.

The **Shark Conservation Fund** drives global shark and ray protection by funding science, policy, and local projects in 50+ countries. Every donation fuels action that strengthens laws, creates protected areas, and gives frontline groups the tools they need to save sharks worldwide.

Acknowledgements

Thank you to the Sapunaoa Aumua family, based in Samoa. The many months you hosted me formed a significant proportion of my research into authentic village life in Polynesia. I will never forget the pristine coral and marine biodiversity near your home, which inspired much of the scenery in this novel.

Also, thank you to my grandmother, Pat Goddard, for always providing a quiet space to write when needed, and keeping me on track.

Finally, acknowledgement to my parents, Helen and Phil, without whom I would not have thousands of memories from around the Pacific to draw from.

About the author

Joshua McKenzie-Brown is a New Zealand author of eco-crime thrillers, inspired by real environmental crime. A former World Champion adaptive sailor, biology teacher, and journalist, he combines scientific insight with a deep respect for nature to craft fast-paced fiction grounded in truth.

He holds a Bachelor of Arts from Victoria University of Wellington and a Postgraduate Diploma in Education from the University of Auckland. A certified Project Jonah Marine Mammal Medic and Coastguard NZ volunteer, McKenzie-Brown brings firsthand experience to every page. His years of international yacht racing, along with teaching experience in the Pacific Islands and Aotearoa, inspire stories set at the intersection of law, nature, culture and crime.

His novels expose the illegal activity destroying our planet, from wildlife trafficking and habitat destruction to industrial exploitation and 'traditional medicine', while delivering the tension and pacing you would expect from Baldacci or Grisham.